"The͟ cabin."

Brigid ͟ ͟ ͟ ͟ ͟ hands, as if checking to see if they were still there—checking to see if they were still hers.

Griffin and Lucas looked at each other, wide-eyed. James, on the other hand, was lost in thought. Then, his eyes widened as well.

You all are gifted. More so than you may realize.

"No way," he whispered. Everyone's attention shifted to James.

"What?" Brigid asked. James looked at her, his mind racing.

You are their leader.

"Try it again."

The Dark Side of the Moon

Reed Piller

The Dark Side of the Moon

Copyright © 2014 by Reed Piller

All rights reserved. No part of this publication may be reproduced, stored in a retrieval system, or transmitted by any means – electronic, mechanical, photographic (photocopying), recording, or otherwise – without prior permission in writing from the author.

Printed in the United States of America
ISBN: 978-1492980759

Cover design by Reed Piller
Pendant in picture designed by MG Artisan Pendants

First edition, 2014.

Learn more information at:
www.reedpiller.com

For Ryan

Without you, Camp Moonstone

would not exist.

1

Five strangers arrived at the bus station at exactly the same time—3pm—just as the letters had instructed. The early August air blew easily through the makeshift structure that had seemingly been dropped in the middle of nowhere. They sat in the uncomfortable silence, none of them quite brave enough to break it.

James Wood surveyed the four sitting with him. Each of them sat at their own bench with their luggage in front of their feet. Two girls, one blonde and one brunette, and two guys, one blonde and the other brunette. They looked vaguely familiar, as if he knew someone that resembled them. But he was sure he had never met them before…except for the dark-haired girl who looked even more familiar than the rest—

"When do you think they'll get here?"

James looked up at the guy with dark hair. By the way he met his eyes, James knew he was the one that had spoken. He was tall, and even though he was sitting, it was easy to tell that he came close to six feet. His eyes were a dark blue, almost navy, and they were kind.

Before James could answer him, the blonde girl spoke. "I don't know," she said, brushing her hair off of her shoulder. It swept across her back, resting only inches away from the bench she sat on. "But if we're stuck here until then, we might as well get to know each other."

James nodded. No one seemed to jump at the chance to speak, so he introduced himself first. "I'm James."

The girl smiled at him, her light blue eyes—the kind of blue that reminded James of a cloudless, winter sky—sparkling. "I'm Brigid," she said.

The dark-haired girl spoke next. "I'm Marah." The name triggered something in James' distant memory as well, but he could not place it. He studied her face; saw for the first time how pretty she was. Her dark brown hair fell in waves past her shoulders, and she wore little makeup. Her eyes were also blue, though darker than Brigid's. He wanted to see if the blonde guy had blue eyes as well—something in the back of his mind told him that five people with the same eye color was not exactly normal. But, he couldn't seem to tear his equally blue eyes away from Marah's.

"Griffin," said the boy who had spoken first. Finally, James looked from Marah, back to Griffin, the tall, dark-haired guy with the endearing smile.

The final member of the group paused for a moment before revealing his name. He didn't seem as eager to share as the others had. His blonde hair came almost to his eyebrows, and as best as James could tell, he was about the same size as James.

"Lucas," he finally said. "But you can call me Luke."

Luke also had light blue eyes, but not as light as Brigid's. James studied Luke's eyes, then glanced between the other four almost imperceptibly. Something about the blue eyes triggered a memory, a recent one, something that suddenly made him uneasy about their small gathering. But the memory never came, and James didn't dwell on the feeling.

"What happened?" Griffin asked. James turned his attention back to Luke, to what Griffin was referring to. There was a small bruise on his cheekbone, right underneath his left eye. Luke seemed startled by the question, but he quickly realized what Griffin was pointing at as well.

"Oh," he replied airily, "I got into a fight."

James figured that that was a regular thing for Luke, and judging by the look that Marah and Brigid exchanged, they had come to the same conclusion.

Griffin paused, studying Luke, before answering.

"Sweet," he murmured.

James smiled. At that moment, a small white bus screeched to a halt right in front of them. The five of them looked up in surprise, but before they could stand, the door to the bus swung open and a man stepped out. He looked to be well over six feet tall, even taller than Griffin, and had dirty blonde hair with only slight traces of gray. He surveyed the five teenagers as they stood and nodded to himself, seeming satisfied.

"Hello," he said, taking Marah's suitcase in one hand and Brigid's in the other. He lifted them into the back of the bus effortlessly, then motioned for James, Luke, and Griffin to do the same. He spoke slowly, seeming to be in no hurry, as he closed the back door and moved back to the front of the bus.

"Good to see you all. We'll be heading to camp now, and we will only stop once. So make sure you have everything. We will not be coming ba—"

He stopped abruptly, and his face twisted, struggling to remain emotionless. James felt that now would be the time to exchange nervous looks with someone. But, he didn't know anyone there well enough to do it. He risked a glance at Marah, but she kept her gaze firmly away from his. The man met each of their eyes, and then continued speaking.

"Looks like we're all set. Take a seat and we'll get going." He slid into the driver's seat, and glanced back at the five of them as they situated themselves in separate seats. He visibly relaxed at the sight of them. He revved the engine, his face finally breaking into a smile.

"No turning back now!" he exclaimed.

They had no idea how right he really was.

* * *

A few hours later, they pulled into a gas station that was just as abandoned as the bus stop they had come from. There was a single street light next to the building, and it was struggling to stay lit, only illuminating the darkness for a few seconds at a time. Their small bus was the only vehicle there, and it looked as if it was the only one that had been there in a while. The man rose from his seat and smiled at them.

"We're just stopping for a minute. I'll be right back," he said. James watched him exit the bus and head over to the small building that looked more like a shack than a gas station. He turned to Griffin, who was seated directly across from him.

"That guy is starting to creep me out," he said.

Griffin snickered. "Dude. Starting? I was creeped out the minute he opened his mouth." Brigid turned to join the conversation.

"This just doesn't feel right to me," she said. Marah shook her head in agreement. They all turned to hear Luke's opinion, but he was staring out the window with headphones in both ears.

Brigid rolled her eyes. "Speaking of people who creep you out," she whispered.

Griffin tried to hold his laughter in. "Now Brigid, let's be nice," he scolded in mock seriousness. All four of them were laughing now, making subtlety impossible. Luckily, Luke never turned around.

Once their laughter had faded, Brigid spoke again.

"So, where are y'all from? And why did we have to meet in Iowa of all places?"

Griffin shrugged. "Isn't the camp in Iowa?" He furrowed his eyebrows. "Is it?"

"I don't even know," James said. "That's just where we were supposed to meet."

"Well, we can't be going too far," Marah said.

"I sure hope not," Brigid said. "My parents and I drove all the way here from Georgia."

Griffin laughed. "Dang. We came from Texas."

"Colorado," James said.

Marah rested her head against the seat and paused, seeming to struggle with the question. Finally, she said, "Missouri."

"Why are there only five of us going to camp? And how did the five of us get chosen?" James asked.

Griffin shook his head and laughed. "I have no clue. My mother told me I was going, and I said okay. That's all I need to know."

Brigid smiled. "There's probably a bunch of other groups going, and we're just a really small one. You know how churches take groups to camp? Like that."

"Yeah, that's probably it," Griffin said, nodding.

James shrugged. "I guess so."

Marah followed the conversation with her eyes, but didn't contribute to it. Brigid and Griffin, who had moved to another animated topic, didn't notice. James, however, grew quiet as well, glancing across the aisle at Marah every now and then. Her dark blue eyes revealed nothing, and he guessed that she wanted it to be that way.

He shifted in his seat, and the circular pendant he had hidden beneath his shirt moved with him. His mother had given it to him the day before; made him promise to wear it. The circle was a mix of white and splotches of grey and black, with a smaller stone in the top right corner.

It was the full moon, she had said. His father's. What the full moon had to do with either of them, though, he had no idea.

After a few minutes, the man returned, a white paper bag in hand. Instead of sitting in the driver's seat, he started towards the back of the bus.

"Pardon me, kids. Just checking on something," he said. James turned his attention from Marah, Griffin, and Brigid and watched the man closely instead, wondering what it was that he could possibly need to check on. When he came to the back of the bus, he reached up and grabbed something off the shelf. James couldn't tell what it was in the darkness. He heard the rustling of what he guessed was the paper bag being opened.

Suddenly, as if a switch in his brain had been flipped, James could barely hold his eyes open. He felt as if he hadn't slept in days, and it was a struggle to stay awake long enough to even see the man pass by him again. A moment later, the engine rumbled to life and James gave into the iron grip that pulled him down into darkness.

2

"Camp Moonstone?" Griffin's loud voice awakened James. He rubbed the sleep from his eyes and looked out the window. He felt as if he had been sleeping for hours, but it was still nighttime. Finally, he saw what Griffin was referring to.

A large sign made of rock was sitting on the ground, surrounded by several bushes. The words, 'Camp Moonstone', were carved into the rock and illuminated by several floodlights in the ground.

James turned to look at Griffin. "What a strange name for a camp," he said.

"I've seen worse," Griffin replied, grinning. The bus pulled onto the gravel road of the camp and parked on a field of grass behind the sign.

Marah peered over the back of her seat to look at James and Griffin. "Shouldn't the other groups be here already?" she asked, "Surely we're not the only ones in the camp!" The engine turned off and the man turned around. He smiled reassuringly.

"Of course not! We just came down a day early. The other campers will be here in the morning," he explained. Brigid stood and stretched. Griffin did the same, his large frame towering over Brigid's. He stepped into the aisle and stood in front of the seat Luke was sleeping in. He tapped on his head.

"Rise and shine!" he shouted. Luke jumped and ripped the headphones out of his ears. He looked up at Griffin and opened his mouth to say something. But, thinking better of it, he sighed and said nothing. Griffin smiled in triumph. Marah turned and looked at James in astonishment. He shook his head, the expression on his face matching hers.

"Looks like we're in for an interesting few weeks," he whispered. Marah laughed quietly and went to the back of the bus to grab her suitcase. James and Brigid followed her. Griffin and Luke glared at each other, as if having a silent battle that neither of them really won, before joining them. The back door swung open and they looked down at the bus driver's smiling face. He started grabbing the suitcases from them and placing them on the grass.

Marah studied him for a moment. "You know," she said, "You never told us what your name is." The man stopped and looked up at Marah, seeming startled. Everyone had stopped what they were doing and were now looking at him expectantly. He laughed nervously and wrung his hands.

"My name. Right. I'm John. John Smith."

Brigid raised an eyebrow and looked down at him skeptically. They didn't believe him, but they were all too tired to question it.

"Yeah, right," Brigid muttered, only loud enough for Marah to hear. Marah shrugged and forced a smile. They carried their bags to two large cabins. In front of the cabins was a large fire pit, and in between them was a path leading into the woods. Mr. Smith told them that the cabin on the left was for the guys, and the one on the right was for the girls. They quickly dropped their bags in the appropriate cabins, glad to be rid of them. As soon as they returned outside, Mr. Smith motioned to the right. They squinted in the darkness and were barely able to make out two buildings. He pointed to the larger one first.

"That's the dining hall. You'll eat all your meals in there." Then he pointed at the smaller one.

"And that's my cabin. See you in the morning!" he said, heading down the gravel path into the darkness. After he was gone, Griffin turned to the rest of them.

"I don't know about you guys, but I'm beat," he said. The others nodded their agreement and headed into their cabins.

James stepped into the guy's cabin and switched on the light. Temporarily blinded by the brightness, he stumbled over to the first bed he saw. He sat down and let his eyes adjust. The cabin was nicer than he had thought it would be. It was large, with wooden floors and three beds lined up against the back wall. Each bed had a dark blue comforter and pillow. There was another door to the left of the one he had come in that he guessed was the bathroom. He stroked the surprisingly soft comforter.

Griffin stood beside him, looking equally impressed. "Nice place," he remarked. James nodded, yawning.

Griffin chuckled. "I'm with you, buddy. Who knew riding in a bus all day could be so exhausting?" he asked, dropping face first onto the bed next to James. Griffin said something, but his words were muffled by the pillow.

"What?" James asked. Griffin raised his head, grinning.

"I said, this is the life."

James laughed and lay back onto his pillow, putting his hands behind his head. All his worries about camp were gone.

* * *

The early morning sun poked through the window, waking James. He rolled over, away from the window, and tried to go back to sleep. But it was no use. Giving up, he stood and stretched. Both Luke and Griffin were still asleep. James headed to the bathroom, enjoying the silence.

He emerged several minutes later. Luke was still asleep, but Griffin was sitting on his bed, not looking fully awake. He shook his head at James in disbelief.

"What time is it?" Griffin asked. James crossed the room and peered down at the small clock on the nightstand next to Luke's bed.

"7:30," James announced.

Griffin stared at him groggily, one eyebrow raised in disbelief. "Do you get up this early every morning?"

James thought for a moment, then nodded. "Basically."

Griffin groaned and fell back onto his pillow. "You're insane. This is way too early for me." James smiled and pulled out his normal attire, a t-shirt and some athletic shorts, assuming it would work for whatever Mr. Smith had planned. As soon as he was finished changing, Griffin reluctantly rose from his bed. He stretched, looking longingly back at it, but continued towards the bathroom. He closed the door and shouted to James without reopening it.

"Hey, James! Would you mind making my bed for me so I'm not tempted to get back in it when I'm done in here?" he asked.

James snickered. "Nice try, Griffin," he replied.

Griffin sighed. "Dang it," he muttered. James heard the water turn on in the bathroom and then turned to see Luke sitting up, staring at the closed door.

Luke scowled. He said nothing, but the look on his face revealed his thoughts clearly enough. James rolled his eyes, but remained silent as well. Better just to leave him alone. The two of them stayed on opposite sides of the room, never meeting each other's gazes. Griffin still hadn't returned by the time James was finished making his own bed, so he decided to go ahead and make Griffin's for him. When he started on Griffin's bed, Luke looked at him in astonishment. James just shrugged, as if to say, why not?

A few minutes later, Griffin finally emerged, tiny droplets of water still clinging to the ends of his dark hair. Luke quickly took over the vacated bathroom. Griffin looked down at his newly made bed, up at James, and back again in surprise. A grin slowly spread across his cheeks, brightening his entire face. He wrapped James in a bear hug.

"I didn't think you really would! Thanks, man! You're awesome!" he exclaimed.

James laughed. "No problem." At that moment, they heard a knock on their door. James opened the door to reveal Marah and Brigid smiling at them. Brigid's long hair was in a neat French braid down her back, and Marah had somehow wrapped a small braid around the top of her head, using it as a headband to pull the rest of her dark, wavy hair away from her face.

"Hey guys!" Brigid exclaimed, "Ready for breakfast?"

"We are, but Luke's still in the bathroom." James said. Brigid sighed. Marah motioned towards the fire pit in front of the cabins. It was surrounded by several large logs for them to sit on.

"Let's wait for him out here," she suggested. The logs were long enough for all four of them to fit on one. They sat down and looked over at the dining hall. It was quiet.

Too quiet.

"When do you think everyone else will get here?" Marah asked.

"Tonight?" Griffin guessed. Marah shrugged.

"I guess we'll have to ask Mr. Smith at breakfast," James said.

Brigid made a face. "You don't think that's his actual name, do you?" she asked. They all chuckled quietly, as if even considering believing him was absurd.

"Of course not," Griffin said.

Marah traced a pattern in the dirt with the toe of her shoe, deep in thought.

"Why would he lie to us?" she asked. The others seemed troubled by her question. No one could come up with an answer. James shifted his gaze towards the small cabin that Mr. Smith had said was his.

"I don't know," he said, "But I'd like to find out."

Luke emerged from the guy's cabin and they headed down the path together. It didn't take long to get to the dining hall. James pushed open the door and they peered inside. It looked like a typical lunchroom; there were several tables lined up in six rows of two. At the front of the room was a buffet with a large chalkboard behind it. They all headed towards the buffet. The food was still warm, so it couldn't have been put there too long ago. But, there was no one in sight.

They loaded their plates with food and sat down at the first table. They ate in silence for a few minutes.

"This is the best breakfast food I've had in my entire life," Griffin said in between bites. The others nodded their agreement. They cleared their plates quickly, and Griffin went up for seconds. When everyone had eaten their fill, they stared at each other contentedly. Something was wrong, though.

"I wonder why Mr. Smith didn't come to breakfast," James said.

"Maybe he already ate? Or...he slept in?" Marah guessed.

Griffin stood up. "Only one way to find out." They followed Griffin out of the dining hall and down the path to Mr. Smith's cabin.

James stepped up onto the small porch and knocked.

"Mr. Smith?" he called, "Are you there?" There was no answer. James looked back at the others, but their faces mirrored his confusion.

"Try again," Brigid suggested. James did, but there was still no answer. He reached down hesitantly and turned the knob. To his and everyone else's surprise, it was unlocked. The door swung open.

Mr. Smith was not inside. Actually, nothing was inside. The cabin was spotless. James stepped in and looked around in disbelief as the others filed in. No one seemed to know what to say.

"Well," Griffin said, standing in the middle of the room, frozen. Luke shook his head and spoke for the first time all morning.

"What *the heck* is going on?"

"I have no idea," Marah muttered. Her face displayed mixed emotions. She looked angry, and at the same time, terrified. She left the vacant cabin quickly. She headed down the path—back to their cabins—without looking back. The others hurried to catch up. She sank down onto the log they had sat on earlier that morning and rested her forehead in her hands. Brigid sat on the ground next to her and pulled her knees to her chest. Luke continued to the guy's cabin without hesitation. James and Griffin looked at each other, at a loss of what to do.

A few minutes later, Luke returned to the fire pit, rolling his suitcase behind him. He spoke quickly, giving the others no chance to respond or protest.

"I don't know what's going on, but I'm not going to sit here and try to figure it out. I didn't want to come to this stupid camp in the first place. I'm going home." And with that, he was gone. They watched him go, too shocked to react right away.

"Well," James mimicked Griffin. Griffin punched him in the arm, his gaze still fixed on Luke. They continued to watch him in silence until he passed the camp sign and turned out of sight. As soon as he had disappeared, the spell was broken. James and Griffin turned around and Marah and Brigid looked up at them. They stared at each other for a moment, waiting to see if anyone else would leave. No one budged. Marah breathed a sigh of relief. Griffin glanced in the direction Luke had gone, and then returned his gaze to James, Brigid, and Marah.

"And then there were four," he said, sinking down onto the log next to Marah. Marah laughed half-heartedly. James sat down on the ground, facing Griffin, and Brigid moved to face Marah so that they could all see each other.

"So," James began, "Obviously, there is something going on here."

"You can say that again," Griffin agreed.

"Did you all get those weird letters inviting you to come here?" Marah asked.

"Yep," Brigid replied. James stared at the ground. There was something bugging him about the letters, but he couldn't remember what it was. Then it hit him.

"You know, the weirdest thing about that letter was that when they addressed the envelope, they put my middle name on it. I mean, people don't usually do that anyway, but I've also never told anyone my middle name," James said.

Marah looked at him in amazement. "I've never told anyone my middle name either. And it was on the envelope."

"This is too weird!" Griffin exclaimed, groaning. "Mine was on there, too, and I've never told anyone."

Brigid took a deep breath and pulled her fingers through her long hair. "Me too."

"Well, what are your middle names?" Brigid asked. They frowned at her, unwilling to share.

"Come on," she prodded, "Maybe it will help!"

Marah sighed. "Fine." She looked away, unsure.

"Artemis," she finally whispered.

James spoke quickly, trying to get it over with. "Anningan," he said.

Brigid looked at Griffin expectantly, but he shook his head.

"No way."

Brigid gave him a stern look and he caved.

"Soma," he said, barely loud enough for them to hear. He immediately turned on Brigid.

"What's yours?" he asked.

"Selina."

Griffin threw his hands up.

"Great. We all have weird names. So what?" No one had an answer for that.

"Did your parents ever say anything about it?" Brigid asked.

"Not really," Marah said. She smiled wistfully. "A friend of mine when I was younger used to tell me that I had a different name because I was the long lost princess of a kingdom somewhere."

"Maybe that's why we're here," Brigid laughed.

"If we were kings and queens, I would think they would have dropped us in a castle instead," Griffin said.

"Summer camp isn't all that royal," James added.

Marah shrugged. "You never know. It has to mean something that we all have unusual names."

"Maybe we're science experiments. We might be genetically altered humans and they left us here to do some tests," Griffin said.

James stared at him for a moment. "I think I like the princess idea better."

Brigid laughed. "I don't know about you guys, but I don't think there's anything genetically special about me."

"We do all have blue eyes. That doesn't seem like much of a coincidence," James said.

Griffin nodded enthusiastically. "See! I'm right. Maybe we're not even humans. We're just blue-eyed aliens that look like humans."

"I wouldn't go that far," Marah said.

15

"I highly doubt we're aliens," Brigid agreed. "But it is weird that we have so many similarities."

James sighed. "There has to be a reason."

"How are we supposed to find it? We've been abandoned in a random camp in the middle of nowhere!" Griffin exclaimed.

"Maybe Mr. Smith will come back?" Brigid guessed.

"He doesn't seem all that reliable," Marah said.

James nodded in agreement. "He wouldn't even tell us his actual name. I wouldn't count on him coming back for us any time soon."

By that time, the afternoon sun was high in the sky, and the heat bore down on their small gathering. James stood and stretched. He turned slowly, surveying the entire camp. He stopped midturn and squinted, convinced he had seen something. His eyes widened.

"Is that Luke?" The others followed his gaze. Marah gasped.

"It is!" she exclaimed.

"What's he doing back here?" Griffin asked. Luke looked exactly the same as he had when he had left. He was still dragging his suitcase behind him, and his shoulders were slumped over. James guessed that it was either from exhaustion or disappointment.

It turned out to be a little bit of both. When Luke finally reached the cabins, he dropped his suitcase in front of them and dropped onto one of the logs. He caught his breath before meeting the four expectant gazes.

"You are not going to believe this," he said, breathing in loudly. It sounded like he had run most of the way back to camp. Judging by the look on his face, he probably did. His eyes were wide, and he started motioning wildly with his hands.

"I was going to walk until I found some place that I could stop at and call someone to pick me up. So, I'm walking down this path and it looks like it goes on for miles when I slam into a wall," he explained. James studied Luke. He wasn't making any sense.

"Are you sure?" James asked hesitantly.

"Yes!" Luke exclaimed, nodding violently. "There's like a barrier or something around this place. But it's made to look like the path keeps going." The rest of them looked at Luke skeptically.

"How would we have gotten in here then?" Griffin reasoned.

Luke shrugged. "I don't know! You tell me," he demanded.

"*I* don't know. I fell asleep when we stopped at that gas station."

Luke stared at Griffin in surprise. "So did I."

"Wait a second. *I* fell asleep at the gas station," James said. All three guys turned to Marah and Brigid.

"Yep," they responded together.

"This is too weird..." Griffin whispered.

Brigid quickly shifted her attention to Luke, remembering something.

"Luke!" she exclaimed, "What's your middle name?"

"What?"

"Your middle name!" Marah exclaimed. They were all looking at Luke intently. He shifted his weight and started to mess with his t-shirt.

"I-I don't really want to-"

"Dude, just tell us what it is," Griffin said, cutting him off.

Luke sighed.

"Khons."

They all reacted at the same time: Marah groaned, James closed his eyes, Griffin muttered "Awesome", and Brigid whispered "You too?"

"What?" Luke demanded.

James took a deep breath. "Was your middle name on the letter they sent you about this camp?"

"Yeah, but-"

"Have you ever told anyone your middle name?"

"No..."

"We all have weird middle names, too," James finally explained.

Luke raised his eyebrows.

"No way."

"Way," Griffin said, sitting back down on the log.

Brigid shook her head in disbelief. "Something tells me we're the only ones invited to this camp."

3

They sat by the fire later that night, trying hopelessly to make sense of their situation. They caught Luke up on the only two things they had established: they all had unusual names and blue eyes. Griffin made sure to add his genetic experiment theory to the story. Luke frowned in frustration.

"My mom always told me that Khons was a family name," Luke said.

"It would have to be a really old family name then," Griffin said.

Luke scowled at him. "There's always the chance it means absolutely nothing and we're wasting our time."

"I don't think they would have closed us in this camp if it meant nothing," Marah said.

"But what could it possibly mean?" Luke asked. "Maybe we all just happen to have parents with blue eyes that like weird names."

"My mom doesn't have blue eyes," James said.

Luke sighed. "Maybe your grandparents did. You get my point!"

"Five people left in the same camp? All with unusual names and the same eyes?" Brigid countered. "I don't think that just happened on accident."

* * *

At breakfast the next morning, they found fresh, hot food in the buffet.

"How did this get here?" Griffin asked, perplexed.

"Who knows," Luke muttered. They all sat down with their food, and the question was forgotten as the conversation turned to the more pressing matter—they had been left alone.

"Well, we can't just sit around for two weeks waiting for someone to show up," Brigid said.

James nodded and frowned, deep in thought. "Wasn't there a path into the woods in between our cabins?" he asked.

Marah stared at him for a moment before nodding. "Yeah, I think so," she said.

Griffin raised an eyebrow. "Let's check it out then. Couldn't hurt," he reasoned. The others agreed. They finished their food and headed back to the cabins. Brigid and Marah changed their shoes before meeting the guys in front of the path. It led straight into the woods; as far as they could see, there was nothing but trees.

Brigid hesitated. "Are you sure about this?" she asked, eyeing the path that looked as if it led to nowhere.

"We have to do *something*," Griffin said.

James nodded. "It'll be fine. And we might be able to figure out what's going on," he reassured her.

Brigid sighed. "Alright." They all stepped into the shadow of the trees with James leading the way.

The forest was eerily quiet. Besides the sound of their footsteps on the ground, it was silent. The trees stood completely still, their leaves unmoved by wind. The sun was hidden from view. Only small pieces of the clear, blue sky were visible through the treetops.

They continued in silence for what felt like miles. Finally, they came across a small path that split off to the left of the main path. They stopped, unsure of whether to turn or continue straight. James turned to the others, shrugged, and started down the small path. They followed it for a while, until the forest ended abruptly and opened up to a large field.

The field was a huge circle, surrounded by more forest. In the center was a baseball diamond. Griffin grinned. He jogged over to the diamond and picked up a baseball bat lying on the ground beside it. He took a practice swing and looked back at the others.

"Let's play!" he exclaimed.

James smiled, but shook his head. "There's no ball!" he yelled back, "Let's look around some more and try to find the equipment."

Griffin's shoulders drooped. He reluctantly agreed and dropped the bat. They headed back into the woods and onto the main path. They had only walked for a few minutes when they found another small path, this time going off to the right. They followed the new path, and once again, it opened up to a large, circular field. This time, there was a large, dark blue barn in the middle.

James grabbed the handle and slid one of the doors to the side. His eyes widened in shock as he took in the room. Up on the lofts, instead of hay, there were swords and other weapons lining the walls. In the center of the room, there was a large wrestling mat. Punching bags lined both side walls, and weights lined the back one.

"Wow," James finally said.

"Some gym," Luke agreed. Brigid and Marah said nothing, still shocked by all of the weapons in the lofts.

"Ahh, air conditioning," Griffin said. They all laughed and separated to examine the equipment. Griffin and Luke headed straight to the weights and punching bags. James headed up the ladder to look at the swords. Brigid and Marah sat down on the wrestling mat and watched the guys explore. The three of them circled the gym, occasionally commenting on the equipment.

When they were finished, they rolled the door back into place and headed back down the path. They found two more side paths, one to the right and one to the left, just like the first two. The left path led to a large lake with two canoes resting in the sand next to it. The path on the right led to a large field with five targets. Next to the last target was a large wooden container with bows and arrows. Finally, they reached the end of the main path, and what they found in the clearing was the last thing they expected.

* * *

The five of them stared at the scene in front of them in amazement. In the middle of the clearing, there were five small cabins arranged in a circle around a large fire pit, just like the one in front of the first cabins. This fire pit, though, was surrounded by five tree stumps. At the top of each cabin's door, there was a different phase of the moon carved into the wood.

All five of their hands went to their necks at exactly the same time. They all pulled a necklace out from underneath their shirts, looking at each other in bewilderment. Their necklaces were almost identical: a long black cord, with a circular charm that had a small gemstone in the top corner. But, there was one difference.

Each charm was a different phase of the moon.

They walked slowly, hesitantly, towards the cabin that corresponded with their charm. James had the full moon, Luke had the new moon, Marah had the crescent moon, Brigid had the half moon, and Griffin had the gibbous moon. They turned the knobs simultaneously and turned to look at each other before stepping inside.

James looked around the small room. A bed almost identical to the one he had slept in the night before was positioned in the back right corner. Beside the door, on the same side of the room as the bed, was a dresser. And on the other side of the room was a desk. What caught his attention first, though, were the words painted at the top of the back wall, right above the window.

Anningan-Inuit god of the moon.

James stared at the words. He read them again and again, trying to wrap his mind around it. The god of the moon? Anningan was his name, but he was no god.

He sighed and tried to clear his head. All he had seen that day was starting to run together. It was a lot to digest, and it didn't help that he didn't know what most of it meant. He sat down at the desk and discovered the most shocking news he had received all day. All week. Heck, his entire life.

It was only four words, scribbled across a small slip of paper. The handwriting wasn't the best, but the four words were completely clear.

You are their leader.

The hair on the back of his neck stood straight up. He instinctively looked towards the door. Who had put this here? Was he supposed to be the leader of four people he'd just barely met? And, he thought, why him?

He stood slowly and pushed the door open. He stepped out into the clearing and looked at each cabin in the circle. No one had come out yet; it was completely, painfully silent.

James walked over to the cabin with the gibbous moon carved into the door, which if he remembered correctly, was Griffin's. He knocked on the door and Griffin opened it immediately, his face white.

"Is this some kind of joke?" he asked. He closed his door and went to sit on one of the stumps around the fire pit. Eventually, the other three emerged from their cabins, looks of fear and confusion on each of their faces. They each sat on a stump, looking at each other across the unlit fire. James glanced down at the small piece of paper hesitantly before finally lifting it up.

Luke's eyes widened. "You got a note, too?" he asked. James nodded. Luke stood and hurried towards his cabin.

"I left it in my cabin!" he called out. Griffin, Marah, and Brigid also returned to theirs. After only a few moments, they had all returned to the stumps, notes in hand. They looked at each other, afraid to know what the other notes might say. Brigid cleared her throat and jump-started the conversation once again.

"Well, we might as well get it over with and find out what they all say," she pointed out. Her proposition was met with silence. She sighed.

"Fine, I'll go first. But if we're going to do what mine says, you guys are going to have to start talking more." She eyed the others before continuing. She lifted the paper to her face and cleared her throat.

"It says, 'The four others you are with are your team members. Get to know them.'" Brigid looked at the others, her new team members, expectantly.

"What kind of a team?" Griffin asked, "Capture the flag?"

Luke snorted. "I doubt it."

Griffin shrugged. "Mine says, 'You only have one week in this camp to prepare. Use it wisely.'" James raised his eyebrows.

"Good news, guys," Griffin said, "We've got a week to train for capture the flag."

James rolled his eyes, chuckling. "I highly doubt that we were ditched at this camp so that we can learn how to play *capture the flag*," he pointed out.

Luke nodded in agreement and lifted up his slip of paper. "Mine says, 'All five of you are gifted. More so than you may realize.'"

"Maybe...we're all extremely gifted at capture the flag?" Griffin offered weakly.

Marah smiled at Griffin. "Mine says, 'Your necklaces are of great importance. Protect them. They will be of great help in times of trouble,'" she said.

James frowned. "Huh?" he asked.

"No idea."

"What's yours say?" Griffin asked, looking at James.

James looked down at his slip of paper sheepishly. "You are their leader," he said, barely loud enough for them to hear.

Griffin's eyebrows shot up.

"Whoa," he whispered.

* * *

They sat in front of the fire pit, reading the notes over and over again. No one knew what to make of them. No one knew where to begin. They looked at each other hopelessly, willing each other to come up with something. Anything.

Luke shook his head. "I give up for today. I'm going to bed." He rose and stretched, but before he could walk away, James spoke up.

"Hey Luke, could I keep your note for tonight?" he asked. Luke gave him a strange look but handed the paper over anyway.

Marah and Brigid retired to their cabins soon after Luke had gone.

James looked at Griffin and voiced what had been on his mind all night. "I didn't ask to be the 'leader' of whatever this is. I don't want you guys to think I'm...better or anything like that." Griffin rolled his eyes, a smile tugging at the ends of his lips.

"We don't think that, man. Quit worrying," he said. James looked away, unconvinced.

"Look, James. That's the least of our problems right now," Griffin said. He stood up and handed his note to

James. He looked down at him sympathetically before nodding towards his cabin.

"I'm going to get some sleep," he said. James nodded and gathered the five notes in his hand. Griffin disappeared, leaving James alone with his thoughts.

* * *

The fire was dwindling. James added a few more branches and then continued to read and reread the notes. What did it all mean?

His thoughts were interrupted by a loud scream from Marah's cabin. He jumped up and burst through the door. Griffin and Luke came in only moments later.

Marah and Brigid stood in the middle of the room, facing each other, both their eyes wide with surprise. Neither of them seemed able to give an explanation for what had happened.

"What's going on?" James asked.

Brigid shook her head. "I don't know. I just...really wanted to talk to Marah. And I was imagining standing in her cabin. Then, the next thing I knew, I *was* standing in her cabin." She looked down at her hands, as if checking to see if they were still there—checking to see if they were still hers.

Griffin and Luke looked at each other, wide-eyed. James, on the other hand, was lost in thought. Then, his eyes widened as well.

You all are gifted. More so than you may realize.

"No way," he whispered. Everyone's attention shifted to James.

"What?" Brigid asked. James looked at her, his mind racing.

You are their leader.

"Try it again."

4

They all, Brigid especially, looked at him like he had gone mad.

"Try it again," he repeated.

"But, I don't even know how I did it the first time!" Brigid protested.

"You said you imagined being in Marah's cabin, right?" James asked, "Just imagine where you want to go, and see what happens."

Brigid looked apprehensive, but finally decided to try it. She took a deep breath, closed her eyes, and disappeared. Marah gasped and glanced around the room. Then, just as quickly as she had gone, Brigid reappeared, sitting cross-legged on Marah's bed.

Griffin's stared at her in disbelief. "What the...?" he asked.

Brigid giggled. "That's fun!" she exclaimed. They were all too shocked to speak. Brigid continued to disappear and reappear in different places, her laughter echoing through the room even when they couldn't see her.

Luke sank down onto the bed and chuckled nervously. "Now we know what they meant by 'gifted'."

"There is no way..." Griffin muttered, following Brigid's movements with his eyes. Marah lowered herself down onto the carpet and hugged her knees to her chest. Marah, Luke, Griffin, and James met each other's helpless gazes. Brigid wove through them, making her reappearance faster each time. She appeared beside Marah and then disappeared again.

But, unlike the previous times, she did not reappear right away. James glanced around the room.

"Brigid?" he called.

"Brigid!" Marah exclaimed. Suddenly, Brigid reappeared, barely an inch away from Griffin. He yelped and jumped backwards.

"Good *night*, Brigid! Don't do that!" he exclaimed. Brigid laughed in delight and disappeared again. Moments later, she appeared sitting on the floor next to Marah. She placed her hands on the floor behind her and leaned back on them, breathing heavily.

"Done already?" Luke asked, a teasing smile on his face. Brigid gave him a challenging look, but was unable to keep a straight face for long. The corners of her lips curved slowly upward, and she finally gave in.

"It's harder than it looks!" she exclaimed.

Luke shook his head, yawning. "I'm going back to bed," he said. Everyone agreed and slowly filed out of Marah's cabin. Brigid lingered behind, finally looking at Marah once the guys had gone. Marah smiled at her encouragingly.

"Well," Brigid began, "I just wanted to talk. And since you're the only other girl here..."

Marah laughed. "Sure! What's up?"

Brigid bit her lip and thought for a moment before answering.

"It's just making me nervous. We can't call home, we don't know what's going on, we're the only ones here!" she exclaimed, throwing up her hands. "And then this happened!"

Marah nodded. She took a piece of hair in her hand and slowly twisted it around her finger. She shrugged. "I wish I knew. But I'm as lost as you are."

Brigid sighed. "Why did I even come here?" she asked, knowing she wouldn't get an answer. Marah sat down on her bed and set her pillow in her lap, running her fingers over the five phases of the moon stitched in the middle. Finally, she returned her attention to Brigid.

"I think..." she began, "I think there's a reason we're all here. Something bigger than we could imagine. And as much as I hate to say it, we're going to have to stay here and figure out what it is."

Brigid breathed out heavily. The sick feeling in the pit of her stomach told her that Marah was right. Something big was going on here. And it was up to them to figure out what it was.

* * *

James sat up in bed and looked around the room. He was disoriented for a moment, but quickly remembered where he was. He groaned as the events of the previous night came back. Brigid's strange new ability confused and scared him, if he was honest with himself. He stretched and pushed it from his mind, choosing to deal with it later. He dressed quickly and stepped out into the cool morning air. No one was outside yet, so he sat on one of the five tree stumps to wait.

He did not have long to sit and think. Luke emerged from his cabin only a few moments after James sat down. He sat next to James and thrust his hands in his pockets, staring off into the distance.

"This doesn't bother you?" Luke finally asked.

"What?"

"*This*," Luke said, swinging his arm out in front of him.

"Yeah," James said, "But there's nothing we can do about it anymore. We're alone, we can't leave..."

Luke sighed. "Then, what? Just go along with it?"

"I guess. Might as well, until we figure out what's really going on here." James said. Luke didn't respond. They sat, both lost in their own whirlwind of thoughts, until the rest of the group came outside. They greeted each other in silence; it looked as if none of them had gotten much sleep the night before. Marah and Brigid dropped down onto two of the stumps, struggling to hold their eyes open.

James stood and held back a yawn. "Breakfast?" he asked.

Marah groaned and stood back up. As Griffin walked by, Brigid held out her arms. He shook his head.

"No way. Why don't you just 'teleport' there, or whatever you call it?" Brigid dropped her arms and cocked her head, as if the thought had not occurred to her until that moment. She raised an eyebrow.

"Can I go that far?" Brigid asked. They all shrugged.

"How should we know?" Luke asked.

"Worth a try," James said.

Brigid frowned in thought, considering this. "Okay, I'll try. But I'm going to come straight back, so wait for me," she said. Then she disappeared.

Marah, Luke, James, and Griffin stood in silence, staring at the spot where Brigid had just been.

"That is so unfair," Griffin muttered.

Luke chuckled. "Only if it works," he said. Just a second later, Brigid reappeared. Her eyes sparkled with excitement.

"It works!" she exclaimed. "See you there!" Then, she disappeared again.

Griffin sighed and looked at the rest of them.

"Like I said. Totally unfair."

The four of them began the long trek through the woods to the dining hall. They walked most of the way in silence, but halfway down the path, Griffin spoke up.

"So when do *we* get cool superpowers?" he asked. Marah laughed.

"Good question," James said.

Finally, they emerged from the woods and found Brigid sitting on one of the logs in front of the cabins they had used the first night at camp. She smiled brightly at them.

"What took you so long?" she asked.

Griffin shook his head. "Not all of us have magical abilities."

Marah grinned. "We had to use the old fashioned method of transportation."

Brigid joined them and they walked down the path to the dining hall together. Once again, the room was completely empty, but the buffet was filled to the brim with freshly cooked food. The five paused and glanced at each other. They dismissed the unsaid question; having too much on their minds already. Unfortunately, they all knew that the surprises were far from over.

They sat down with their food and talked about nothing important. After they had finished and the buffet emptied itself, they noticed the large chalkboard behind it for the first time. It was blank and spotless; it looked as if it had never been written on. There was an eraser and a single piece of chalk sitting on the tray. Griffin picked up the chalk and tried to write on the board but nothing showed up. He looked at the others, bewildered.

He rubbed the chalk on his hand and then tried again. But, like the last time, the chalk refused to appear on the board. Suddenly, large, white letters began to appear at the top of the chalkboard. Griffin dropped the piece of chalk and stepped away quickly. They all watched as more letters formed, unable to take their eyes away.

Finally, the writing stopped and they read the message left on the board.

Training: Day 1

The gym: weightlifting, hand-to-hand combat

Griffin's eyes widened. "And I thought nothing else would surprise me..."

James shook his head, at a loss for words.

Brigid, who was in much better spirits than the others, shrugged her shoulders as if the whole thing was completely normal.

"Let's go to the gym then," Brigid said. Griffin, Luke, and Marah began to leave, but James was still studying the chalkboard. They turned to watch him as he picked up the now broken piece of chalk from the floor. He tried again on the front side, but nothing appeared. So, he flipped the board to reveal another side, identical to the first. He tried the chalk on that side, and it worked. He wrote his name in all capital letters in the middle of the board, amazed that the chalk would write so flawlessly on one side, and not at all on the other.

Griffin shook his head. "I don't even want to know," he said.

"Let's take it down to the cabins," James suggested.

Griffin gave him a strange look. "Why?"

"In case we need it."

Griffin sighed. "Alright." They unlocked the wheels and rolled the large board outside and down the path. When they got it to the clearing, they placed it in between James and Griffin's cabins. James disappeared into his cabin as soon as the board was in place. He returned moments later with five scraps of paper in his hand. He erased his name off of the board and took the chalk from the tray, writing each of their names across the top. Small, white magnets that they had not noticed before were also sitting in the tray, and he used those to attach each of the notes they had received the night before under each of their names.

Under Brigid's note, he wrote: 'Teleporting'. He turned to Brigid.

"That's what you call it, right?" he asked.

She shrugged. "I guess. I have no idea." He put a question mark beneath everyone else's note. He surveyed his work and placed the chalk back down, satisfied. Then he turned to the others.

"Let's go."

* * *

James pushed open the door and switched on the light. The gym was exactly as they had left it. They looked around hesitantly, not sure of where to begin.

"So...weightlifting or hand-to-hand combat?" Griffin asked.

Luke shrugged. "Whatever."

"I vote we start with weightlifting," Brigid said, "Sounds less dangerous." Marah quickly agreed.

Griffin laughed and headed towards the back wall. "Sounds good to me!"

They all started curling fairly small dumbbells, going heavier if their first choice was too easy. Marah and Brigid both stayed with 10 pound dumbbells, and James and Luke used the twenty-fives. Griffin picked up the twenty-five like James and Luke, but exchanged it almost immediately for something heavier. He continued to exchange them until he got up to 100 pound dumbbells. He looked at the others, amazed.

"I lifted back at home all the time, and I never curled anywhere close to this," he said. "And this isn't even that hard!"

Luke's jaw dropped. "That's insane."

"I know!" Griffin exclaimed. "I don't know what's going on."

James smiled. "I think you just found your cool superpower." Griffin looked at James, then back down at the weights. The corners of his mouth started to turn up as he realized what James was saying. He lifted one of the weights above his head and the grin spread all the way across his face.

"Awesome!" he exclaimed.

After a few minutes, they returned their weights to the rack and headed over to the large wrestling mat in the middle of the floor.

Griffin pretended to crack his knuckles. "Who's ready for some hand-to-hand combat?"

Luke chuckled. "There is no way I'm fighting you now," he said.

Griffin's face fell. "Aww, why not?"

James raised his eyebrows. "You can curl over 100 pounds, Griffin. Why in the world would we want to *fight* you?"

"Oh, right. Good point," Griffin said. "Then who am I supposed to fight?"

"Me," Brigid said, a mischievous gleam in her eyes.

Griffin looked down at her. "No offense or anything, but *you?*" he asked incredulously. Brigid nodded, confident.

Griffin, on the other hand, was hesitant. "You sure?" he asked. The others looked at Brigid, just as surprised as Griffin.

"Positive. We're the only ones with 'powers' so far, so we have to fight each other," she said. Griffin frowned, considering this. He finally consented, still wary about the whole thing.

Griffin and Brigid stepped into the middle of the mat, and the others sat on the edge. They were tense, waiting to see what would happen.

Griffin raised his arms slowly into the defensive position. Brigid did the same. Griffin threw a half-hearted punch, and Brigid easily dodged it.

"Is that all you've got?" she asked, obviously provoking him. Griffin relaxed and raised his eyebrows competitively. He threw another punch, this one harder, barely missing Brigid.

They continued like this for a few minutes, Brigid dodging Griffin's punches and occasionally throwing a punch of her own, which was easily blocked by Griffin.

They stood still for a moment, eyeing each other—daring the other to make the first move. Suddenly, Brigid disappeared. Griffin was taken off guard. He glanced around wildly, waiting for her to reappear.

She appeared, crouched down next to Griffin, just as he took a step. He tripped over her outstretched leg before he even realized she was there.

He grunted as he hit the ground. Brigid disappeared as quickly as she had come, and reappeared almost immediately, sitting cross-legged on Griffin's back. She smiled in triumph.

Marah, James, and Luke were speechless. Griffin groaned. Brigid slid off of his back and helped him up. He scratched his head, looking embarrassed.

"Told you I could fight you," Brigid said.

Griffin chuckled. "Yeah. You sure showed me," he admitted, settling down on the ground next to James.

James couldn't hold it in any longer—he began to laugh. He was almost immediately joined by Marah, Luke and Brigid. Griffin looked at James in amazement, but eventually began to laugh as well.

Soon, their laughter died down.

Griffin raised an eyebrow and glanced around at the others. "So," he said, "who's getting their butt kicked next?"

James and Luke both shook their heads.

Marah shrugged. "Probably me," she said.

Griffin laughed. "I think we should let these two big shots fight each other," he said, motioning towards James and Luke. Neither one looked as confident as before. They eyed each other warily before standing up.

"Alright." James said. He and Luke stepped into the middle of the mat and held up their fists like Griffin and

Brigid had done. Luke started to lunge, but James stepped back quickly, holding his hands up.

"Wait! Just please don't give me one of those," James said, motioning towards the bruise on Luke's cheek that was now barely visible.

Luke chuckled good-naturedly. "I make no promises."

James lifted his fists once again. They threw a few punches back and forth, every one blocked. A few minutes into the fight, it was obvious that their fighting skills were equally matched. The fight could go on forever.

Griffin leaned back onto his hands and yawned.

"Come on," he said, "call a truce or something!" Neither one would give in. James and Luke continued to fight, until finally Luke was caught off guard and James knocked him to the ground. James smiled down at Luke.

"Gotcha," he said. Luke glared back up at him.

James raised his hands. "Hey, it was just for fun. No big deal," he said. He held out his hand to help Luke up, but Luke refused and got up on his own. James raised his eyebrows and mouthed 'What's his deal?' to Griffin. Griffin shrugged.

Luke walked quickly off of the mat and sat down, refusing to meet any of their questioning gazes. They sat in an awkward silence for a few moments.

Finally, Marah rose and brushed off her hands. "Might as well get this over with," she said. James smiled at her and raised his fists just as she stepped in front of him. She raised hers as well, looking slightly nervous.

James threw a light punch and purposely missed. Marah grinned and raised one eyebrow. She threw a light punch, and James blocked it with his arm. James threw one, then Marah, then James. Marah punched a little bit harder the next time, and James stumbled backwards. He gave an obviously fake yelp and fell onto his back. Marah laughed and walked over to stand above him. She held out her hand to help him up. He took it and pulled her down on top of him.

They stared at each other, their faces only inches apart.

Marah finally tore her eyes away and rolled off of him. They both were breathless, trying to decipher what had just happened.

Griffin cleared his throat.

"Shall we leave you two alone?" he asked. James rose and chuckled nervously. He helped Marah up and they held each other's gaze for longer than intended. They both glanced quickly away. Griffin snickered, enjoying the scene. James ran a shaky hand through his hair and cleared his throat.

"Who's next?" he asked.

Griffin stood up and slapped James on the back. "I'll go." He stepped out onto the mat and looked at the others.

"Who wants to fight me?" he asked. Before anyone could answer, though, a trapdoor in the floor in front of him swung open. A long pole with a bright white dummy attached rose up out of it.

Griffin stared at it, astonished. "What is that?" he asked.

"Your new fighting partner." Luke said. Griffin lightly punched it in the stomach, testing it. Nothing happened, so he relaxed and started to punch it again. Before he could do so, it began to shake.

Griffin jumped back. The dummy shook out its limbs and then stepped off of the pole it had been attached to. Griffin's eyes were wide. He had backed away so far that he tripped over the edge of the mat.

The dummy stopped in the middle and raised his fists, just as they had been doing. Griffin stepped hesitantly back onto the mat and moved slowly towards it. Finally, he raised his fists as well.

The dummy swung at him. He blocked it easily, and seemed to relax. He swung back and barely missed, starting to get into the fight. It lasted for only a few minutes, until Griffin's fist finally came in contact with the dummy's head. His fist went straight through and the head disintegrated.

The now headless dummy stood still for a moment.

Griffin stared at it, his eyes wide. "Oops," he said. Marah's hand flew to her mouth and she tried to hold back a laugh.

The dummy finally moved, lifting its hands to feel the place where its head had been. Its shoulders slumped, and it reattached itself to the pole. The pole began to descend back underneath the floor and the trapdoor closed. They all stared at the spot in the floor, waiting for something else to come up. But nothing did.

"Is it just me or was that a little weird?" Griffin finally asked.

* * *

When they had returned to their cabins for the day, James went immediately to the chalkboard. He erased the question mark below Griffin's name and wrote 'Super Strength'.

Griffin grinned at James and then disappeared into his cabin. Brigid yawned and headed over to hers.

"Good night," she said, closing the door behind her. Luke entered his and closed the door without saying a word.

Only Marah and James were left. James stood, staring at the board. Marah came up behind him. He glanced back at her and placed the chalk back in the tray.

"Do you understand any of this?" he asked desperately.

Marah shook her head. "No. None of us do." James sighed and turned towards her, finally taking his eyes from the board.

"I just wish..." he said. He didn't finish the thought, though. He didn't know what he wanted.

Marah smiled at him sympathetically.

"Me too," she said.

"I'm supposed to be the leader. And I don't have any more knowledge of what's going on than the rest of you do."

"No one expects you to. You're doing the best you can."

"I could do better."

"Don't beat yourself up about this, James."

He nodded, and turned his attention back to the chalkboard. Marah moved along the back of the board, tracing the tray as she went. She stopped in the middle, closed her eyes and let the memories she had suppressed for so long resurface.

Her family had moved every year or two. Different cities, states. Different faces. After the first few places, she had just stopped paying attention. The people would be gone soon enough. Every now and then, though, there would be someone she'd remember; someone she would let herself get to know. And then they, too, were gone. The only solace was in her father's arms, where she could forget the world. Eventually, she could forget all of the names, all of the faces. All of the relationships that never lasted long enough to matter. But there was one face that never left her.

The one little boy, with the dark brown hair and the bright blue eyes, that she had met on the first day of first grade. The little boy with the beautiful, innocent smile.

His parents and hers, they had acted as if they didn't know each other, but the alarm on their faces had been clear. And Marah had moved again, the very next day.

She hadn't let herself believe it, but now she knew that it was true.

After all these years, that little boy was once again standing right in front of her.

Marah hesitated. "James?" she asked, barely loud enough to be a whisper. She started to say it again, but somehow he had heard her.

"Yeah?"

Marah circled the chalkboard; came to face him again.

"We moved around a lot when I was little," Marah said. She paused, but James nodded for her to continue.

"I remember one place, it was the fastest we'd ever left a city. I didn't even get to come to the first day of school, just the day where the parents meet the teacher. But I met someone that day...."

"A little boy, with dark hair and blue eyes," Marah paused again. "It was you, wasn't it?"

James stared at her, unbelieving. "That was you?"

5

The next morning, they awoke to a new message on the chalkboard. It said:

Training: Day Two
Archery Field

"Cool," Griffin said.

James chuckled. "Let's go then," he said.

Griffin shook his head. "No way." They all looked at him strangely.

"Why not?" Marah asked.

"I need food first." They laughed, and headed down the path to the dining hall.

Their breakfast was brief, but by the time they made it to the archery field, the day had warmed noticeably. The clouds had cleared, and there was no trace of the cool morning breeze they had enjoyed earlier.

They each grabbed a bow and a couple of arrows from the crate on the right side of the clearing. Then, they lined up on the chalk lines which were positioned several feet away from each target.

Brigid awkwardly inserted her arrow into the bow. She pulled it back slowly and focused on the target. She released the arrow and it began to fly.

Her face brightened...until it dropped only halfway between her and the target. Her shoulders drooped and she lowered the bow.

"That was only my first try," she said in defense. Luke chuckled and raised his bow. He released the arrow and it hit the left side of the target.

Brigid glared at him.

He raised his hands in surrender. "I've done it before!" he exclaimed.

Griffin rubbed his hands together. "My turn," he said, moving his bow into position.

As soon as he pulled it back, the entire thing snapped in half. He stared down at the pieces, and then glanced around at the others.

"Oops," he muttered. Marah laughed and handed him another bow. He lifted this one delicately. He exaggerated the whole thing, using only his thumb and forefinger to hold the bow.

Finally, he released the bow and the arrow flew straight to the target.....and right over the top.

Griffin sighed. "Apparently my gift is also a curse."

James lifted his bow, trying to hold back a laugh. He released, and the arrow landed in the same spot as Luke's had—just on the right side of the target.

Marah lifted her bow last. She looked at the others apprehensively.

"I've never done this before, so..." she said. She pulled the arrow back and released it quickly. It flew through the air faster and straighter than anyone else's had gone. Then, it hit the target. Dead in the center.

Marah's mouth dropped open.

"How did you *do* that?" Luke asked. Marah shook her head, unable to speak. She looked down at her hands and the bow.

"I have no idea," she said.

"Maybe you're just lucky," Griffin said.

Luke shrugged. "Try it again."

Marah lifted her bow and released another arrow. It landed as close to the first arrow as possible, and they both shuddered at impact.

Griffin grunted. "Guess we found her power," he said. Marah raised her eyebrows.

"Umm...Marah?" James pointed down at her feet. They all looked down at the ground. The chalk line that Marah had been standing on was faintly glowing.

She jumped off of it and watched as it slowly disappeared. A moment later, another chalk line began to appear a few feet behind the first.

They all exchanged glances. Griffin scratched his head.

"Magical chalk lines. Yeah, of course. Totally saw that one coming," he muttered. Brigid giggled. James patted Griffin on the back and then met Marah's eyes. He motioned towards the new line.

"I guess you have to shoot from there now," he said. Marah nodded and stepped onto the line. She looked at the other four—still arranged in a straight line in front of her—before raising her bow.

She released the arrow and it landed right next to the first two. Luke shook his head and looked at James and Griffin.

"We're getting smoked. By a girl," he said. They all laughed and then looked back at Marah, raising their bows competitively. She lowered hers as the line beneath her began to disappear.

"Be my guest," she said. James sent his arrow flying first. It landed closer to the middle this time, but it was still on the outer edge of the target. He lowered his bow in defeat at the same time Luke released his arrow. Luke had about the same result as James had had. Finally, Griffin raised his bow and gingerly pulled it back. He released, and the arrow skimmed the top of the target, landing on the other side.

"Dang it."

Marah laughed and moved backwards another few feet.

She continued to shoot arrows to the center of the target, until they could no longer see her or the chalk line.

But, they could see her arrows flying out of the trees—and straight to the middle of the target.

At least three more arrows came through the trees before Marah finally emerged.

"How did I do?" she asked. Luke, James, and Griffin just stared at her. Brigid grinned and gave her a thumbs up.

At dinner that night, the conversation revolved mainly around their new abilities.

"If we have these 'special abilities' why are we just now figuring it out? Wouldn't we have noticed before now?" Marah asked.

The others fell into silence.

Griffin drummed his fingers on the table. "She's got a point," he said, "I've weight-lifted before. You would think I would have noticed that I'm abnormally strong."

Brigid pursed her lips.

"I've wanted to be somewhere else plenty of times. But I've never actually appeared there," she said. James rested his forehead in his hands and stared down at his food.

Luke slid down in his seat and leaned his head back. "Somehow, maybe, we didn't have the powers until now?" he guessed.

Marah fidgeted in her seat, twisting the cord to her necklace absentmindedly. "But how is that possible?" she asked. James shook his head and looked up at the rest of them.

"I don't know," he said, "It seems like whenever we look for answers...we just find more questions."

Griffin sighed. "There are so many things that we *don't* know, I can't keep track of it all," he said.

Luke pushed his food around with his fork. "Is there anything we *do* know?" he asked. They looked at each other, trying to think. Griffin scratched his head.

"We know what Luke's note meant by 'You are all gifted'," James said. Marah and Brigid nodded.

"Good point," Griffin said, "But we still don't know what everyone's gifts are."

James sighed. "Well...close enough."

They finished eating and returned to the cabins. By that time, the sun had begun to set and the moon was clearly visible in the sky.

Marah looked up wistfully and voiced what had been bothering her all day.

"Do you think our parents knew about all this? When they sent us here?" she asked. The question rendered the others speechless, motionless.

They stared at each other, horrified at the truth that had just dawned on them. Why else would their parents have insisted so adamantly that they all come?

"I guess they had to have known," Luke finally said.

"Then they knew about our...abilities, too?" Brigid asked. Marah's eyes widened.

James took a deep breath. "Why wouldn't they have told us?"

6

Training: Day Three
The gym: sword fighting

They were growing used to the chalkboard directing their activities. However, Marah and Brigid were less than excited about the training for the day.

The guys, on the other hand, were ecstatic.

"Real sword fighting," Griffin said, "This is awesome! Do we get suits of armor too?" James laughed. He, too, was grinning ear to ear. "Doubt it," he said.

"Oh. Well, let's go!" Griffin exclaimed. Griffin, James, and Luke took off, practically running, down the pathway. Marah and Brigid followed much more slowly, in no hurry to get there.

"Sword fighting!" Brigid exclaimed sarcastically.

Marah laughed. "Not exactly my idea of fun," she said.

"I think I'd rather do archery again," Brigid said, "And that's saying a lot."

They arrived at the gym a few moments later. Griffin, James, and Luke were already inside. They were crowded around a small table that hadn't been there before. Curious, Marah and Brigid tried to peer over their shoulders.

"What's so interesting?" Brigid asked. Griffin turned around, noticing them for the first time. He stepped aside, allowing them to see the table.

It was small and rectangular, with each of their names carved in the wood across the bottom. Above each of their names was a sword. Griffin and Luke had regularly sized swords, Marah's was slightly smaller than theirs, and Brigid's was a small dagger. Each of the swords had the phase of the moon that corresponded with its owner's necklace carved into the hilt.

Above James' name, though, there was only an outline of a sword. He had not taken his eyes off of it, not even to greet Marah and Brigid. Looking closer, the two girls noticed words carved in the middle of the wood.

You will create your sword yourself.

Brigid's eyes widened. "*What?*"

James shook his head. "I have no idea."

All of a sudden, another sentence formed beneath the first. The letters appeared one at a time, at an agonizingly slow pace. Finally, the entire sentence was revealed.

Concentrate-Imagine your sword.

"Great. That helps," James muttered.

Marah studied the words. "What does that even mean? *Imagine* your sword?"

Before anyone could answer her, yet another sentence appeared.

Picture the sword-will it to become real.

James turned to the others. "Seriously?" he asked, "What is this?"

Griffin shrugged, his eyes wide. "Might as well try it," he said. James frowned, hesitant.

"Come on, James," Luke said, "What've you got to lose?"

James considered this, finally turning back to the table. He put both hands on the edge to steady himself and closed his eyes.

Only a second later, he reopened them and looked down at the table.

"It didn't work," he said.

"You didn't even try!" Griffin exclaimed.

"Do it again—longer this time," Marah suggested. James sighed, but closed his eyes again. The others waited anxiously, refusing to take their eyes from the sword's outline. Nothing happened at first.

They glanced at each other questioningly. James' eyes remained closed.

Suddenly, the outline on the table began to glow. Griffin, Marah, Luke, and Brigid jerked their attention back to the table. The hilt of the sword began to form, slowly growing taller, until the entire sword was visible. The glowing faded, and they all stared at the sword that had just...appeared.

Griffin reached out to touch it—see if it was actually there. His outstretched hand met cold metal. He ran his fingers down the blade, shaking his head in amazement. He looked over at James and saw that his eyes were still squinted shut in concentration.

Griffin tapped on his shoulder. "Uh...James? You might want to look at this," he said. James opened his eyes and looked down at the table. The light bounced off of the blade—the blade that had not been there the last time he had looked.

James stared at it, speechless. "How did I do that?" he asked, crossing his arms to keep his hands from shaking. He stared down at the hilt of the sword. All five phases of the moon were carved into it, making a straight vertical line down the front. He touched the carving delicately.

Luke shook his head and wandered away. "This is crazy," he whispered. James lifted the sword and stared at it reverently.

"Wait...can you make *anything* appear? Just by picturing it?" Griffin asked. James put the sword down and looked at Griffin, his eyes wide.

"I don't know," he said.

Griffin raised his eyebrows. "Well? Try!" he exclaimed.

James shrugged. "Alright...what should I picture?" he asked.

"A chocolate bar," Brigid said, grinning. James laughed and closed his eyes. He held out his hand and, to their amazement, a chocolate bar materialized out of thin air.

James opened one eye and peered down at his hand. He grinned when he saw the chocolate bar. He unwrapped it and broke off a piece for each of them.

"That is *so* unfair," Griffin said. They laughed and James divided the rest of the bar into five pieces.

Brigid took a bite out of hers and frowned. "My power seems so much less exciting now," she said, "I want to be able to make chocolate bars whenever I want to!"

They quickly polished off the chocolate. Much to Griffin's dismay, James did not make another one. They grabbed their swords and moved over to the wrestling mat.

"I guess this is where we're supposed to sword fight?" Griffin asked.

Marah shrugged. "Probably," she said.

Brigid looked down at her dagger, and then over at James' long sword. "How exactly are we supposed to do this?" she asked, "Isn't it kind of...dangerous?"

James nodded. "Yeah..." he said, "These swords seem awfully sharp."

Luke chuckled. "Swords are supposed to be sharp," he said.

"Not when we're supposed to be fighting each other!" Marah exclaimed. They all stared at each other for a moment, unsure of what to do.

Griffin lifted his sword and swung it around a few times, eager to try it out. "We'll be careful," he said. Marah and Brigid stepped off of the mat at the same time.

"We're not going first," Brigid said, holding her hands up. Griffin turned to James.

James held up his hands as well. "Sorry, buddy. Still not too keen on the idea of fighting a guy with super strength," he said.

Griffin chuckled. "Fair enough." He turned to Luke. "Guess it's you and me," he said, lifting his sword.

Luke lifted his, the excitement evident on his face.

"Bring it on."

They clashed swords, lightly at first. But as the fight progressed, they became more confident and began taking fairly hard swings at each other. Marah and Brigid watched nervously. Marah hugged her knees, hiding her face behind them for most of the fight. Brigid squealed every time their swords collided with a loud bang. James kept his attention on Griffin and Luke, struggling not to laugh at Brigid.

After a few minutes, Griffin jumped back and held his hands up in surrender.

"Okay, okay, you win," he said, breathing hard. Luke smiled.

"That's harder than I thought!" Griffin exclaimed. Luke nodded in agreement. They stood in silence for a moment, trying to catch their breath.

Griffin and Luke exchanged glances in silent communication. Marah, Brigid, and James looked at each other and raised their eyebrows. Whatever the two of them were thinking was most likely not good.

They turned to Marah and Brigid, a mischievous gleam in their eyes. Both Marah and Brigid's eyes widened in fear. Brigid stood and started running in the opposite direction. Marah, however, was not fast enough. Luke grabbed Marah and dragged her, against her will, to the middle of the mat. Griffin quickly caught up to Brigid, picked her up, and slung her over his shoulder.

Brigid pounded her fists on his back. "Let me go!" she exclaimed. Griffin only laughed. He carried her over to Marah and set her down. She brushed the strands of hair that had escaped from her braid out of her face and glared at Griffin. He chuckled and went to sit with James and Luke.

Marah and Brigid stared at each other.

"I really don't want to do this," Marah said.

Griffin laughed, enjoying their discomfort. "Too bad. Got to do it sometime," he said. Marah frowned at him and awkwardly raised her sword. Brigid raised her dagger. She looked at Marah's sword.

"This is unfair," Brigid protested. Luke sighed and handed her his sword. She started to raise it up, but was surprised with its weight. She put her other hand on the hilt and used both to lift the sword. She turned to face Marah, and they looked at each other, neither wanting to make the first move.

Finally, Marah half-heartedly clanked her sword against Brigid's. They continued like that for several moments, their swings getting harder each time, but never going above a light hit.

Suddenly, a trapdoor opened right next to Brigid's foot. She shrieked and jumped backwards. They all stared at the hole, waiting.

"Not again," Griffin groaned. Sure enough, the same white dummy from two days before rose out of the floor. But this time, when it stepped off of the metal pole it had been attached to, the pole descended back into the floor and the trapdoor closed.

James looked at the place in the floor where the opening had been. "Didn't it stay open last time?" he asked nervously. Luke nodded.

They heard the same sound—wood scraping wood—but on the other side of the room. Another dummy rose out of the floor near the doorway. Then, more dummies began appearing, one after the other, all over the room, until there were about twenty of them.

James, Griffin, and Luke jumped to their feet. They met Marah and Brigid's fearful gazes. No one had the chance to say anything, though, because at that moment, the dummies began to advance upon them. Brigid quickly slid Luke's sword across the floor to him, and he did the same with hers.

They formed a tight circle, their backs to each other. They faced the oncoming dummies, waiting with their swords ready. As soon as the dummies were close enough, they began to fight. They were quickly separated.

All five of them were spread out throughout the room, close enough to see what was happening to the others, but far enough away to force all of them to fend for themselves.

The dummies were tougher to defeat than expected. James pierced through the cotton of a dummy's stomach, but it continued to attack him. A few seconds later, the hole James had made was completely sewn up. Shocked, and at a loss of what to do, he called to the others, "If you hit them, they sew back up!"

"Then how do we get rid of them?" Luke called back desperately. At that moment, Griffin came in contact with the side of the dummy he had been fighting, slicing straight through. The two separated parts of it fell to the floor. Griffin stared at the pieces, expecting them to reconnect themselves. But, they only lay there, motionless. He grinned and kicked the broken dummy to the side.

"You have to cut them in half!" Griffin announced.

Brigid looked at her small dagger. "Wonderful!" she yelled.

Dummies began falling left and right. Because they finally knew how to defeat them, the dummies that had surrounded Marah, Griffin, Luke, and James quickly lay in pieces on the floor. The only one still fighting was Brigid. She was surrounded.

"Help!" she called, "I can't cut all the way through!" The others ran to her aid. As soon as they began fighting, Brigid disappeared and reappeared on the opposite side of the group of dummies. They fought the dummies from both sides until they too lay in pieces. Brigid smiled in relief.

But, before she could join the others, the lumps of cotton began to move. They all came together between Brigid and the rest of the group, growing taller and taller, until it was a tall mound with makeshift arms and legs. Marah, James, Griffin, and Luke jumped backwards, their eyes wide.

"Brigid?" James called, "Brigid!"

Brigid tried to come around the large object, but it turned towards her and swung one of its arms. Brigid screamed and jumped just out of its reach. It reached towards her again, and this time, it grabbed Brigid, lifted her off the ground, and swung her around. Brigid screamed.

Marah gasped. "We have to do something!" she exclaimed.

Griffin looked up at Brigid. "Teleport, or whatever you call it!" he yelled. Brigid brightened and closed her eyes. The others watched her, but to their dismay, she remained where she was.

Brigid opened her eyes and a look of absolute terror crossed her face. "It's not working!" she screamed. Marah, Luke, Griffin, and James looked at each other, bewildered.

"Help!" Brigid exclaimed, snapping them back to focus. They all charged at once, attacking the large object from the bottom.

They continued cutting away pieces until the arm holding Brigid was almost to the floor. Marah hurried over and cut her free. Brigid gave Marah a quick hug and took a deep breath to compose herself before joining in the fight.

When the "monster" was nearly gone, yet another trapdoor opened beneath it. The remaining pieces fell into the large opening before it quickly closed.

The gym was eerily silent. They looked around, tense, waiting for something else to come. But, nothing did. They finally relaxed and settled onto the wrestling mat. They stared at each other, still saying nothing.

Then, they all burst into laughter.

"We were fighting dummies!" Griffin exclaimed, in between laughs. This made the others laugh even harder.

When they had all settled down, Luke spoke up. "What *was* that?" he asked.

James looked around the room. "Who knows," he said.

Marah shook her head. "Things just keep getting weirder," she said.

Griffin snorted. "That's the truth."

After dinner, they returned to their cabins and congregated around the fire pit.

"I want to know why Brigid's teleportation wouldn't work this morning," Griffin said. They all agreed.

"I have no idea," Brigid said.

James sighed. "Well, it can't just work sometimes and then not other times," he said.

"There must have been a reason it didn't work," Marah said.

Brigid nodded slowly. "So...we just have to figure out...when it works and when it doesn't?" she questioned.

"Yeah," Luke said, understanding dawning on his face, "We just have to try different things and see if you can teleport."

"Oh! Good idea," Brigid said, "What should we try?" James started to say something, but stopped himself.

Brigid looked at him curiously. "What?" she asked.

He bit his lip. "You're not going to like this, but we should probably try tying you up or something."

Brigid sighed. "Alright."

"So we need some rope...and a chair?" Griffin asked.

James nodded. "I can get the chair from my desk. But I don't know where we can find rope."

Griffin pursed his lips. "I think I might have seen some in my closet last night," he said. "I'll check."

James and Griffin disappeared into their cabins. James kicked his door open a second later and carried the chair out. He placed the chair in the grass, and Brigid sat down, looking slightly nervous.

James smiled at her. "It'll be fine," he reassured her, "We'll untie you as soon as you're finished." Brigid nodded, not looking completely convinced.

Griffin came out next, the coil of rope wrapped around his arm. He smiled. "Found it!"

"In your closet?" Marah asked.

Griffin shrugged. "*I* didn't put it there."

Brigid stared at the rope in Griffin's hand. Then, she turned to James. "You were right."

"About what?" James asked.

"I don't like this."

James laughed. "It'll be fine." Brigid frowned, but let Griffin tie her to the chair anyway.

Once she was securely fastened to the chair, James and Griffin stepped away. They all looked at her, and Luke nodded. Brigid took a deep breath and closed her eyes.

Marah, James, Luke, and Griffin watched her closely, anxious to see what would happen. Nothing did—a few moments later, Brigid reopened her eyes and frowned.

"It didn't work," she said.

James nodded thoughtfully. "So, you can't teleport if you're tied up, or...contained, I guess," he said, as if checking it off of a mental checklist.

Brigid nodded impatiently. "Can you please untie me now!" she exclaimed. Startled, Griffin and James hurried to untie her. Brigid stood up and shook out her already stiff arms.

"Let's not do that again, please," she said.

James chuckled. "No problem," he said.

"Alright! Next test," Griffin said, grinning. James stared off into the distance, trying hard to concentrate.

"Umm," he began, "We know she couldn't teleport when that...*thing* was holding her, but we need to see if she can when something that's...more normal sized is holding her."

Griffin nodded and furrowed his eyebrows. "So that means...?"

James laughed. "That means that you need to wrap your arms around her and see if she can teleport."

"Oh!" Griffin exclaimed, wrapping his arms around Brigid. She stood there awkwardly for a moment, then finally closed her eyes. She squeezed her eyes shut, trying to concentrate, but once again nothing happened. She opened her eyes and sighed, getting frustrated.

"That didn't work either," she said.

James pursed his lips. "Okay, now grab Marah's hand and see if you can do it," he said. Now it was Marah's turn to look nervous. Brigid grabbed Marah's hand and closed her eyes. Marah stared at her, waiting.

Griffin, James, and Luke jumped in surprise when both Marah and Brigid disappeared. They looked around wildly. Finally, they reappeared a few feet away from where they had originally been standing. Brigid looked happy, but Marah stumbled away from her, clutching her stomach.

"Oh no," James said. He grabbed Marah by the shoulders and guided her to one of the tree stumps. She sat slowly and stared at the ground between her feet. The rest of them watched her nervously.

After a few minutes, Marah sat up, still looking pale.

"Are you okay?" James asked.

Marah nodded. "I'm fine. I felt like I was going to pass out, or throw up, or something," she said, "Apparently, it's a lot harder for us to teleport than it is for Brigid."

"I'm really sorry, Marah," Brigid said, "I didn't know that was going to happen."

"No, it's my fault. I told you to do it," James said. He looked back at Marah, still looking concerned. "Are you sure you're okay?"

Marah smiled. "I'm fine, I promise."

Griffin looked at Brigid. "I want to try!" he exclaimed. Brigid stared at him.

"Are you crazy?" she asked.

"No!" he exclaimed. Then, "Well...maybe." They all laughed, and Brigid held out her hand.

"Alright..."

Griffin grinned. "Yes!" They both disappeared and reappeared a few feet away. Griffin nodded happily.

"I feel-" he began, but then slapped his hand over his mouth. He shook his head and ran around to the back of his cabin. The rest of them looked at each other, and Luke snickered. Griffin returned a few minutes later. He sat down on one of the stumps without meeting anyone's eyes.

"I'm fine," he finally said. James shook his head, smiling.

Luke walked over to Brigid next. "My turn," he said, holding out his hand.

Brigid stared at him. "Seriously," she said.

Luke smiled. "Seriously."

Brigid shook her head and grabbed his hand. "If you say so."

She closed her eyes, and so did Luke. James, Marah, and Griffin exchanged glances. Brigid and Luke disappeared, and then reappeared just like everyone else had. Brigid opened her eyes and looked over at Luke nervously. He still had his eyes squeezed shut.

"Luke?" Brigid asked. Luke opened one eye and looked around. He relaxed and opened the other, completely unfazed. Griffin's mouth dropped open.

Luke grinned. "Looks like you don't get sick if you close your eyes," he said. Griffin shook his head. James nodded, looking impressed.

Marah just sighed. "You couldn't have figured that out *before* I went?" she asked.

Luke chuckled. "Sorry."

Brigid looked pleased. "This is great!" she exclaimed.

Griffin nodded. "Yeah it is," he said, "I don't have to walk to breakfast anymore!" Brigid giggled. James and Marah rolled their eyes.

Luke motioned to the chalkboard. "We forgot to add Marah and James to the list," he said. James rose and walked over to the board. He erased the question mark beneath Marah's name and his own. Underneath Marah, he wrote 'Archery'. He stared at the space beneath his name then turned to the others.

"What would you call mine?" he asked. They frowned in thought. No one offered a name for a few minutes.

Finally, Griffin spoke up. "I guess...materializing? Or something like that?" he guessed.

James shrugged. "Works for me," he said. He added 'Materializing' underneath his name. He surveyed what they had on the board so far.

"Everyone has their ability except for Luke," he said. Luke only shrugged.

"Maybe tomorrow?" Marah offered.

Luke nodded. "Hopefully."

7

When James woke up the next morning, the sun had barely begun to rise. He got dressed and went outside, thinking he would be the first one awake. But, when he stepped out of his cabin, he saw Luke already sitting on one of the trunks. He had one of the long sticks from the fire, and was tracing invisible patterns in the grass. He had not noticed James.

James approached silently and sat down next to Luke. Luke only glanced up when he sat down. James rested his arms on his knees and wrung his hands.

"Up already?" James asked.

Luke looked up at him. "Morning person," was all he said. James nodded, not knowing how to start a conversation.

"Do you want to be here?" he finally asked.

Luke stared at him and raised his eyebrows. "You do?" he asked skeptically.

James thought about this for a moment. "Well, no, I didn't choose to come here. But it's alright now—I'm not completely against it," he said.

Luke continued to stare at the ground, dragging the stick back and forth in front of him. "Are you saying that I am?" he asked.

James winced. "No, you don't seem open to the rest of us. You just...keep to yourself, I guess," James said. Luke still didn't meet his eyes. He stopped dragging the stick and sat in silence for a moment before answering.

"Always have," he said. James didn't know how to respond, so he just nodded. They both sat there, saying nothing, for what felt like ages—until Marah joined them outside.

"Good morning," she said, giving each of them a warm smile.

James returned the smile. "Good morning," he said. Luke mimicked James, but did not look up at Marah. She frowned at him, looking concerned. She didn't have time to say anything, though. Griffin and Brigid emerged from their cabins at about the same time and everyone headed to breakfast.

Luke was the last to follow the group down the pathway, and Marah hung back to talk to him. Brigid was in front of them, and James and Griffin walked together at the front of the group. James watched Marah and Luke from the corner of his eye, unable to make out what they were saying.

Griffin stopped midsentence, noticing that he didn't have James' full attention. He glanced back to see what James was staring at. He smiled knowingly at James.

"What?" James asked.

Griffin smiled. "Oh, nothing," he said.

James sighed. "What?" he asked again. Griffin snickered and glanced back at Marah and Luke.

"I'm onto you," was all he would say. James sighed, but knew it was no use to protest.

Arriving at the dining hall, the five of them grabbed their food and sat down.

Griffin immediately dug in. "I never knew that camp food tasted this good," he said in between bites.

Brigid giggled. "I wonder where it all comes from," she said. The rest of them shrugged simultaneously.

"Yet another question we don't have the answer to," Luke said. James sighed.

Griffin just shrugged. "I'm not complaining about this one," he said, grinning. Marah laughed. They cleared their plates easily, and a little while later, they were headed back down the pathway.

They went immediately to the chalkboard to see their training for the day.

Training: Day Four

The baseball field—take a break from training, and have some fun

Griffin laughed aloud. "Yes!" he exclaimed. James grinned. Marah and Brigid were, for the first time, excited about the plans for the day. Even Luke joined in the celebration.

They set off for the field right away. When they arrived, they found two bats and three baseballs lying on the ground.

"When did those get there?" Griffin asked.

James just looked at him. "Are you expecting an answer?" he asked.

Griffin sighed. "Never," he muttered.

Luke picked up a baseball and tossed it into the air. "Who cares?" he asked, already in much better spirits.

Griffin grinned. "I agree. Now...let's pick teams!" he said.

Marah laughed. "We'll be uneven!" she protested. Griffin frowned, considering this. He pointed to Brigid, a small, playful smile growing on his face.

"She'll teleport and play both teams," he said.

Brigid smiled. "Sounds good to me."

Griffin laughed and turned to Marah. "Problem solved."

"And for the rest of us?" Luke asked.

"Right. Well, Marah and I will be team captains," Griffin said. Before Marah could say a word, he exclaimed, "I call James!"

Marah chuckled. "Okay, I guess I pick Luke," she said. James walked over to Griffin, giving him an awful look. Griffin raised an eyebrow. Then, his mouth formed into an 'o'.

"Oops," he whispered.

"Who wants to bat first?" Marah asked, interrupting James and Griffin.

"We will," Griffin said. Luke positioned himself on the pitcher's mound, while Marah and Brigid went on either side of the outfield. Griffin picked up one of the bats and tossed a ball to Luke. Luke wound up his pitch and grinned at Griffin.

"Ready?" he asked.

Griffin returned the smile, his eyes shining. "My friend, I believe the question is: are *you* ready?" he said. Luke shook his head and pitched the ball as hard as he could. There was a loud crack as Griffin's bat came in contact with the ball. It soared through the air...and kept going until they could no longer see it.

Luke sighed. "Oh, come on!" he exclaimed.

Griffin grinned at him, then dropped his bat and took off running.

Halfway to second base, he shouted, "Home run!"

James stepped up to bat next. Luke wound up once again and released the ball. James hit the ball, sending it right in the middle of Marah and Brigid. The next thing he knew, Brigid had appeared directly underneath his ball, allowing it to fall right into her outstretched hand.

Griffin and James stared at her in shock. Recovering quickly, Griffin yelled, "Brigid! You're on our team too, remember?" Brigid shrugged, smiling innocently. Luke laughed.

Brigid appeared again next to James, ready for her turn to bat. Luke pitched the ball to her, and she hit it just hard enough for it to go over Luke's head. Marah began to run for the ball, but Brigid appeared underneath it first. She held out her hand...then stepped away at the last second. She shrugged, her eyes twinkling.

"Oops," she said. Luke shook his head. Brigid disappeared and reappeared at first base, then second, third, and home. Griffin cheered.

Luke sighed. "Is that really allowed?" he asked.

James shrugged. "I guess so," he said. After a while, James, Griffin, and Brigid received their third out. They switched, Luke and Marah at bat, and Griffin and James in the outfield. Brigid began in the outfield with Griffin and James. Griffin ran straight to the pitcher's mound and picked up the ball.

Luke motioned for Marah to go in front of him. "Ladies first," he said, grinning. Marah sighed and stepped up hesitantly. She picked up the wooden bat from the ground and held it up. Griffin raised an eyebrow and she nodded. He released the ball.

Marah swung at the ball, but she didn't hit it. The ball went straight through the bat. Griffin's jaw dropped. Marah held the bat up and looked at the round, smoking hole in the middle of it. Luke snickered.

"Um, I think maybe I should pitch from now on," James suggested.

Griffin sighed. "When will my superpower ever be *useful?*" he asked. He wandered away, slowly making his way towards the side of the outfield opposite of Brigid. Luke picked up the spare bat and James pitched the ball to him. Luke hit it, and it flew straight at Griffin.

Everyone realized, too late, that Griffin wasn't paying attention to the game. The ball was only a few feet away, still headed for his face, and he hadn't even noticed.

"Griffin!" Marah screamed. He looked up, and before anyone knew what had happened, he caught the ball—his hand barely an inch away from his face.

"How in the world?" Luke asked. Griffin shook his head, speechless.

James stared at him, trying to comprehend what had just happened. "How did you even react that fast?" he asked. Griffin shrugged, still saying nothing.

Brigid cocked her head. "Would that be considered another superpower?" she asked.

Griffin brightened. "You think?" He turned to James. "Is it?"

James shrugged. "I don't know! I guess," he said.

Griffin grinned. "Sweet," he said.

Luke frowned. "Wait...how come he gets two?" he asked.

"Oh, yeah," Marah said, "Why is that?"

Griffin shrugged, still smiling. "Like I know!"

James nodded. "Now we've got teleporting *and* super fast reflexes on our team," he said.

Marah sighed. "Unfair. My talent isn't helping at all!" she said.

Marah turned to Luke. "You need to hurry up and figure out what yours is," she said.

Luke grinned and gave her a mock salute. "I'll do my best," he said. Marah shoved him playfully.

"Well, try harder. We're losing," she said. James watched their banter in silence. He turned slightly to look at Griffin. Griffin raised his eyebrows. James sighed and turned back to Marah and Luke. He tossed the ball in the air, waiting.

"Who's batting next?" James finally asked, interrupting them.

"Oh, me!" Brigid exclaimed. She appeared next to Luke and picked up the bat. James pitched it to her and she hit it—right back to him. James caught it, and only a moment later Brigid appeared next to him. She pushed the ball out of his hand before James could even get a good grip on it. James stared at her in surprise, then chuckled, shaking his head good-naturedly.

"Alright then," he began. Brigid looked down at the ball, then back up at James.

"Darn," she said, "You missed it."

James laughed. "If you say so."

They continued to play for several hours, eventually losing count of points. Finally, Luke held his hands up.

"My arms are going to fall off if I have to pitch another ball," he said.

James laughed. "Agreed," he said. The five of them stretched out in the grass. The sky was cloudless, so the moon was clearly visible, even in the middle of the day. James stared up at it, grasping the small moon around his neck.

"What does the moon have to do with anything?" James asked. No one said anything for a moment.

"It must be important, if it's on all of our necklaces," Marah finally said.

"And our cabins," Griffin said.

"When do you think we'll find out?" Brigid asked. The question brought an uncomfortable silence.

James rested his head on his hands and stared up at the sky. "Soon, hopefully," he said.

"If ever," Luke muttered. Brigid propped herself up on her elbow. Her eyes were wide. She looked at Luke.

"You don't think we're going to be left here by ourselves...*forever*, do you?" she asked. Luke shifted his weight and glanced away.

It was something they all had thought about, but no one had had the courage to ask until now. And no one had an answer.

When they returned to their cabins after dinner, the sun had already begun to set. The shadows were growing longer. The conversation from earlier that day still had everyone on edge.

Brigid yawned. "I'm about to fall asleep standing up," she said. Marah laughed and quickly agreed. They both retired to their cabins, leaving the guys alone. Griffin sat down on one of the tree stumps and stared up at Luke and James. Luke yawned and motioned towards his cabin.

"I guess I'll go to bed, too," he said. James nodded.

Griffin looked at James. "I'm not really that tired yet," he said.

James met his eyes. "I couldn't sleep if I wanted to."

Griffin nodded slowly. "Want to go see if the magical buffet has late night snacks?" he asked.

James laughed. "Sure."

They headed down the darkened path. Moonlight pierced through the treetops, giving them a small amount of light to see by. They followed the familiar pathway mindlessly, both lost in their own thoughts.

They said nothing until they arrived at the dining hall. After being outside in the darkness, the bright light of the building was shocking. Sure enough, the buffet was full...of ice cream. And every topping imaginable.

Griffin's eyes lit up. He stared at the ice cream, almost overwhelmed.

"This. Is. Awesome," he said. James laughed, just as shocked—and excited—as Griffin was. The two immediately dug in. James filled his bowl with chocolate, and Griffin piled in scoop after scoop of rocky road.

Next, they made their way down the sides, both of them taking a small sample of every topping available. By the time they were finished filling their bowls, the ice cream towered high above the edge of the bowl.

James started towards their normal table, but Griffin shook his head.

"What?" James asked.

"We sit there every day. It's too boring," he said.

James snickered. "Alright, where would you like to eat then?" he asked.

Griffin pursed his lips, thinking hard. "I don't know, where haven't we been yet?"

"We haven't gone to the lake," James offered.

Griffin nodded. "Yeah, good idea!"

They left the dining hall and headed back down the pathway. They passed the two familiar side paths, leading to the baseball field and the gym, and turned left onto the path leading to the lake. It was the only place they had not revisited that week.

They stepped up onto the dock and sat down with their bowls. The water was clear, and they could see the moon's reflection in the middle of the lake. Griffin immediately stuck a spoonful of ice cream into his mouth. He closed his eyes and smiled.

"Mmmm. Heaven," he said. James laughed and took a spoonful of his.

James paused between bites and looked over at Griffin. Griffin met his gaze and looked at him questioningly.

"I know we just met a few days ago," James said, "But I feel like I've known you all my life."

Griffin smiled. He swallowed his ice cream and said, "Weird, right? I feel the same way."

James chuckled. "I used to think my life was boring. Then this happened."

"None of it makes any sense," Griffin said, shaking his head. James stared out at the water.

James sighed, and returned his attention to Griffin. "But why the five of us?"

"Cause there's only five phases of the moon," Griffin said, smiling. James raised his eyebrows.

"I'm kidding," Griffin said, "How should I know?"

"You could be right though," James said. Griffin shrugged.

"Why would our parents send us here so willingly?" Griffin asked.

James frowned. "What do you mean?" he asked.

"They've never pushed me to do anything, go anywhere. They always say that it's my choice. But this time, they were all over the camp thing. They asked if I wanted to go, but I knew I really didn't have a choice. Your parents didn't do that?" Griffin asked.

"My mom lets me make my own choices, but she wants to be involved with everything. So I wasn't surprised when she told me she thought I should go. It was only weird because it seemed so important to her," James said.

Griffin nodded. "They must have known."

"Known what?" James asked.

"Everything. Why we're here, what's going on here. Everything we don't know."

James' eyes widened.

"No..." he began.

"How else would you explain it?" Griffin asked.

James sighed. "I guess it can't be that bad, then. If they knew and still sent us here," he said.

Griffin shrugged. "Let's hope so."

The two of them grew silent, thoughts of their parents weighing heavy on their minds. James polished off his ice cream and set it aside. Griffin stuck his spoon in his mouth and sighed. He pulled it out and dropped it back in the bowl.

"Anyway," he said.

"Hmm?" James asked, distracted.

"I know what you're thinking about," Griffin said, teasing. James cut his eyes at him.

"What?" he asked.

Griffin snickered. "Marah."

James jerked his attention back to Griffin. "No I wasn't."

"You were," Griffin argued.

"Wasn't."

"Were."

James sighed. "Whatever."

"Knew it," Griffin said, chuckling. James glanced away, an unreadable expression on his face. Griffin furrowed his eyebrows, staring at James, but the moment passed and James returned his gaze to Griffin.

"What is it?" Griffin asked cautiously.

"Nothing. It was...nothing," James said, "Why would I be thinking about Marah?"

Griffin raised his eyebrows. "You're not as slick as you think."

"Oh, really?" James asked, the corners of his lips turning up.

"Really. Someone's got a little love interest," Griffin teased.

James rolled his eyes. "Doesn't matter. She and Luke..."

Griffin snorted. "Her and Mr. Mysterious? Yeah, right." James said nothing.

"Look, if it's supposed to happen, it'll happen," Griffin said. James raised his eyebrows and smiled.

"Thanks."

Griffin grinned. "Didn't know I could be deep, did you?" James shook his head, chuckling softly.

"Never would have guessed."

"I know," Griffin said. He smiled. "I guess we should head back."

James looked up at the sky and nodded.

"Probably."

8

The next morning, when James emerged from his cabin, he found Griffin already outside. He was studying the chalkboard intensely. James walked over to him and peered over his shoulder.

"What are you looking at?" he asked.

Griffin glanced back at James. "There's nothing there," he said.

James shrugged. "We never look at it this early. The training's always there after breakfast," he said.

"Oh, right," Griffin said, not looking thoroughly convinced. He tore his gaze from the blank board and followed James over to the fire pit. They sat down on two of the tree stumps.

James wrung his hands and looked up at Griffin. He opened his mouth to say something, but before he could, Luke joined them outside. He stretched and gave them a crooked smile before sitting down.

Griffin looked him over. "Someone's in a good mood," he said.

Luke shrugged. "I guess," he said, smiling. Marah and Brigid came out of their cabins soon after Luke. Both yawned as the guys stood up to walk to breakfast. No one said much—they were all still worn out from the day before.

They soon arrived at the dining hall and sat down with their food.

"Wonder what we're doing today," Griffin said.

Brigid shrugged. "Who knows. What else is there to do?" she asked. The others grew silent.

"I can't think of anything," James said, "Maybe we'll do something at the lake?"

Brigid nodded quickly. "I forgot about the lake!" she exclaimed, "That's probably what we're doing."

James shrugged. "It was just a guess," he said.

Marah smiled. "I guess we'll just have to wait and see."

They finished their food quickly, but when they returned to the cabins, there was nothing to see. The chalkboard was still blank.

James frowned. "That's weird," he muttered.

Brigid looked nervous. "Why isn't there anything on it?" she asked. They all stared at the board in silence—unsure of what the absence of a training schedule meant and afraid to find out. They were so absorbed in their thoughts that none of them noticed the man appear behind them on one of the tree stumps.

Brigid was the first to turn around. She screamed when she saw the man.

Everyone else spun around, immediately seeing what Brigid had seen. The shock was evident on all of their faces.

"*Mr. Smith?*" Griffin finally asked incredulously.

The man smiled. "Yes. But you should probably know my real name now," he said.

"Knew it," Brigid muttered. The man stepped off of the tree trunk and then sat down on it. He motioned for James, Griffin, Luke, Marah, and Brigid to sit as well. They clustered together—James, Griffin, and Luke on three of the tree stumps, and Marah and Brigid on the ground between them. Marah was between Luke and James, and Brigid was between James and Griffin. They looked to the man expectantly. He cleared his throat.

"Well, for starters, my name is actually Wane," he said.

"Wane?" Luke asked.

Wane sighed. "Yes, Wane. I live on the moon. The moon wanes. My father thought it was just *hilarious*."

"I take it you don't like it?" Griffin asked.

"Could be worse. I could be wax," Wane said. He cracked a smile.

"Wait," Marah said, "Did you just say you lived *on the moon*?"

Wane nodded. The others looked at him expectantly.

"Yes. But I guess I'm getting a little ahead of myself, aren't I?" he said.

Marah smiled slightly, encouraging him to continue. He thought for a moment.

"Oh my. There is a lot to tell you. I guess I must start there," he said. James raised his eyebrows, but said nothing.

"Yes, I live on the moon," Wane said, "But so do your parents. And all of you did, at one point."

Griffin's stared at him, slack jawed. The other four were too shocked to react.

"Wait, no," Griffin said.

"Yes," Wane said, "You see those necklaces you all have on?" Griffin lifted his, a charm of the gibbous moon. James, Luke, Marah, and Brigid reached for theirs as well.

"They belonged to your parents. And to their parents. And so on," Wane said, "They are what gave you your new abilities. And they gave your parents their abilities."

"Our parents have superpowers, too?" Griffin asked.

"Oh, yes. Where did you think yours came from?" Wane asked. Griffin shrugged sheepishly.

"And," Wane added, "You see those small stones in the corner?" James touched his and nodded. Wane pointed at him.

"Okay, everyone else let go of your necklace," he said, "And James, press on that stone and think about something, anything." James obeyed.

All of sudden, Griffin, Luke, Brigid, and Marah heard James' voice echoing through their minds.

This guy is a nut.

Brigid giggled. Marah looked at James, her eyes wide.

"It worked?" Wane asked. Luke nodded slowly. Griffin reached for his necklace next. He pressed the stone down and thought: *How cool is this?*

James raised his eyebrows. "Whoa."

Wane smiled. Brigid pressed down her stone.

Should we trust him?

Marah met her eyes and pressed down the stone on her necklace.

I think so, yes.

Luke pressed his next.

No.

They all glanced at him and he shrugged. Aloud, he said, "Well, I don't."

Wane looked at him questioningly.

"How do we know we can trust you?" Luke asked. James winced.

Wane looked surprised, but then he smiled. "Ah, smart boy," he said.

"Your mother told me about you. Just like your," he paused for a moment. "Grandfather."

Luke said nothing. "Anyway...proof you can trust me," he said. He pulled a small picture out of his pocket and unfolded it. He gazed down at it and smiled. Then, he handed it to Luke.

"All of you, with your mothers. I believe all of you were around one year old," Wane said. Luke looked down at the picture and his eyes widened. The others craned their necks to see. Luke recognized his mother, holding a much younger version of himself, and four other women, holding much younger versions of Marah, Brigid, James, and Griffin. They were standing in the grass, in front of a building he didn't recognize. Beside them was a sign that said, *Holy Church of Jericho.*

Marah's hand flew to her mouth. They stared at the picture of themselves in silence. This was the last thing they had expected Wane to show them.

Finally, Brigid spoke up. "What is Jericho?" she asked.

"That is our city," he said, a wistful smile on his face.

"On the moon?" Brigid asked.

Wane nodded. "On the moon." Brigid shook her head and sank back down on the ground.

Griffin drummed his fingers on his chin. "Haven't the politicians been talking about starting one? A city on the moon?"

Wane chuckled. "Little do they know there's already been one for over sixty years."

James laughed. "They don't know?"

"Of course they don't know! You think they'd be able to find us?" Wane asked.

James shrugged. Brigid pursed her lips. "If they do start their own…won't they find us then?"

Wane shook his head. "I highly doubt that will happen. But if they did start their own, they still wouldn't find us. For one, our city is on the dark side of the moon—the side you never see."

Griffin nodded. "Cool."

"And," Wane said, "The barrier around both our city and this camp make them invisible to the outside world."

James nodded. "That's convenient."

"So how did this all happen? How could you have a city on the moon for over sixty years when the government hasn't even figured out how to start one?" Marah asked.

Wane cleared his throat.

"We figured out how to *get* to the moon before they did," he remarked. "But let me start from the beginning."

"A long time ago, in the 1950's, each of your great-grandfathers worked for the same company. All five of them were incredibly smart, each in their own unique way. The main thing they all had in common, though, was their fascination with the moon.

"The president at the time, President Truman, started a secret task force to build a civilization on the moon. It was soon after the end of World War II, and Truman felt that Americans needed another place to go if another World War were to happen. Your great-grandfathers were chosen to lead the project, and eventually, the city itself.

"During the construction of the city, they discovered large amounts of a light blue gem, moonstone, and saved it for future use. As a gift to celebrate the new city, James' great-grandmother designed a full moon necklace with the moonstone for her husband. Soon, he started to develop abilities like yours that they linked to the moonstone in his necklace. Your great-grandfathers used the moonstone to build four more necklaces so that each one of them had one that corresponded to a different phase of the moon. They experimented with different forms of the moonstone to strengthen the necklaces and their powers.

"These necklaces, when worn for a long period of time, would eventually cause the wearer to inherit a weak, permanent form of their ability. Once this happens, you must work to strengthen your ability so that it is the same with or without the necklace on. Your great-grandfathers did this once they passed their necklaces down to their children—your grandparents. And your grandparents did the same when they passed the necklaces to your parents. Also, once each generation receives the necklace, they inherit their own, unique ability. No one, except for the parent that gives their child the necklace, knows what that ability will be."

"Wow," Griffin said.

"I thought you said the government didn't know," Brigid said. "But a president started it?"

Wane nodded. "They don't know anymore. Each president after Truman was told about the city, until the power of the necklaces was discovered. At that time, John F. Kennedy was president and he believed that that kind of power needed to be kept secret. Because of this, he delayed telling anyone about the city. He did not have the chance to give the information to a successor before he was assassinated, so the secret of our city died with him."

"And now no one knows?" James asked.

"Only the few remaining members of the task force. And the inhabitants of the city."

"The task force still exists?" Luke asked.

"Yes," Wane said. "Those still on Earth work to keep the secret protected."

They sat in silence for a moment, trying to process all that Wane had said.

Then, "How is that even possible?" Brigid asked, "A city on the moon? There isn't any air on the moon!"

Wane smiled. "No, but like I said, your great-grandfathers were very smart men. They built a barrier around the city—just like the one around this camp—that kept the city just like a normal one on Earth: oxygen, rain..."

Luke smirked. "You couldn't have told us that before?"

"Now what fun would that have been?" Wane asked.

"Really, though. Why did you wait to tell us all this? Why not from the beginning?" James asked. Wane did not answer for a moment. He stared off into the distance before meeting James' eyes again.

"Because...I couldn't just tell you. You had to figure it out on your own. It made you—and your abilities—stronger," he said.

Luke looked at him skeptically. "That didn't work out too well," he said.

Wane looked alarmed. "What do you mean?" he asked.

Luke sighed. "I don't even have a power," he said.

Wane cracked a smile. "Ah. That's because you haven't been looking in the right place," he said. Luke raised an eyebrow. Wane scanned the area. His eyes settled on a fallen branch a few feet away. He picked it up and placed it on the stump he had been sitting on. He motioned towards it, looking at Luke expectantly.

"What?" Luke demanded.

"You have no idea?" Wane asked. Luke shook his head, exasperated. Wane motioned towards the branch once again.

"Focus on the branch, Luke. Move it to the next stump over," he said. Luke stared at him as if he'd suddenly grown another head. Wane only nodded encouragingly. Luke sighed. He stared hard at the branch.

Nothing happened.

Luke let out a burst of air. "Nothing," he muttered.

"Try it again," Wane said. Luke looked annoyed, but did as he was told. He focused on the branch again. After several moments, the branch lifted into the air. Luke's eyes widened, and the branch fell back down. He looked over at Wane.

"How...?" he asked.

Wane smiled. "That's not all," he said, "Focus on the branch again. But this time, imagine that it is the one thing you hate most. Direct all of your anger towards it."

Luke nodded slowly, disbelief written clearly on his face. He stared at the branch again. This time, looking downright...menacing. Nothing happened for a moment, so Luke frowned harder.

All of a sudden, the branch exploded into flames. Luke—and everyone else—jumped.

Griffin chuckled softly. "Awesome," he whispered. Wane grinned. Luke stumbled backwards, stunned.

"No way," Luke muttered.

"Oh, but there is," Wane said, "I'm assuming everyone else figured out what their ability is?" James, Griffin, Brigid, and Marah nodded simultaneously. Wane nodded. He pointed to James.

"What is yours?" he asked.

James studied him. "Don't you already know?" he asked.

"Of course. I'm making sure *you* know."

"Oh," James said, "Materializing?"

"You're not sure?" Wane asked.

"No, I'm just not sure if that's what it's called," James said.

"You can call it whatever you want to," Wane said, "Show me."

James raised an eyebrow. Wane continued to stare at him expectantly, so he complied. He sighed and held out his hand. A moment later, a baseball appeared on the palm of his hand. He tossed it up into the air and smiled at Wane.

Wane nodded in approval. "Impressive," he said. Wane looked to Griffin next.

"And yours?" he asked. Griffin grinned and flexed his arms.

"Super strength!" he exclaimed, "And reflexes."

Wane smiled. "Very nice."

He looked to Brigid. "Teleporting," she said.

"Show me," Wane said. Brigid grinned and disappeared.

She reappeared right next to Wane. He jumped in surprise.

Griffin shook his head. "She likes to do that," he said. Wane chuckled. He turned to Marah.

"Archery," she said.

Wane raised an eyebrow. "And?" he asked.

Marah shook her head, looking perplexed. "That's all," she said.

Wane shook his head. "No it's not. You know it isn't," he said.

Marah eyes widened.

"No, I—" She stopped midsentence and shook her head.

"Yes, Marah," Wane said gently, "You've known for a while."

James stared at Marah. Griffin raised an eyebrow.

"What is it?" Brigid asked.

Marah sighed. "I can...see things...before they happen," she said.

Griffin's mouth dropped open. "Seriously?" he asked.

Marah looked down. "Seriously."

"You knew I was coming, didn't you?" Wane asked.

Marah nodded, looking pained. "Yeah."

James studied her. "Why didn't you tell us?"

Marah shrugged. "I...I don't know," she said, "It only happens in my dreams."

"No, it doesn't," Wane said.

Marah's head shot up. "But..."

"You can do it when you're awake," Wane said, "You've just never tried."

"But, I," Marah stumbled.

Wane shook his head and interrupted her. "Just try it," he said, "Close your eyes and concentrate."

Marah was hesitant, but she closed her eyes. The others stared anxiously at her.

Several moments later, Marah's eyelids flew open. Her shock was evident. She stared at nothing, staying silent for a minute.

"What did you see?" Wane asked softly.

Marah met his eyes. "A woman," she said, "A woman I've never seen..."

She stopped.

"Wait. Yes I have. Where's the picture you showed us?" she asked. Wane was shocked. He furrowed his eyebrows and handed Marah the picture. She scanned it quickly, then focused on one person. She pointed to her excitedly.

"That's her!" she exclaimed. The rest of them leaned in, straining to see who Marah was pointing at.

Griffin's eyes widened. "My mom?" he asked.

Wane sighed. "Abigail..." he muttered.

"Where was she?" Wane asked. Marah pointed to the vacant stump next to James. Wane rubbed his temples with his fingertips.

They all stared at the stump, waiting.

Sure enough, a dark haired woman appeared, standing on the stump.

Wane glared at her. "Abigail. What did we talk about?" he demanded. "You can't be here, you know that."

Abigail shrugged and smiled apologetically. "I'm sorry. I just had to see him," she said. She scanned their faces, soon landing on Griffin's. Her grin grew wider.

"Hey baby," she said.

Griffin's face turned bright red. "Mom..."

Abigail grinned. "Sorry, Wax. Just had to see him," she said. Wane frowned. James and Luke covered their mouths, trying to stifle a laugh. Abigail pulled some type of dust from her pocket, and threw it into the fire pit. At the same time as Abigail disappeared, an enormous bright blue flame erupted from the pit.

Wane shook his head. James and Luke exploded into laughter.

"It's not funny, boys," Wane muttered.

Marah chuckled. "Wax?" she asked.

Wane sighed. "Your parents are watching—have been watching, actually—from up on the moon. Apparently, Abigail heard me explain my name," he said.

Wane frowned again. "She will never let me live that one down," he muttered.

"Wait a second," Brigid said, "Our parents have been watching us...*this whole time?*"

Wane nodded. "Every second."

Griffin sighed. "Well, that puts a damper on things."

James chuckled. "Like they were bright and sunny to begin with."

"That's the truth," Luke muttered.

"So, why are we here anyways?" Marah asked.

"Good question," Wane said.

James stared at him. "You don't know the answer?" he asked.

Wane smirked. "Of course I know the answer."

"Once again," Wane said, "I'll start from the beginning."

"As you've probably figured out, one of each of your parents has special abilities, just like you do. The other doesn't. Citizens of Jericho can marry within our community, or they can return to Earth to attend college and meet someone.

"Anyway, your necklaces belonged to one of your parents—the one who has an ability. Marah: your dad is the one who has the abilities, Brigid: your mom is the one, Griffin: your mom."

Wane paused before saying the last two. A shadow crossed over his face; his expression was unreadable.

"James: your dad, Luke: your dad."

Luke stared hard at Wane, his expression a mixture of shock, confusion, and disbelief. James stared at the ground. Griffin eyed them both curiously. No one said a word.

Wane continued with his story.

"Your parents had just gained control of the city. The leadership was passed down from their parents to them—

it happens when the time is right...with every generation. And we lived peacefully for several years under their rule.

"There are several people that work closely with your parents. I am one of them. Another one—a very close friend of mine and of your parents...he..."

Wane's voice broke. Marah, Luke, James, Griffin, and Brigid looked at him nervously. Soon, he composed himself and continued.

"Our friend, he betrayed us. We never...we never saw it coming."

Wane paused again.

"We imprisoned him immediately. It was the only thing we could do. But, only a few days later, he escaped and fled to Earth."

Brigid gasped. Wane nodded slowly.

"You five were only two years old. And you were next in line to rule. We had to keep you safe. We didn't know if there were others...friends of his...still living in the city. So, we sent all of you—with your parents—down to Earth and separated you...where he would not be able to trace you."

"Why bring us together now?" James asked.

"Because...sixteen has always been the year that the necklaces are passed down to the next generation. Even in times of trouble, we do not break tradition." Wane cracked a sad smile.

"But, there is another reason. You needed to discover your powers, develop them. Because you are the ones that will fight him."

"Wait..." Brigid began.

"No..." Marah protested.

"Why..." Luke said.

"Whoa..." Griffin muttered.

"What?" James asked.

9

Wane chuckled softly. "You heard correctly. Your parents have been searching for him all of these years—to no avail. But they could not fight him anyway. He knows their powers—he knows their weaknesses. It is your battle now."

All five of them started talking at once. Wane wandered away, off in his own world. James, Griffin, and Luke continued to talk over one another. Brigid and Marah just stared at each other—neither one knew what to do or how to react.

Griffin and Luke's protests soon turned into a heated discussion. James turned away and watched Wane. He had made his way over to James' cabin. He brushed his fingers against the full moon carved into the door. He stared at it, lost in thought. James watched him closely. He had no idea what was so important about his particular phase.

Brigid spoke up, breaking James and Wane's concentration. "What are we going to have to do?" she asked softly. Wane turned towards her. He scratched the back of his neck and studied the ground. He looked up again, obviously pleased that someone was willing to help.

Griffin and Luke grew silent, looking desperately to Wane. Hoping that their tasks wouldn't be as terrible as they were imagining.

"First, we have to find him," Wane said.

"You don't even know where he is?" Griffin demanded.

Wane sighed. "No...he keeps...disappearing."

"Disappearing," Luke repeated, skeptical.

"Yes. As soon as we find him, he drops off the grid again. So, the first order of business is locating him again."

No one protested this time.

"Then what?" James asked.

"Depends on what we find," Wane said, "But, as much as I don't want it to come to this, most likely you will have to fight him at one point. He will not go down without a fight—that much is certain."

Marah sighed. James dropped his forehead into his hands.

"But, you said only our parents have powers. So, it can't be that difficult. We have powers. He doesn't," Griffin said. Brigid brightened.

Wane nodded slowly. "Yes, that's what I said. But he is powerful, nonetheless."

Griffin nodded, looking much more confident. James lifted his head, Marah's face was now calm, Luke had the beginnings of a smile on his face, and Brigid was deep in thought.

Wane studied them. "One step at a time," he said, "We'll take it one step at a time."

Night was growing closer. The sky was alive with the bright colors of the afternoon sun. James raised an eyebrow, noticing something for the first time.

"If there's a barrier, how come we can see that?" he asked.

Wane looked up at the sky. "An illusion," he said, "Personally, I like it better that way." He stood and stretched out the stiffness in his back. He stepped back up onto the stump and smiled down at the five of them.

"I'm going back up for the night. But I'll be back in the morning," he said. Then, as an afterthought, he stepped back down and pulled a small disc from his pocket. He handed it to James. James took it and looked at Wane curiously.

"What is it?" he asked.

Wane smiled, stepping back up onto the stump. "Watch them if you want. They're..." he paused, searching for the right word. "Home videos." He threw the same dust Abigail had had into the fire. The blue flames erupted with a roar, and he was gone.

Marah jumped. "What *is* that?"

Griffin shrugged. "Who knows. But it's pretty cool."

James held up the disc. "Home videos," he repeated. He shook his head. "This is crazy."

"Totally. That means we have to watch them," Griffin said, grinning.

Marah frowned. "How are we supposed to watch them? There's no TV here," she said.

Luke sighed. "You're right."

"Maybe there's one in our rooms we didn't notice," Brigid said, "Wane knows what's here. He wouldn't have given us something we couldn't watch."

James nodded. He walked to his own cabin and swung the door open. Inside, in the middle of the room, was a small television on a stand. He turned to the others.

"Okay, I *know* that wasn't there before," James said.

Luke shook his head. "Who knows. Who cares anymore. Wane probably did it somehow. I wouldn't be surprised."

"I wouldn't be surprised if it was aliens at this point," Griffin muttered.

Marah giggled. "I wouldn't go that far."

James pushed the stand up against the wall and pushed the disc in. They all sat together on the deep blue carpet in the floor. James turned out the light and joined them.

"I feel the need for popcorn," Griffin whispered. James held out his hand. A small bowl of popcorn appeared and Griffin stared at it in amazement.

"I could totally get used to this," he said, shoving a handful of the popcorn into his mouth.

Static appeared on the screen, and then a light blue carpet. The movie had begun.

The camera shook, then turned on two young boys. James recognized one as himself and the other as....Griffin? Griffin chuckled. "Dude."

The two of them sat a few feet away from each other. Baby James was sitting up, spinning dials on some type of generic baby toy. Griffin was lying on his back, a small yellow ball in his hand. Each time he squeezed the ball, it would let out a small squeak. And each time it squeaked, little Griffin would giggle hysterically.

Griffin groaned. Luke snorted, trying to hold back a laugh.

They grew silent again as a new figure came on the screen. It was Abigail, Griffin's mother. She took the ball away, much to little Griffin's dismay, and sat him upright. Then she took the toy away from James. James stared up at her, looking confused. Abigail moved out of view again.

"Play with *each other*," Abigail said. Griffin looked over at James, seeming to understand what Abigail had said. But, James was looking forward, a stoic expression on his face. He still seemed traumatized by the loss of his toy.

They heard the sound of footsteps echoing in the background.

"There you are, Emily," Abigail said. "Were you able to get him?"

"No," Emily sighed. James looked up and grinned at the sound of his mother's voice. But she was unable to pay him much attention. Before she could say anything else, the doorbell rang.

The camera shook a little. "Who could that be?" Abigail asked.

"I don't know," Emily said, sounding nervous. The camera moved closer to James and Griffin and was placed on the table in front of them.

They strained to hear the noises in the background. First, Emily and Abigail walking in the opposite direction—towards the door, most likely. Next, the door squealing in protest as it was swung open. Then, a man's voice.

At that moment, little Griffin stood up and walked over to the small table. He stuck his face in the camera so that the video only showed his eye. He started giggling again.

Griffin groaned. "Come on, little me! Move! We can't hear!"

Griffin, the one in the video, did not stop playing with the camera until the sound of the door closing interrupted him. He grew quiet, staring at something behind the camera.

All of sudden, the silence was broken by a loud sob. The sobs continued as Abigail moved onto the screen. Her eyes red, she picked up Griffin and held him on one hip. Then she lifted James onto the other. She drew a ragged breath and shut the camera off.

The screen went black.

"What was *that* about?" Griffin asked.

James shook his head, stunned. "I have no idea."

Their conversation was cut short as another video began. This time, all five of them, at about two years old, were in the video. They were sitting in the grass, in front of the same sign from Wane's picture.

"It's their last day together," Abigail said from behind the camera.

"They won't see each other for another fourteen years," Emily said sadly.

"Hard to believe." It was another woman, one they had not heard yet.

"Mom," Brigid breathed.

The women stopped talking and focused the camera on Luke, James, Griffin, Marah, and Brigid. They were playing together quietly, unaware of that day's importance. Marah and Brigid sat together, pulling at the grass. James began to walk towards them, and as soon as he did, Griffin grabbed a chunk of Luke's hair and pulled it down. Luke shrieked.

The camera shuddered as it switched hands. Abigail and another woman, Luke's mom, moved onto the screen.

"Griffin! No!" Abigail said. Griffin looked up at her, his eyes wide in a 'who, me?' expression. Luke's mother picked him up and stroked his hair. Griffin stared over at Luke and his mother, then returned his gaze to Abigail. Then his face broke into a grin. Abigail sighed. She returned to her place behind the camera and said, "He's too cute to yell at."

Emily chuckled. "Gotta love him."

And just like that, the video was over. The screen remained black for several minutes, so James shut it off.

"I guess that's all," James said.

"I was a bad kid," Griffin muttered.

Luke laughed and stroked his own blonde hair. "Just don't pull my hair again."

"I'll try," Griffin said, returning the smile.

Brigid stared at the blank screen. "I guess that was the day they brought us to Earth," she said.

"Hard to believe we've known each other since we were born. Then we get here and think we've never seen each other in our entire lives," Marah said.

"We were best friends back then," Griffin said softly. He and James exchanged a look. Luke noticed their expressions. "What?" he asked.

"We were just saying, the other day, that we'd only just met, but we felt like we'd been friends for forever. Looks like we have been," James said.

"Crazy," Brigid whispered.

"I wish we could remember at least some of it. Being there," Marah said.

"Maybe then we'd *really* know what was going on," James said.

"We'd at least know what all the sobbing was about," Griffin said, referring back to the first video.

"Oh, yeah," Luke said, "What *was* that about?"

Griffin shook his head. "No idea. Maybe they found out their friend was evil? Or that he escaped? Whichever."

"That's probably what it was," Brigid said, "Didn't seem like too far before the second video."

James nodded slowly, saying nothing.

Brigid stood and peered into the darkness outside the window. "I guess we should go ahead to bed," she said, "Who knows what Wane will make us do tomorrow."

Griffin smiled. "Good point." He stood and stretched. Everyone else followed suit. They filed out the doorway, one at a time. Griffin was the last to leave. He held the door open and turned to James.

"Night," Griffin said.

James smiled at him. "Good night."

"Pretty successful day, don't you think?" Griffin asked.

James chuckled, then grew somber. "There's still questions."

Griffin nodded. "At least now we have some answers."

10

When the five of them awoke the next morning, Wane had not yet arrived. They met outside to wait. Marah motioned towards the chalkboard.

"I guess that's not going to tell us what we're doing anymore," she said.

Griffin nodded. "Kind of sad, actually. I'm going to miss it."

James chuckled.

Wane appeared on one of the tree stumps and smiled at them.

"Good morning!" Wane exclaimed.

The five of them returned the greeting.

"What's the plan for today?" Griffin asked.

Wane smiled. "Well, I thought I'd show you something."

James and Griffin exchanged glances. Marah looked at Wane curiously.

"What?" Luke asked.

"You'll see," Wane said. He led them down the pathway they, by now, could walk down with their eyes closed. He turned down one of the side paths and came up to the lake. They all stared at the lake, then at Wane.

"What's so special about it?" Griffin asked.

Wane grinned. He pulled a small remote control from his pocket and pressed a button. All of sudden, the dock began to lift up, revealing a flight of wooden stairs beneath it.

The five of them stared at the staircase in shock. None of them knew what to say.

Wane chuckled. "Pretty cool, huh?" He led them down the staircase, their heads swiveling back and forth in curiosity as they made their way down.

"Are we going *under* the lake?" Brigid asked.

"Yes," Wane said.

Marah stopped abruptly. "Isn't that dangerous? What if the ceiling collapses?"

Wane smiled up at her. "No need to worry. It's perfectly safe."

Marah sighed, but followed him farther down. Finally, they reached a door at the bottom of the stairs. Wane swung it open, and once again, the five of them were rendered speechless.

Wane had led them to a large, circular room. It was completely filled with television screens, computers, and technology they had never seen before. Directly across from them was a huge screen that stretched from the ceiling to the floor. It was several feet wide—it would probably have filled the entire wall of a rectangular room.

Marah looked up and gasped. James was standing beside her, so she gripped his arm and pointed. The ceiling was clear. They were able to see the water and all of the fish in the lake. Brigid's eyes widened.

Wane chuckled. "I promise, it is completely safe."

James stroked Marah's arm comfortingly. She reluctantly let go of his arm. She took a deep breath and stepped into the room, trying not to look up. Once they had all filed in, Wane closed the door. He flipped a switch, and all of the computers hummed to life. The large screen in the back blinked on, and a message box popped up. It said: 'Welcome! Please enter your password.'

Wane walked over to the screen and opened up a virtual keyboard. He typed in a string of letters that the five of them were not quick enough to see. He turned to them, as if a thought had just occurred to him.

"If you ever need to get into this and I'm not here, the password is 'Moonstone'," he said.

"What is 'Moonstone' anyway?" James asked. "Why is it so important?"

"Well," Wane said, "It's what your necklaces are made out of. Dust from a moonstone is what I use to go back and forth between here and Jericho. And, we just like it."

Luke chuckled. "Okay then."

The screen loaded quickly. On it was a map of the entire Earth, with small red dots in various places. It was, apparently, the last thing Wane had been doing on the screen.

"What is that?" James asked.

"It's where he—the man we're trying to find—has been," Wane said. He pointed to a red dot in almost the exact center of Canada. "That's where he was spotted last. And then he just...disappeared."

"We'll find him," Brigid said softly.

Wane smiled at her. "I know you will."

* * *

Several hours later, Brigid was still seated in front of one of the many computer screens. Luke, Griffin, and James were sprawled out on the beanbag chairs in one corner of the room. Marah had found a kitchenette behind one of the doors in the main room and was busy making lemonade.

They had found out that Brigid had another skill—she knew everything and anything about computers. Wane sat beside her, watching her work in amazement.

She turned to him. "What if he changed his name again?"

Wane sighed. "I thought of that. But, all we have to go by right now is that he went by Michael Roth in Canada."

"And that's not his actual name?" Brigid asked.

"No."

"What is it then?"

Wane paused. "Marcus."

Brigid returned to her research. James stood and made his way over to them.

"Sorry I couldn't be of more help," he said. Brigid looked up at him and smiled.

"That's fine. At least you tried." She motioned towards Luke and Griffin. "Maybe you can go get those two bumps on logs to do something."

James grinned. "Sure thing."

Marah poked her head out of the kitchen. "Lemonade, anyone?"

Brigid looked over, nodded and smiled, then continued working.

James nodded. "Thanks."

Griffin and Luke lifted their thumbs in agreement. Marah chuckled and shook her head. "Coming right up."

Marah brought two cups of lemonade out at a time. She handed the first two to Wane and Brigid, the next two to James and herself, and the last two to Luke and Griffin. Griffin took a tentative sip.

"This is great!" he exclaimed.

Marah laughed. "Thank you," she said. "Now help Brigid, would you?"

Griffin stood and bowed to her playfully.

Luke frowned. "I'm technologically impaired," he protested.

"Nice try. I'm useless with computers too, and I'm making lemonade," Marah said. "You can find something."

All of sudden, Brigid shrieked in delight. Luke jumped up.

"You found him?" he asked.

"Yes!" she exclaimed. "Well, maybe."

"Pull it up," Wane said. Brigid typed something into her computer and the information appeared on the large screen.

"There's a Michael Roth that just moved to Texas," she said.

James smiled. "Impressive."

Griffin stretched. "Well, that wasn't so hard, was it?"

Brigid shot him a look and turned back to the screen.

"Do you have a picture of him?" Wane asked.

"Yes, I just found it," Brigid said. She pulled up a picture of a middle-aged man with short, light brown hair. She looked at Wane expectantly.

"Is that him?"

Wane's face fell. "No. It's not him."

Brigid sank back down into her chair. "Oh."

Marah sighed. "Looks like this is going to take a lot longer than we thought."

Brigid nodded, her frown growing deeper. She looked exhausted.

Marah looked at her, concerned. "Maybe we should just call it a day," she offered.

Brigid nodded gratefully.

"I agree," Wane said, "Get some dinner and take the evening off. We're starting more training in the morning."

Griffin groaned. "Haven't we done enough?"

Wane shook his head, his expression serious. "You can never be too ready."

* * *

Griffin yawned. "I thought we were done with training!"

It was the next day, and he and James were sparring in the gym. Luke sat across the room, half-heartedly curling with one arm.

James swung at Griffin, hardly paying attention to the fight. Griffin took advantage of James' lapse of interest and tripped him, sending James crashing to the floor.

James sat there for a moment, then fell back with a sigh. He tossed his sword aside and curled up into a ball.

"Wake me when he comes back," James said.

Griffin lowered himself to the ground as well. He glanced over at Luke, whose curls were growing further and further apart.

"I believe I said to train, not sleep!" Wane boomed from the doorway. James shot up, his eyes red. Griffin stood up slowly and rubbed his eyes.

"I don't know what you're talking about," Griffin said. He stifled a yawn.

Wane smirked. "I'm working with Marah and Brigid right now." He paused, surveying the three of them. "You're next."

Luke nodded, his eyes only halfway open. "Cool."

"Look, kids," Wane said. "I know you're tired, but you need to take this seriously. It's only a matter of time before we find him. And you need to be ready."

Wane shook his head and closed the door. As soon as he was gone, James and Griffin collapsed back onto the floor.

"I can't do this for much longer," Griffin muttered. "It's unnatural to wake up with the sun rise."

James rolled over. "Get used to it."

* * *

Marah and Brigid stood together, facing Wane, in front of one of the targets on the archery field.

Wane lifted an arrow that had its tip removed. "Battle techniques. We'll use these so I don't hit you with an actual arrow."

Brigid stared at him. "You're going to be shooting arrows at us?"

Wane grinned. "Pretty much."

"Stay there," Wane said. He jogged to the line of trees and turned to face them again. He lifted his bow and one of the disassembled arrows.

"Dodge these!" he shouted. Marah and Brigid glanced at each other. Wane shot the first arrow straight at Marah. She stepped to the side and easily dodged it.

The next was aimed at Brigid. She too dodged it easily. Brigid smiled at Marah. "Not as hard as we thought," she said.

As soon as she had finished speaking, Wane sent over twenty arrows raining down on them. They both shrieked and tried to dodge them, unsuccessfully.

"Hey!" Brigid shouted. Wane shrugged. He loaded another oversized group of arrows into the bow and shot them in Marah and Brigid's direction.

But, they were ready this time. They both dropped to the ground, allowing the arrows to pass over them. Marah stood, brushed her hands off, and smiled at Wane. Wane grinned back, and nodded in approval.

Next, he loaded a single arrow into the bow. Marah raised an eyebrow and exchanged glances with Brigid. Brigid shrugged. Wane aimed the arrow for Marah and let it go.

Marah tried to step away, like she had with the first arrow, but this one followed her. Her eyes widened. She tried to change directions again, but the arrow continued to follow her. She stopped, and let it hit her. She picked up the arrow from the ground and looked over at Wane. He moved closer.

"Specialized arrow. Once its set on a target, it will follow it until it hits it."

"Then how do you *not* get hit?" Marah asked.

"Destroy the arrow before it hits you," Wane said.

Brigid sighed. "Right. Easy enough."

"That's the spirit!" Wane exclaimed. He moved back to his place by the trees and pulled out another arrow.

"Let's try this again," he announced. Both Brigid and Marah took a deep breath. Wane aimed it for Marah again and let it fly.

Before Marah or Wane had a chance to react, Brigid had disappeared, reappeared beside the arrow, pulled it out of the air, and snapped it in half.

"Like that?" she asked.

Wane's eyes widened in surprise. "Yeah," he finally managed to say.

Marah shook her head and laughed. "I'm staying with her during battle," she announced.

Wane chuckled. "I might have to agree with you on that one."

Wane motioned for Marah and Brigid to join him.

"I think that's good for today. Go do some work in the gym and tell the guys to come out here."

They nodded and headed down the path.

"Good job!" Wane called after them.

"Thanks!"

* * *

When Marah and Brigid arrived at the gym, they found Luke, Griffin, and James lying on the wrestling mat— sound asleep.

Marah laughed softly and shook her head. Brigid grinned, amused. They glanced at each other and tip-toed over to the edge of the mat.

Griffin began to snore, and Marah struggled not to laugh. She reached for the sword lying next to James and picked it up. She motioned for Brigid to do the same with the sword next to Griffin. Marah held up the sword and acted out her plan to Brigid.

Brigid grinned and nodded. They both held up their swords, and Marah counted down on her fingers. 3, 2, 1...

Both swords clattered to the ground.

All three guys jumped up and looked around wildly. Marah and Brigid burst into laughter.

"Not cool," Griffin said, his voice thick with sleep. James tried to tame his hair—which had begun to stick out in every direction.

Brigid grinned. "Rise and shine," she said.

"Ha, ha. Very funny," Luke muttered.

"It's your turn with Wane," Marah said.

Griffin groaned. "Great."

They staggered towards the door, still hardly awake. James was the last to leave. He held up his hand and nodded at Marah and Brigid. "Wish us luck," he said.

Brigid laughed. "Have fun!"

As soon as the guys were gone, Brigid and Marah turned to look at the empty gym. They stood, silent and unmoving, for a while.

"What are we supposed to do?" Brigid asked.

Marah carefully lifted one of the swords. She handed it to Brigid, and then took the other for herself.

"I guess we teach ourselves how to sword fight," she said.

Brigid stared at the weapon in her hands. She twisted it left and right, watching as the light bounced off of the metal. "Should be...interesting."

* * *

On the other side of the trees, Luke, James, and Griffin were just arriving at the archery field. They were less than enthusiastic about the whole situation.

Wane, who was kneeling down beside the box of arrows, turned at the sound of their approach. He motioned for them to join him.

The three of them knelt down beside Wane.

"What are you doing?" James asked. Wane was in the process of pulling the sharp tip off of one of the arrows.

"Removing the tips," Wane said.

Griffin raised an eyebrow. "We got that part. *Why* are you doing it?"

Wane smiled to himself. He pulled the tip off of the arrow and set it in the box. He held up the rest of the arrows for them to see.

"I'm taking off the sharp part so you don't bleed when I hit you with it," Wane said.

Griffin furrowed his eyebrows. "Say what?"

"You'll see," Wane said. He jogged over to the line of trees, beside the path, and held up his bow. James, Luke, and Griffin stood beside the targets, facing him. They glanced at each other, looking skeptical and slightly nervous.

All of sudden, Wane sent a cloud of arrows down on them. They jerked in surprise, trying to avoid getting hit, but it was no use.

"Uncalled for!" Griffin shouted.

Wane raised his bow again. Griffin dropped to the ground and covered his head with his hands. Wane lowered his bow back down, the hint of a smile on his face.

"I haven't even shot at you yet!" Wane yelled at Griffin.

Griffin looked up. "I'm being proactive!" he shouted back.

Luke glanced over at James, then looked down at Griffin.

"Do you even know what that means?" Luke asked.

Griffin stood up and brushed the grass off of his shirt. "Not really. But it sounded right."

James chuckled. Wane sighed and walked back over to them.

Wane lifted up one of the arrows. "I'm going to shoot these at you."

"I'm still not entirely comfortable with that," Griffin interrupted.

"You didn't let me finish," Wane said, trying to hide his smile. "I'm going to shoot these at you, and you have to dodge them. I'm preparing you for battle. And Griffin, it will not hurt if it hits you."

"Well, that's good news. But...battle?!" Griffin asked, his eyes wide.

"Just in case. It's a...precaution. Have to be prepared," Wane said. He let out a weak chuckle and returned to his place by the trees.

"Alright," he shouted, "Just dodge the arrows!"

Wane shot a single arrow in Griffin's direction and he side-stepped it easily. He raised an eyebrow at Wane. Griffin looked warily at James, who shrugged.

Wane loaded another arrow, this time aiming it in Luke's direction. Luke tried to step aside, as Griffin had done, but the arrow followed him. The arrow followed his movements, no matter which direction he went in. Luke took off running in the opposite direction.

After a few moments, Luke turned around and started jogging backwards. He faced the arrow, a look of concentration on his face. Griffin and James looked at him curiously, unable to figure out what he was doing. Then, the arrow burst into flames.

"Oh," Griffin said.

Wane jogged over to the three of them, arriving at the same time Luke did.

"Well, I guess we don't have to do that again. You figured out the trick the first time."

"What *was* that?" Luke asked.

"Specialized arrow. Set it on a target and it will follow it until it hits it."

Griffin sighed. "Fantastic."

Wane chuckled. "Isn't it?"

* * *

Marah and Brigid turned at the sound of the guys coming through the door. James came in first, but he didn't see Marah and Brigid right away. He looked around, confused. Griffin and Luke wandered in after him.

"Where are they?" Griffin asked.

"Up here!" Marah called. James, Luke, and Griffin looked up at the same time. Marah smiled and began her descent down the wooden ladder. Brigid followed close behind.

"What were you doing up there?" Luke asked.

Brigid smiled. "We gave up on sword fighting...so we decided to look around. There's a lot of cool stuff up there!"

"Did you enjoy dodging arrows?" Marah asked, a teasing glint in her eye.

James laughed. "Sure."

Griffin lowered himself slowly onto the wrestling mat. Brigid sat next to him, and Marah next to her. James sat down next to Marah, and then Luke sat next to him, completing the circle. Brigid leaned back on her hands and yawned.

Griffin nodded. "I agree."

Luke ran a hand through his hair, looking distracted.

James studied him. "What is it?" he asked.

"I don't know. It's just..." Luke paused. "Something's been bothering me."

Brigid leaned forward. "What's wrong?"

Luke now had everyone's full attention. He looked uncomfortable. "It's probably nothing," he said.

James shook his head. "No, it's something," he said. "Tell us."

Luke sighed. "It's just that I don't think that my dad is the one that should have powers."

Griffin raised an eyebrow. "Why not?"

"Because...I don't even know my dad. He left my mom and me when I was a kid."

"I'm sorry," Marah said.

Griffin frowned. "He just...left?"

"Yeah. I don't really know why," Luke said.

"Your mom never told you?" Brigid asked.

Luke shook his head.

"And you don't find that strange?" Griffin asked.

"No. Why else would he leave?"

"I don't know..." Marah began.

Luke interrupted her. "It was his choice. And I've always hated him for it."

"Have you asked Wane about it?" James asked.

Luke stared at him. "No. Why should I?"

"We just found out today that the first two years of our life were spent *on the moon*," James said. "Who knows what else they haven't told us?"

"What are you saying?" Luke asked.

"I'm saying that it might not have been your dad's choice to leave you."

Luke stared at his hands. "I don't know."

"You should ask him," Griffin suggested.

Luke still looked skeptical. "Why would he have to leave though? All of your parents came down to Earth with you. What's so different about mine?"

No one had an answer for that.

Griffin scratched his head nervously. "I don't know, man. But I'm sure Wane could tell you."

Luke sighed. "I guess I can ask him tomorrow."

Griffin groaned. "Tomorrow. He's going to make us train more tomorrow, isn't he?"

"Most likely," James said, laughing.

Griffin stood up slowly. "I'm going to bed now, then."

11

Early the next morning, Brigid stood in front of her bathroom mirror. She stared at herself, trying to figure out where the dark bags under her eyes had come from—and why they wouldn't go away.

She pulled on one of the few clean t-shirts she had left. It was still warm out, but summer was almost over. Would they be out of here before winter? Or, she thought, was this the new normal? Brigid shuddered at the thought. She wondered if she would ever see her old home again.

She tried to push the fears from her mind. Focus on the positive. That was what she had always told herself—even as a little girl. But it had been easier then.

Brigid sighed and pushed the door open, stepping out into the fresh morning air. Luke sat on one of the tree stumps, not too far away.

"Sleep well?" she asked, sitting down beside him.

"Not at all."

"You didn't sleep well? Or you didn't sleep at all?" Brigid asked.

Luke looked up at her. He smirked. "I didn't sleep at all."

Brigid frowned. "Because...of what you told us yesterday?"

"Yeah, pretty much," Luke said. He stared at the ground.

"Are you going to ask him?"

Brigid gained his attention back. He met her eyes and sighed. "I don't know."

"You should."

Luke cracked a smile. "Oh, really?"

Brigid blushed. "Yes. Don't you want to know?"

"I thought so. But..." Luke paused.

"But, what?"

"But...I don't know what I want anymore."

Brigid nodded. "I know what you mean."

They sat in silence for a moment. Both of them staring forward, deep in their own frustrations.

"It still couldn't hurt to ask," Brigid said.

Luke chuckled. "I guess you're right."

Brigid smiled triumphantly.

"I'll think about it," Luke said.

Brigid's face fell. Luke laughed aloud.

"I will," he said.

"Promise?"

"Promise."

* * *

Several hours later, Luke and Griffin stood back to back, breathless. They were in the middle of a mock battle Wane had put together.

Griffin sucked in a breath of air. "Ask him," he said, before sprinting away. Luke was caught off guard; he lost focus for only a second.

"Luke!" Brigid shrieked from a few feet away. He dropped to the ground just as three arrows whizzed over his head.

"Good!" he heard Wane shout. There was an explosion behind him. He dodged a few more arrows. Another explosion. More arrows.

Now was not the time.

The problem was, Luke couldn't seem to convince himself that anytime was right. There had been several instances that day where he could have asked. But he didn't.

The smoke lifted. Luke looked around in surprise. He spotted the others quickly, who looked just as stunned.

"Not what you expected, was it?" Wane said, seeming to appear through the smoke.

Brigid shook her head slowly. The five of them began picking their way through the rubble, towards each other. Wane led them to a patch of untouched grass. He motioned for them to sit.

"Rest," he said. They sat down gratefully. Wane allowed them a few moments of silence as the ringing in their ears began to fade.

Marah gasped, startling everyone. She pointed at Griffin's leg. Blood was trickling down the side of it. Griffin looked down in alarm, but when he realized what she had been referring to, he relaxed.

"No big deal," he said. Wane pulled a bandage from his pocket and tossed it to Griffin.

"No really, I don't-"

"Just in case," Wane said.

"I had to show you what battle would be like. But even this is nothing compared to what a real battle can be like," Wane said. He motioned towards Griffin's leg. "There are a lot worse things that can happen. And Marcus will stop at nothing to make sure of it."

The mood grew solemn, even more so than it had been a moment before.

James spoke up. "How are we supposed to win? We've only started training...and Marcus is..." he hesitated.

"Experienced," Griffin finished.

Wane nodded. "You'll be ready."

He nodded again, as if trying to convince himself. "Well," he said, "That's all for today." He turned and strode away.

Griffin eyed Luke. "Wait, Wane!" he shouted. Luke stared at Griffin, his look of surprise turning quickly into a glare.

Wane turned around. "Yes?"

"Luke has something to ask you," Griffin said. Luke shot Griffin another hateful look. Wane raised his eyebrows expectantly.

"Um," Luke began, "What...what training will we be doing tomorrow?"

Wane stared at him for a moment, almost seeing right through him. Luke held his breath. Then, Wane smiled. "You'll have to wait and see," he said. He turned and walked away. Luke sighed in relief.

Now, Griffin glared at Luke. "Why won't you ask him?"

Luke said nothing for a long time. Finally, he stood up.

"I don't know," he said. Then he disappeared down the pathway.

Griffin shook his head. "What's so hard about this?" he asked. "Why won't he just ask already?"

Marah only shrugged.

"It's his deal. There may be more we don't know about," James said.

Griffin sighed. "Whatever. But if he doesn't hurry up and ask, I will."

James chuckled.

"He'll ask. When he's ready," Brigid said softly. Griffin looked at her in surprise.

"And how do you know this?"

Brigid smiled and shrugged. "I just know."

12

"How are we supposed to get in?" Griffin asked, staring intently at the wooden dock.

"No clue. Didn't he have some kind of remote?" James said.

A twig snapped behind them. The five of them turned their heads at the exact same time. Wane gave them a slight wave.

"Good. You're all here," Wane said. "I was going to suggest we start in here today."

"I wanted to ask you about something," Luke blurted out. Brigid and Griffin exchanged shocked glances. James studied Luke, trying to find the drastic change between the night before and this morning. Wane looked at Luke curiously. He said nothing at first, only pulled out his remote and pressed the button. The dock lifted up, and they filed down the staircase. Luke followed directly behind Wane, and the others drifted a little farther behind. Griffin turned to them, his eyes wide. "That was fast," he murmured. When they made it to the room, Wane turned to Luke.

"What did you want to ask me about?" Wane asked.

Luke had grown hesitant again. Griffin nudged him forward. Wane walked over to one of the computers and Luke followed him. Wane leaned down, opened something up on the computer, then paused and looked back at Luke.

"What is it?" Wane asked.

Luke paused. "My dad can't be the one with powers."

Wane stared warily at Luke. He raised a cautious eyebrow. "And why not?"

"He left my mom...she said he left her."

Wane sighed. "She said that?"

"Yes. Is it true?"

"You know she did what she did to protect you. She couldn't tell you then where you were from. She couldn't tell you all that you know now."

"I know that," Luke said. "But what about my dad? Why couldn't he come with us?"

Luke motioned towards Griffin, Marah, James, and Brigid. "Their parents did."

Wane shifted his gaze to the four of them. He stared at them for a long time, saying nothing. Finally, he turned back to Luke.

"That's something your mother needs to tell you," he said.

Luke frowned. "But, why can't you—"

Wane pounded his fist on the table. Luke jumped back, startled. Luke, Griffin, Marah, Brigid, and James had the exact same looks on their faces—complete shock, confusion...and the expression that, for the past few days, none of them could seem to mask. Fear.

Wane met their eyes. He looked ashamed. He stared at the floor and took a deep breath. Finally, he looked up at Luke.

"It's something she has to do. She'll tell you when she's ready."

"Can't you just tell me?" Luke asked.

"Luke...it's not my place. I'm sorry." Wane sighed heavily and turned back to the computer screen.

Luke stood still, staring at him. He didn't know how to react.

Finally, he turned around. James searched his face, trying to figure out what he was thinking. Marah tried to reach out and console him. But Luke didn't see either of them. He had a faraway look in his eyes—he was somewhere else entirely.

Luke passed Marah and James without acknowledging either of them. Griffin and Brigid tried to reach out for him next, but he passed them too. He came to the wall and turned around to lean against it. Slowly, he slid down into a sitting position. He still had that look on his face: shock mixed with hurt, glossy eyes fixed on nothing in particular.

Marah started to go over to him, but James stopped her.

"Leave him," he said softly. "He needs to deal with it himself right now."

Marah met James' eyes. She sighed and nodded slightly.

Griffin shuffled his feet. With Luke and Wane lost in their own worlds, the rest of them were at a loss of what to do. They stared at each other, waiting for something to happen.

Nothing did.

Brigid sighed and moved over to one of the computers. She pulled out the chair and sat down. Marah, James, and Griffin followed, gathering behind her chair. She looked up at them and shrugged.

"Might as well do something," she said. Griffin nodded in agreement.

James studied Griffin, noticing for the first time how tired he looked. Surprised, he turned to Marah. She too looked tired—it looked as if she had aged five years overnight. Suddenly, his vision narrowed and the room seemed to close in around him.

He couldn't take it anymore.

He glanced at Luke, saw the expression on his face that could only mean that his world was crashing down around him. And he knew that it was only a matter of time before it happened to one of the others—before the news was worse, before the things they loved were gone and sanity was no longer an option.

James backed away from the group without them noticing. He moved quietly to the door, pulled it open and started up the stairs. Once he knew that he was out of earshot, he took off running and didn't stop until he was back out in the open. He gulped in the fresh air, relishing in the harsh wind that whipped at his face.

He stopped and tilted his face towards the sky. He closed his eyes and breathed in slowly.

James opened his eyes and looked down at his shaking hands. He continued to take deep breaths, attempting to calm himself down.

Everything was going too fast. And he could tell that the situation was taking a toll on all of them.

He wanted to go back to the simplicity of life with his mother, life where school—which had never truly been that difficult for him—was his only worry. Life where he could see the real sun, where he knew his own home. Life where he didn't have to worry for the lives of himself and his friends. But he couldn't think about that, couldn't think that way. Not yet.

He steadied himself and started back down the stairs.

Wane's words came back to him, and he repeated them over and over.

"One step at a time," he told himself. "One step at a time."

* * *

Marah turned at the sound of James' return. She gave him a knowing look. Though he didn't know it, she could clearly read every emotion on his face. She put a comforting hand on his shoulder. He smiled at her, then pressed a hand on the back of Brigid's chair.

He forced a smile. "What are we working on?"

Brigid looked back at him. He saw the concern on her face before she quickly forced it away. She focused back on the computer screen before answering.

"Searching everything possible that could help us find him," Brigid said.

"Sounds complicated," Griffin said.

Brigid nodded. "It is."

"Do we even know what this guy looks like?" James asked.

Brigid shook her head, a grim expression on her face. "Not really. The last time they found him he had brown hair. But apparently, the time before that he was a blonde."

"Fantastic," Griffin muttered.

James stared at the computer screen. "So...we have pretty much...nothing to go on."

Brigid sighed. "Exactly."

13

"Are you sure you're alright?" Marah asked. She and Luke were seated next to each other at the dinner table. The others turned their focus to the two of them, waiting for Luke's answer.

Wane was not present; he had decided to retire to his cabin early.

Luke nodded slowly. He pushed the food around on his plate. "Yeah. Fine."

"You haven't eaten a single thing yet," Marah interjected.

"Sorry, mother," Luke said, sticking a bite of chicken in his mouth.

"Hey," Griffin said, "She's just trying to help you."

Marah nodded. Her face had hardened, she refused to say anything else.

"Like I said. I'm fine," Luke said.

The rest of them didn't argue with him any further. Silence fell over the table. Finally, Brigid stood, her chair scraping against the tile floor.

"This is stupid," she announced. "We only have each other right now. And if we're fighting each other already, we'll never win against...against whoever it is we're fighting."

Griffin sighed. "You're right."

James and Marah nodded in agreement.

"Sorry," Luke mumbled.

Brigid nodded. "Good." She sat back down. At the same time, Luke stood up and walked out of the dining hall. The door slammed behind him. The remaining four stared at the door in a shocked silence.

Brigid sighed heavily. "Or not."

"It was a good try," James said.

Griffin shook his head. "I don't get him."

"I don't think anyone does," Marah said. She stood up and brushed the long waves of brown hair off of her shoulder. "I guess we should go ahead and head back."

The others followed her out the door. It was already dark out, but the moon offered enough light to see by. Marah stared up at it. James followed her gaze, then looked at her expectantly. She met his eyes.

"Isn't it weird? Thinking that our parents are up there right now?" she asked.

James smiled and nodded. "We've looked up at it all of our lives. But I never would have thought that I was born there."

"Seems impossible," Griffin whispered.

"Everything that's happened since we got here seems impossible," Brigid said.

Griffin chuckled. "True."

They continued down the pathway to their cabins. Brigid passed by Luke's cabin on the way to her own. The room was dark, but she could see movement inside the window. She stared at the closed door for a long time before finally moving on to her own.

Brigid turned and met the eyes of Griffin, Marah, and James. She offered a weak smile.

Marah returned the smile. "Good night," she whispered.

* * *

The camp was enveloped in darkness. There were still several hours until the sun would rise. But, Luke was wide awake.

He had only gotten minutes of sleep at a time, and he had finally given up completely. Now, he sat on the end of his bed, staring at the shadows on the floor.

The darkness reminded him of home. The electricity came and went, and it had stopped bothering him by the time he was old enough to understand why. It was the same with his mother. She was always there physically. But emotionally...not nearly as often.

The responsibility of taking care of the house, and taking care of her, usually fell on him. So, he did what he had to do and no more than that. Then he got as far away as he could, running daily through the woods behind the small house, going as long as his body would allow. But for some reason, he had always come back.

This time...he probably wouldn't. Probably couldn't.

Luke pushed off the bed slowly. He walked mindlessly around the small room, finally deciding to stop at his open suitcase on the floor. He unzipped one of the pockets and pulled out the small piece of paper. It was a note his mom had stuck in the bag before he left—he had found it on the first night.

He unfolded the paper and read it again.

Have a great time. I love you. -Mom

Luke sighed and crumbled the note in his hand. He shoved it back into his suitcase. What else hadn't his mom told him?

He didn't know what to do anymore. He didn't know what to believe anymore. He didn't know who to trust.

He pushed his door open and stepped out into the darkness. He scanned the row of cabins. It was completely silent, except for a light snoring coming from Griffin's cabin. Luke smirked. He sat down on one of the stumps and stared at the fire pit. He stared hard at the embers, willing a flame to appear.

Nothing happened.

Luke blew out a gust of air, exasperated. He tried again, and a small flame appeared, but it was immediately extinguished. He gritted his teeth and focused harder.

A larger flame appeared this time, and it remained for a few moments before going out.

He created several small bursts of fire, one after another. He stopped, breathing heavily, and rested his forehead in his hands.

A few feet away, James lay in bed, staring at the ceiling. He had just awoken from only a few hours of fitful sleep. He couldn't slow the whirlwind of thoughts in his mind. It had grown stronger each day, and it seemed that the more he found out, the more he realized he didn't know.

James took a deep breath and closed his eyes. But he knew it was useless. Sleep would not come.

He swung his legs over the side of the bed, sitting up slowly. The night was warm—and silent. James had grown to hate the silence.

The sound of flames crackling startled him.

He turned his head to the sound. It was silent again. Had he imagined it? Then...there it was again. He rose and peered through the window.

Luke was seated on one of the tree stumps by the fire pit, his back to James. Sparks from small flames rose up every few seconds. James guessed that Luke had been unable to sleep, like James had, and decided to practice.

Luke stood up abruptly, just as James began to step away from the window. Luke walked purposefully towards his cabin.

James furrowed his eyebrows and waited.

A few moments later, Luke returned. He stood over the fire pit, his fists clenched. He lifted one and let a small, crumpled piece of paper fall. Luke stared at the paper. James could see the conflict in his eyes. Luke took a deep breath, stared down at the paper, and it burned.

14

Early the next morning, Griffin pounded on Luke's door. James, Marah, and Brigid stood behind him. Receiving no answer, Griffin turned to the others.

"I have very little patience left," he said. James shook his head and stepped in front of Griffin. As soon as he had lifted his fist to knock, the door swung open. A disheveled, red-eyed Luke stared out at them. Without a word, he closed the door behind himself and pushed past them. Griffin watched him go, his mouth agape.

Marah sighed and started after him. They followed Luke all the way to the dining hall, never quite closing the distance between themselves and him. Wane met the group at the door.

He frowned before speaking. "I'd like to apologize for yesterday," Wane said. "I wish I could tell you everything, but it's not important right now. We need to focus on your training, and I have to do everything I can to make sure you are ready."

The five of them nodded. Wane smiled.

"Eat a good breakfast," he said. "Long day ahead." He gave them a slight wave and took off in the opposite direction.

Griffin sighed. "Yay."

They filed into the building and filled their plates. They sat in the same seats they had used since the first day. It was the only sense of normalcy they had left—and they clung to it.

Marah picked at the food on her plate. She looked around at the others. They were doing the same.

"Wonder what it is we're doing," she said.

Brigid shrugged.

Griffin took a piece of his bacon, folded it in half, then stuck it in his mouth. He chewed it slowly and eyed the others, deep in thought. He swallowed and cleared his throat.

"Well, it's obviously not going to be fun if we're acting like this," he said. "No, it's not exactly my idea of fun, but we have to do it. And we're just making it worse by being all depressed about it."

James cracked a smile. "I agree."

Marah nodded in agreement.

Brigid sighed. "You're right." She nudged Luke with her elbow. He lifted his head and looked around.

He cut his eyes at Brigid. "Mhmm."

"Good," Griffin said. "It's settled then. We will have fun."

James chuckled. "Sounds good to me."

Conversation picked up, and they finished breakfast in much better spirits. They stepped out into the sunshine to find Wane waiting for them.

"Ready?" he asked.

"Ready," the five of them answered simultaneously.

Wane raised an eyebrow. "Well, good."

He led them down the pathway and towards the baseball field.

"We're playing baseball again?" Griffin asked incredulously.

Wane chuckled. "You will see."

They arrived at the field a few moments later. The five of them looked around at the vacant field, then at each other. A gust of wind rustled the leaves on the trees surrounding them. They looked at Wane questioningly.

He pulled the remote out of his pocket—the same one he had used to open up the lab under the lake.

"Oh great," Griffin muttered. James raised an eyebrow.

"I mean, oh great!" Griffin whispered. James chuckled. They both turned back to Wane and waited to see what he would do with the remote.

Wane pressed a button and looked up. The five of them turned to the sound of metal sliding against metal. They watched in amazement as the two halves of the baseball diamond slid away from each other. Giant boulders that looked more like small islands floated up from the space underneath the field. They floated upwards until they were several hundred feet above their heads, and stopped, suspended in mid-air. Luke, Marah, Brigid, Griffin, and James gaped. Wane only smiled.

More things came up from the vast space underneath the baseball field. Two pillars rose up to the right of the boulders; they had spinning blades attached to the top.

Brigid whimpered.

On the other side of the rocks, what seemed to be a starting platform rose up. Then, more boulders appeared on the other side of the spinning blades. Finally, at the end of the rocks, there was a tall concrete wall with barbed wire along the top.

The five of them stared at the course in shocked silence. Griffin's mouth dropped open. Marah looked over at him.

"You call this fun?" Marah whispered. Griffin shook his head slowly, his eyes never leaving the sharp blades above him—they were spinning at least one hundred miles an hour.

"Alright," Wane announced. "This is your obstacle course. Good luck!"

They all turned and stared at him.

"You're joking, right?" Brigid asked.

"Not at all," Wane replied calmly.

Still, no one moved.

Wane sighed. "Here," he said. He pulled the remote out of his pocket and hit another button. A net that spanned the length of the course rose out of the hole and came up halfway between the rocks and the ground. Wane pressed yet another button and the ground closed back up again.

"Better?" he asked.

"Not really," Griffin said.

"Go," Wane said.

They shuffled over to the starting platform, grumbling the whole way there. James reached the platform first. He looked up, craning his neck to see the top.

"How do we get up?" he shouted.

"Other side," Wane shouted back.

By that time, the other four had arrived at the platform. They followed James to the other side. They stared at the rope ladder that hung down the length of the structure.

Griffin groaned. "You have *got* to be kidding me," he muttered.

James heaved a sigh and started up the ladder. The others followed suit. Several minutes later, all five of them were standing on top of the platform, staring across the field at the rocks.

"Take it slow," Wane shouted. "Work together."

James took a deep breath and jumped onto the first rock. It shook, and James steadied himself before slowly standing up. Griffin steeled himself to jump.

"Wait!" James shouted.

Griffin looked up, startled. "What?"

"We have to figure out how we're going to do this. If we all just jump on, the rock is going to tip."

"Just balance the weight every time another person jumps on," Brigid said.

Griffin looked over at her in surprise. "Oh," he said. "Good idea." He looked over at James. "Can I jump now?"

James nodded. "Sure."

Griffin backed up to get a running start. Then he leapt onto the rock. It shook even harder than the first time. James crouched down to keep from falling. He and Griffin moved slowly towards opposite sides until the rock was balanced. They stood up, and Griffin let out a breath. He motioned for someone else to jump on.

Marah, Brigid, and Luke glanced at each other.

"I'll go," Luke said. He took a few steps back, ran, and jumped onto the rock. It took them a lot longer this time to steady the rock. Once they had, they stayed crouched down, their hands grasping onto the rock for support.

Marah jumped next. The rock shook, and she stumbled backwards.

"Marah!" James shouted. Griffin, Luke, and Brigid cried out at about the same time. But no one was able to help her. Brigid was too far away, and if Luke, Griffin, or James moved, everyone would fall off.

Marah tottered for a few moments.

No one breathed.

Just in time, she fell forward onto her knees. She breathed a sigh of relief. Her hands shook as she grabbed onto the rock. The four on the rock stared at each other in shock.

"There is no way I'm jumping after that," Brigid announced.

Griffin looked over at her. "Teleport then," he said.

Brigid brightened. She disappeared and reappeared in the center of the rock. Surprisingly, the rock didn't move.

Wane chuckled. "Good idea," he shouted. "But you have to jump next time."

Brigid stared down at him, her eyes widened in fear.

"But—" she protested.

"But nothing," Wane replied. "You can do it."

Marah, Griffin, Luke, and James stood up slowly.

"Alright," James said. "It's going to be a lot harder this time."

Marah stared at the next rock. "You go first," she said.

James smiled. He motioned for the rest of them to crouch back down and jumped.

As soon as James' feet had left the rock, it shook violently. The others scrambled to balance it again.

All of a sudden, the rocks started to shift back and forth. James' rock shook again. He clung to it and looked down at Wane desperately.

"As soon as you get comfortable, things change," Wane said. "Learn to expect it."

James sighed and looked towards the others. The distance between them was growing larger and larger. Then, the rocks paused and started back towards each other.

"Griffin!" James shouted. "Jump when I say!"

Griffin nodded and readied himself. The rocks moved closer. Griffin tensed, waiting.

"Now!" James shouted. Griffin jumped as hard as he could. He landed right next to James and they steadied the rock as fast as they could. Griffin smiled at James, breathing hard.

"This isn't too bad," he said.

James smirked. "Speak for yourself."

The rocks moved away from each other again.

Brigid stood up. "I'm coming next!" she called to James.

"Okay," he called back. "Be ready!"

They waited what seemed like forever. Finally, the rocks came close again.

"Now!" James and Griffin shouted. Brigid jumped and landed on the rock, her eyes closed. The rock lurched even harder and James and Griffin struggled to steady it again. Once it was still, Griffin laughed and patted Brigid on the back.

"You made it," he said.

Brigid opened a hesitant eye. Seeing the rock beneath her and Griffin beside her, she breathed a sigh of relief and opened both eyes. She giggled. "I made it!"

James looked over at Marah and Luke. "It's a lot harder to steady the rock with us jumping so hard," he said to Griffin.

Griffin nodded. "It's not going to work with another person."

"Exactly," James said. "So what do we do?"

"How can we get them on here lightly?" Griffin asked.

"Help them over?" James guessed.

"Do we get close enough?"

"I don't know."

"Worth a try," Griffin said. He spoke loud enough for Marah and Luke to hear him. "Who's coming next?"

Luke pointed to himself, and Marah pointed at Luke.

Griffin chuckled. "I guess it's settled then."

"Luke," James said, "When we get as close as we possibly can, Griffin is going to help you over. We can't risk any more jumping."

Luke frowned. "I don't need help."

"The rock is going to tip if he doesn't help you over," James said.

Luke said nothing. He moved to the edge of the rock, as close as he could get to the others, and Marah moved to the back to balance the rock out.

The two rocks moved closer.

"Wait for it..." James said.

At just the right moment, Griffin stuck out his hand.

But Luke refused it.

He completely ignored Griffin and jumped on his own. Everything happened at once.

Luke's jump sent Marah flying forward onto the rock. She twisted halfway down and landed on her back.

As soon as Luke landed on the other rock, it shook violently.

"Luke!" James screamed.

Brigid stumbled and fell. The rock tipped, sending her over the edge. She screamed. Griffin dove for her and barely caught one hand.

"Balance it!" James screamed again. He and Luke slid to the opposite side of Griffin and Brigid as quickly as possible. The rock steadied. Griffin tightened his grip on Brigid's hand.

"Hold on," Griffin said.

"Use your super strength!" Brigid yelled.

Griffin smiled. "Forgot about that."

He started to pull her up, but nothing happened. He looked at Brigid, then down at Wane, panic clearly written on his face.

"Why isn't it working?" he shouted desperately.

"All powers come with restrictions," Wane said. "Try both hands."

Griffin looked down at Brigid. "Give me your other hand."

She held it up, and he grabbed it. As soon as he had both hands, he was able to pull her up easily.

Wane nodded thoughtfully. "I guess in that position you need both hands."

"Good to know," Griffin said.

"That is why we train. To learn our restrictions," Wane said.

Griffin looked over at Brigid, who still hadn't let go of him. He smiled and put his hand on top of hers. "You're okay," he whispered.

At his comforting words, Brigid recoiled and ducked away from his grip. Then, she realized what she had done. She tried to smile, to pretend nothing had happened, but

Griffin had seen it. He studied her, searching her light blue eyes for the secret to what he had done wrong. But there was nothing.

James looked over at them. "Everyone okay?"

Griffin paused for only a moment. "Never better," he finally said, giving James a thumbs-up.

James met both of their eyes, concern clearly written on his face. But he let the moment pass. He turned and looked over at the rock with only Marah left on it. It was moving farther and farther away.

"Marah? You okay?" James called.

Marah groaned and sat up. "I'll be fine," she said.

"Are you ready to come over?" he asked.

"If I must," Marah said.

James smiled. "I'll help you over." He glanced over at Luke. "Please no more jumping."

Marah stared hard at Luke before giving James a distracted smile. "Not a problem."

As soon as the rocks were close enough, James took Marah's hand and helped her over. The rock shook, but not nearly as hard as the time before. Marah breathed a sigh of relief.

Griffin glanced over at the next rock and groaned. "This is going to take *forever*," he said.

"This is the last one before—" James paused, staring at the spinning blades. "*Those*."

They all stared at the forbidding blades and shuddered.

James tore his gaze away. "Let's just get to the next rock."

Brigid looked thoughtfully at Luke. "Can't you move things with your mind?" she asked.

Luke nodded slowly. "Yeah..." Then, he understood. He looked over at the monstrous boulder next to them. "Oh."

"What?" Griffin asked.

"He can move the rocks for us," Brigid said. "So we don't have to jump."

Griffin raised his eyebrows. "And we just now figured this out?"

"Can you move something that big?" James asked.

Luke's gaze had not left the rock. "I don't know."

"Try it," Marah murmured.

Luke took a deep breath. He focused on the rock, his eyes squinted almost shut.

The rock didn't move.

"It's okay. We can—" James began.

Luke cut him off. "No. I can do it."

He focused even harder than before. Finally, the rock began to float slowly towards them. Marah sighed in relief. Brigid had to stop herself from crying out in glee.

The rock moved until it was right up next to the one they were on.

"Go," Luke whispered, his voice rough. Marah and Brigid stepped on first, then James and Griffin. Luke stood up slowly, his eyes never leaving the rock. Then, he stepped over and fell to his knees.

The rocks separated again, taking their original courses. Marah put a hand on Luke's shoulder and knelt down next to him. "Are you okay?"

Luke sucked in a breath of air. He nodded.

"Thank you," she whispered.

"Another restriction you have to remember," Wane's voice boomed. "Use your power too long or too much and it'll drain you."

"What's the point of powers if you have so many restrictions?" Griffin muttered.

James looked at him. "More than most people have."

Griffin snapped his mouth closed. Then, he looked around. "I'm not sure I want them anymore."

Luke stood up and took a shaky breath.

"Better?" Marah asked.

"Yeah," Luke said.

Marah turned to look at the sharp, spinning blades that were now right in front of them.

"This should be fun," Luke muttered.

They stood in silence, staring.

"Wait," Marah said. She pointed at a small, circular button about halfway down one of the pillars. "That might turn it off."

"Or it might make them spin faster," Griffin said.

James couldn't help but laugh. Marah looked at Griffin in amazement. "Way to be positive," she said.

Griffin shrugged. "You never know."

Marah shook her head. She looked back down at the button. "If I had an arrow, we'd be able to find out."

James tapped her on the shoulder. She turned, and he grinned at her, a single arrow in his hand.

She returned the smile. "How convenient."

She took the arrow and turned it over in her hands. She nodded her approval. "Can your magic hands make a bow?"

He bowed to her playfully. "Of course!"

A thin, wooden bow appeared in James' hand. He handed it to Marah with a smile. She delicately placed the arrow in the bow and pulled it back. She aimed for the button and released, sending the arrow straight to the button. A loud *click* sounded and the blades on the top of the pillars slowed to a stop.

Marah lowered her bow and smiled. Griffin patted her on the back. "Nice job," he said.

She smiled at him. "Told you it would stop them."

Griffin held up his hands. "I stand corrected."

"We still have to get over them," Brigid said.

Marah frowned. "True."

Griffin raised an eyebrow. "Maybe Brigid can transport us one at a time?"

James brightened. "I forgot she could do that. That'll work."

"As long as we remember to keep our eyes closed," Marah said. She grimaced.

James chuckled. "Right."

"Let's do it," Brigid said. She took Marah's hand and they both disappeared. Luke, Griffin, and James watched through the small space between the pillars as Marah and Brigid reappeared on the other side. Brigid vanished almost immediately, returning to the rest of them.

"Who's next?" Brigid asked. Luke stepped forward, and she took his hand. Luke closed his eyes and they disappeared.

James turned to Griffin. "He doesn't trust us."

Griffin sighed. "I know."

James started to respond, but Brigid appeared next to him before he could say anything.

"Ready?" she asked.

He nodded, she grabbed his hand, and they both disappeared.

Griffin tapped his foot, waiting for Brigid. He glanced down and crossed his arms. He knew the silence would only last a moment, but even that moment seemed too long. Finally, Brigid returned.

He let out a breath. "Let's go."

She smiled and took his hand. He closed his eyes, and when he reopened them, he was on the rock with everyone else.

"That is so cool," he whispered. Then, he looked over at the next rock. Everyone else followed his gaze. "Here we go again," he muttered.

James shrugged and steadied himself to jump.

"Wait!" Wane called. The five of them looked down at him in surprise.

"What?" Griffin asked.

Wane stepped closer. He tilted his head up and stared at them. "Don't go to the next one yet." He placed his fingers on his chin, then motioned to Luke. "Jump down."

Luke raised an eyebrow. He stared at Wane like he had gone mad. "Jump down?"

"That's what I said."

Luke stared skeptically at Wane. After a few moments, he shrugged and jumped off the rock. He dropped through the air, seeming to fall in slow motion. Then, he landed in the net. He rolled to a sitting position.

"Why am I down here?" he asked.

But, Wane ignored him. He was still looking up at James, Marah, Griffin, and Brigid. He waved his hand towards himself. "Marah."

Marah's eyes widened. "Jump?"

"Yes."

Marah stepped to the edge of the rock and peered over. "I'm not so sure—"

"Just jump, Marah," Wane called.

Luke looked up at her. "It's not that bad. Just hold your breath."

Marah nodded. She sucked in a deep breath, held it, closed her eyes, and jumped.

She fell through the air, her hair whipping against her face, for what felt like forever. Finally, her body came in contact with the net. Her eyes flew open. She sat up and looked over at Luke.

"What are we doing down here?" she asked.

Luke shrugged. "No idea."

Wane nodded at Luke and Marah, then returned his attention to the three still on the rock.

"Okay," he announced, "You are in an actual battle, and Luke and Marah just fell off the rock. There is no net and you can't see where they fell. What do you do?"

James, Griffin, and Brigid stared at Wane in bewilderment.

Luke and Marah exchanged glances.

"Um, help them," Griffin said, as if he couldn't believe Wane would even ask.

Wane stared at him, his face emotionless.

"Wrong."

"What? Why wouldn't we help—"

Wane interrupted him. "You are in danger. And if you stop and try to help them, not only are they most likely dead already, but you'll end up the same way."

James grimaced. "That's nice," he muttered.

Wane continued. "Get yourself out of the direct line of danger first. Then return to help."

The five of them stood, silent.

Wane pursed his lips. "Not all lessons are good ones. But you have to learn them all. And I'd rather you not learn this one the hard way. You won't get another chance if you do."

They said nothing, avoiding the gaze of Wane—and each other.

After a few moments, they met each other's eyes, their expressions grim.

"This is seeming less and less like a good idea," Griffin muttered.

James nodded. Wane took a deep breath, seeming to break the heavy silence. He looked at Luke and Marah. "Go ahead and go back up," he said. Then he wandered a few steps away.

Marah glanced over at Luke, then up at the rock above them. "How are we supposed to get back up there?"

Luke shook his head. They stared up, at a loss as of what to do, until Griffin leaned over the edge and grinned at them. He lifted up one of his hands and dropped an arrow and a coil of rope. It landed next to Marah, and she bent down to pick them up.

"What are these—" she paused. "Oh."

Luke looked at her curiously. She smiled and looked back up at Griffin. "I need the bow," she called.

"Right!" Griffin replied. His head disappeared. Marah returned her gaze to Luke. He still seemed confused. He studied the rope and the arrow in her hand before it finally dawned on him. He smirked.

"Couldn't he have just held onto the rope and dropped the other end down to us?"

Marah laughed aloud. "That would have been too easy. It's Griffin we're talking about."

"Right."

Griffin reappeared and dropped the bow down to Marah. She smiled her thanks. Then, she tied the rope to the arrow and loaded it into the bow.

"Ready?" she shouted.

"Ready!" Griffin said. "Send it up!"

Marah shot the arrow straight up. It floated towards the rock and disappeared. Griffin stood at the edge and held the arrow where both Marah and Luke could see it. "Come on up!"

Marah glanced at Luke. He waved her forwards. "Ladies first," he said.

Marah smiled and started her ascent. Luke followed as soon as Marah reached the top. Once they were both safely on the rock, Griffin tossed the arrow and rope away.

"And to the next one," he said.

"Which method are we using this time?" James asked.

Griffin looked at James, then back to the rock. "Let's just jump this time," he said. "More exciting."

James chuckled. "Alright."

Marah sighed. "Must we?"

"Yep!" Griffin shouted as soon as his feet left the rock. They steadied the rock, then James jumped, then Luke.

Marah and Brigid were the only ones left on the rock. Marah looked over at Brigid, then held out her hand and closed her eyes. Brigid grinned and teleported them both to the next rock.

Griffin chuckled. "Cheaters."

Brigid smiled. They moved to the next rock the exact same way. Before they could even think about the wall in front of them, Wane stopped them.

"You don't need to worry about that," Wane shouted, nodding towards the barbed wire. "We're finished with this; go ahead and come down."

The five of them nodded and turned to each other.

"We should—" James began. But, before he could finish, Luke jumped off the front side of the rock. The rock shook and the remaining four, unprepared, stumbled backwards. It dipped dramatically, and they fell together off the back.

They landed in the net, unscathed. James glared over at Luke, who had already climbed out of the net and down onto the ground.

Griffin sat up beside James. "I'm going to kill him," he said. James shook his head in disgust.

They climbed out of the net and jumped down to the ground. Luke had walked away without looking back; he was already halfway to the line of trees. Wane was a good distance ahead of him.

As soon as Wane had walked into the woods and out of earshot, James exploded in anger. "What is your problem?" he screamed.

Luke turned and stared at him, his expression as hard as the rocks they had just stood on. "I don't have one."

"You have to trust us," James said, moving closer to Luke. Marah, Brigid, and Griffin stayed behind.

Luke stayed where he was. "Who says I don't?"

"I know you don't."

"Whatever," Luke muttered. He turned to walk away.

James hesitated, then took another step. "We're not your dad," he said.

Luke spun around, his eyes burning with anger. He quickly closed the distance between them. "What did you say?" he growled.

James stood his ground. "I said we're not your dad."

"Don't you dare bring my dad—"

"You can trust—"

Luke's face turned tomato-red. "Just say it! Everyone else has."

James stared at him.

"Oh, Luke's dad left him. Luke can't trust anyone now. Luke needs to get over his trust issues," Luke said, not pausing for a breath. Now, he took several deep breaths. "I'm fine."

James sighed. "Luke..."

Luke backed away from him. "You have no idea what it feels like!" he practically screamed.

James shook his head. "Yes, I do."

"How could you possibly know?" Luke breathed. "James, the leader. James, the smart one. James, the one with the perfect life." His voice escalated. "How could you possibly know?"

James stared at him, his mouth in a straight line. "You don't think I know? I know exactly how it feels, Luke."

"No, you don't."

James could not conceal his disgust. He shook his head and practically spat his next words at Luke.

"My dad is dead."

He walked away, and when he came to the edge of the woods, he ran without looking back.

15

Luke watched him go. He turned and met the disbelieving eyes of Marah, Brigid, and Griffin. His hands shook, and his breaths were short. He closed his eyes. Then he, too, disappeared into the woods.

James ran through the trees, the branches whipping against his face. He didn't know where he was going, and he didn't care where he ended up. He was exhausted, but he didn't stop running.

Why had he let himself blow up like that? Why had he allowed Luke to push him so far?

Eventually, the trees broke and the bright sunlight hit him square in the face. He blinked and looked around. Somehow, he had ended up at the lake. He stepped up onto the dock and sat at the edge. He stared out at the water, at the trees behind it, then at the sky above him. The sky that turned out not to be an actual sky. Was anything here real?

James reached down and brushed his fingertips against the surface of the water. He pulled his hand back up and let the droplets of water drip from his fingertips to the palm of his other hand.

He refused to relive what had just happened. But he knew he would have to.

He didn't notice Marah until she was right next to him. He met her worry-filled eyes. He sighed and glanced away. Neither of them said anything. Marah waited. She knew James would speak when he was ready.

James turned his head from her and studied the trees.

"Why didn't you tell us?" he finally asked.

Marah furrowed her eyebrows. "What?"

"That you could see the future," James said, still refusing to meet her eyes.

The hint of a smile danced across her lips. "When did I become the topic of conversation?"

He smiled, but didn't let her see it. Then he shrugged.

She leaned back on her hands and sighed. "Alright."

"My dad gave me the necklace about a week before I came here. Right after that, I started having...weird dreams. I would dream about something, and then the next day, it would happen. At first I didn't realize it, then I thought it was just a coincidence. But it kept happening. So I asked him about it, and he told me that it was nothing. Then, I got here and we figured out about our abilities. And I realized that my dreams weren't coincidences."

She paused. "I was afraid. Afraid that if I told you, you would think I could look into the future and tell you what was happening, what was going on. And I knew that I couldn't."

James turned to look at her. "We would never have expected you to do that."

She nodded. "I know that now."

They grew silent. Marah pulled her knees into her chest and looked away.

"If you don't mind me asking...what happened to your father?" she asked.

James sighed. He didn't say anything for a moment.

"I'm sorry, you don't have to—"

He stopped her. "No, it's fine. He...he died. In a car crash when I was really young."

"I'm so sorry."

James said nothing.

"He died...after we left the moon, I guess?" Marah asked.

"I guess so."

"That's awful."

"Well...that's the story my mom told me."

Marah studied him. "What do you mean?"

"I mean...I don't know what to believe anymore."

"Why would she lie to you about that?"

"I don't know...but after all this, who knows what they have and haven't told us. You know?"

"Yes, I thought that too. But if we become suspicious of everyone—if we lose trust in everyone—we'll go crazy. We can't hate them for this. They did what they thought was the best for us."

He sighed. "I know. It's just hard to believe sometimes."

"I know."

They held each other's gazes for a long time. James turned so that he was completely facing Marah. He reached out and gently brushed a strand of hair away from her face. They leaned in to each other. Marah's eyes fluttered closed.

"You guys okay?" Griffin called.

Marah smiled, her eyes still closed. James sighed. He turned around. "We're fine."

Griffin studied them. He seemed to realize what he had just interrupted. "Oh. My bad." He grinned. "Carry on."

Marah chuckled and stood up. She held her hand out to James. He shook his head and took it, allowing her to pull him up. He looked down at her.

"Later?" he whispered.

She met his eyes, and it seemed that everything they had just said came rushing in at her at once. Her eyes filled with pain, sorrow, and something else that James couldn't quite read. She dropped his hand as if it had seared her and shook her head slightly.

"Marah?" James asked.

She wouldn't meet his eyes at first. When she did, it looked like she wanted to apologize, but couldn't quite bring herself to do it.

She drew in a quick breath and hurried down the dock, away from James.

* * *

Brigid walked slowly through the night, having opted out of dinner. The others had been concerned, but she didn't have the energy or the words to reassure them. She wondered if Griffin would tell them what she had done. She wasn't sure if she wanted him to or not.

But she knew they could never guess why she had shied away from him—from those words that had triggered memories she had never wanted to relive.

She knew she would have to eventually. The words kept replaying in her mind; sometimes in Griffin's voice, sometimes in the voice of the woman who had first said them so long ago. *You're okay...*

Her parents had hired a sitter for the weekdays, while they were away doing whatever it was that they did. They had done all the necessary background checks, but something about the woman just wasn't right.

Brigid, only five years old at the time, was never comfortable with her. If her parents noticed her discomfort at all, they did nothing about it, assuming that she would get used to the sitter over time.

The woman seemed nice enough at first. Then, she started searching the house, going through her parents' things. And when Brigid got in the way, the woman simply locked her in the coat closet in the hallway.

Somehow, the woman had known where the cameras were installed, and where they couldn't see. So she made a habit of searching the house at least once a week and locking Brigid in a closet that was out of the camera's line of sight.

The darkness in the closet was terrifying. Brigid screamed to be let out, screamed until her voice gave out. But the woman would only whisper those same two words, pretending to help Brigid. Pretending that she wasn't the reason for the screams. *You're okay...*

She hadn't said anything, and probably never would, but Brigid believed that that was where her talent with computers had truly stemmed from. All she had needed to see was the screen of her parents' computer, with the video feed from each camera in the house. Then, she knew to throw the toy, move the camera, and rid herself of the woman forever.

Somehow, Brigid made it back to her cabin. She didn't undress, didn't get ready for bed. She just crawled up to the top corner of her bed and pulled the blankets up to her chin. It was warm in the room, but her body shook, and her breaths grew short as the tears began to fall.

The last thought she had before she fell asleep was one that she could not have known until now.

That woman had been working for Marcus.

* * *

The breakfast table was quiet that morning. James and Luke sat on opposite sides of the table. Griffin, Marah, and Brigid sat in between them, Griffin studying Brigid, and Marah glancing up at Luke occasionally, then avoiding everyone's gaze altogether. No one seemed to know what to say. So much had happened the day before, and it was impossible to decide where to begin.

They didn't have to worry about it for long. Wane entered the dining hall only halfway through their meal. They looked up in surprise.

"We've done about all the training we need to do right now," Wane said. "All that's left is specific training for your individual talents. We'll start that today."

They nodded simultaneously. "How are we going to do that?" Griffin asked.

"One at a time," Wane said. "You'll do specific things to develop your powers. Everyone else will stay in the lab and focus on finding him."

He turned to leave. "Meet me in the lab once you're finished."

Once he was gone, Griffin turned to Brigid. "How much longer do you think it will take us to find him?"

Brigid shook her head. "I have no idea. I've tried almost everything. But we have just about nothing to go on. And he's done his job well."

Marah sighed. "How does he expect us to find him then?"

"I don't know," Brigid said. "I guess we just have to keep trying."

A few minutes later, their plates were clear. They stood to put them away and then left the dining hall.

When they arrived at the lake, the opening to the lab was already visible. They climbed down the stairs and found Wane inside.

He motioned for them to join him at the computer. He pulled up a document and then projected it onto the large screen on the wall.

"List of the places he's been and names he's used. You can start with this," he said. He stepped towards the doorway. "Brigid, you're first."

Brigid nodded and looked at the others. "Good luck."

She followed Wane up the stairs and out onto the grass. He moved a little ways away from the dock and looked around. "Here will do."

"What do you know about your restrictions so far?" he asked.

"Well, I know I can't teleport when I'm tied up or when someone is holding me. But I can take someone with me if they hold my hand."

Wane nodded thoughtfully. Then he held out his hand. "Show me."

"You might want to close your eyes," Brigid said.

He looked at her curiously.

"When I first tried this, they didn't close their eyes. It made them sick."

"Oh," Wane said. He closed his eyes tight.

Brigid smiled. She closed her eyes as well, taking them to the other side of the lake. Once they had safely landed on solid ground, she nudged Wane. He opened his eyes.

"Interesting," he said. "Now let me see you do it without me."

She nodded and disappeared, appeared on the opposite side of the lake, then teleported back to her original spot.

Wane studied her. "You close your eyes?"

Brigid looked at him curiously. "Yes."

"Try not to this time."

"But—"

"Just try it."

Brigid sighed. She kept her eyes open, a look of deep concentration on her face. She exhaled quickly. "It didn't work."

"Because you expected it not to," Wane said.

Brigid raised an eyebrow. "Yes I did."

"No, you didn't. Try again."

Brigid sighed again. She did the same thing as before, but this time she disappeared. A few moments later, she appeared a few feet away. As soon as she appeared, she stumbled and fell onto her hands and knees. She looked up at Wane in amazement.

"I could see where I was going!" she exclaimed. "It was so weird!"

Wane chuckled. "I told you it would work."

* * *

Down in the lab, Griffin, Marah, Luke, and James stood in front of the screen, baffled.

"Where do we even begin?" Griffin asked.

Marah shook her head. "I have no idea."

"I guess we search all the names he's used," James said, moving towards the computer.

"But if he's changed it every time...wouldn't he have changed it again?" Luke asked.

"Yes," Marah said. "We need to know how they found him the other times."

"Good idea," Griffin said. "Until then, though, I guess we just use this."

"What's the point?" Luke asked.

"Well, Wane was there when they found him the other times. If he wanted us to use this, it must be somewhat helpful," Griffin said.

"True," James murmured.

"Worth a shot," Griffin said. James nodded and started typing.

Several hours later, they had exhausted every search possible on the names and places on their list. And still, they had nothing.

Griffin sighed in exasperation. "I give up."

At about the same time, Brigid floated down the stairs at a snail's pace. Her eyes drooped, and it was all she could do to hold onto the railing. She reached the bottom and went straight to the beanbag chairs. She sank down into one of them and her eyes closed immediately.

Wane smiled at her, then moved over to look at the screen. He glanced at James, Griffin, Luke, and Marah. "Find anything?" he asked.

James sighed. "Nothing."

Wane frowned, then shook it off. "Don't worry about it. There's a reason we haven't been able to find him."

"Which is what?" Luke asked.

"He's good at disappearing. And he doesn't want to be found."

"Then how are we supposed to find him?" James asked.

"Find his mistakes. He's made them before, and he's starting to make more."

"He's making more mistakes? Like he wants to be found?" Marah asked.

Wane nodded. "Possibly."

Griffin glanced over at Brigid, then back up at Wane. "What did you do to her?"

Wane chuckled. "She's fine. Just overworked. That's what happens when you use your powers too much." He paused. "It's good to know your limits."

16

The next morning, they met Wane at the lab again.

"Griffin," he said. "You're next."

Griffin groaned. "Already?" He looked over at the rest of them. "I'm sure everyone else would love to take a turn."

Wane chuckled. "Let's go, Griffin. You'll survive."

Griffin sighed dramatically. "Fine." He followed Wane out of the lab. Wane led him down the pathway and to the baseball field. There was a silver pitching machine waiting for them.

Griffin stared at it. "Oh no."

Wane grinned. "Oh yes. Go to second base."

Griffin groaned. He dragged his feet all the way across the field to the base. As soon as he turned to face Wane, Wane had already shot a small plastic ball at him.

Griffin shrieked and batted it away. "What was that for?"

Wane laughed. "I thought you had super reflexes!" he shouted.

"That's James!" Griffin replied, shaking his head.

Wane rolled his eyes. "Just shut up and catch the balls."

"Rude," Griffin muttered.

Wane sent another ball flying at Griffin. This time, he caught it with no problem.

"Mhmm," Wane said, raising an eyebrow at Griffin.

"So maybe I am the one with super reflexes," he called back. Wane shook his head. He hit a button on the pitching machine. It sent balls at Griffin within seconds of each other, with no sign of stopping any time soon. Griffin's eyes widened. As soon as he caught each ball, he would barely have enough time to toss it to the ground and move his hand to catch the next one.

This went on for several minutes. Finally, Griffin dropped his arms and let the balls pelt him. He looked over at Wane. "How long do you plan on doing this?"

Wane shrugged, a mischievous smile on his face.

The balls continued to pelt Griffin.

"Come on!" he shouted.

Wane sighed. "Fine. Try and catch them without looking. Keep your eyes on me."

Griffin raised an eyebrow, but tried it anyway. He missed the first few balls, but after only a few tries he was catching them without a problem.

Wane smiled. "Good. Now dodge them."

Griffin sighed. He stepped out of the machine's range and smiled over at Wane. Wane raised an eyebrow. He returned to his position behind the machine and aimed it at Griffin. Griffin sighed and jumped out of the way. Wane continued turning the machine towards Griffin, and Griffin continued dodging the balls, just barely missing them every time.

Wane picked up a pile of arrows from the ground and placed them in the machine.

Griffin shook his head. "No way."

"They're dull," Wane said. "And this is why you're really training. This is what you'll actually be dodging."

Griffin swallowed hard, still looking uneasy. "Alright."

Wane started by shooting only one arrow at Griffin. He caught it easily and tossed it aside. He did this for the first few arrows, but once they started coming faster, he gave up on catching them and focused on getting out of the way. He dropped to the ground, jumped back up, dodged side to side, and got away from groups of arrows when it seemed impossible.

Finally, Wane turned the machine off. He nodded, impressed. "Good work," he said.

Griffin grinned, breathing hard. "Thanks."

Wane motioned for Griffin. "Let's head back."

Griffin followed him down the pathway and back to the lake. They climbed down the stairs, and suddenly, Griffin knew exactly how Brigid had felt. He barely made it down the stairway before crashing in the beanbag chairs.

James chuckled. "You okay over there?" he called.

Griffin groaned. "I feel like I just ran into a brick wall."

They all laughed aloud. Wane moved over to stand in front of one of the computers.

"Any luck?" he asked.

Brigid shook her head. The others frowned, looking hopeless.

"Nothing."

* * *

"James."

James looked up from the computer. "My turn already?" He smiled.

Wane smirked. "You'll sleep well tonight." He turned to the others. "Keep looking."

They nodded. Wane led James up the stairs, and they stepped out into the sunshine.

"Where to?" James asked.

Wane paused. "Here will do." He turned to look at James. "Materializing, huh?"

James nodded.

"Show me," Wane said.

James held out his hand, then looked over at Wane. "What do you want?"

Wane considered this. He smiled. "A chocolate chip cookie."

James chuckled. He focused on his hand, and a cookie appeared a moment later. Wane grinned and took the cookie from James gratefully. He took a bite and nodded in approval.

"Have you ever materialized something somewhere other than in your hand?" Wane asked.

"The first time I ever did it. I materialized a sword onto a table."

"Good. Anything bigger than that?"

James shook his head.

Wane nodded thoughtfully. "Okay. Make a bookcase appear a few feet away."

James focused on the ground that Wane had pointed to. Slowly but surely, a bookcase began to appear.

"Now make one appear over there," Wane said, pointing to the opposite side of the lake.

James raised his eyebrows, but did as he was told. He stared at the ground on the other side, and a bookcase began to appear, even slower than the first time.

Wane watched until the entire bookcase had been formed. He looked over at James. "By the time we're finished, that bookcase will appear in an instant. And you won't have to focus on the spot like you do now. Deal?"

James smiled. "Looking forward to it."

Several hours later, James was able to do just that.

"Last thing. Then we're finished," Wane said. He sent James to the right side of the dock.

"Run to the other side," he called, "And when you're halfway there, make that bookcase appear on the other side of the lake."

James nodded. He steadied himself, then took off running.

Halfway to the other side of the dock, James glanced over at the opposite shore of the lake. And, just like that, a bookcase appeared on the other side. Wane cheered. And as soon as James reached the other side of the dock, he slowed to a stop and collapsed onto the ground.

Wane stood over him. "Great job, James."

James grinned up at him. "Thanks."

Wane reached down and helped James up. They started down the pathway back to the lab.

"What are we going to do when we find him?" James asked.

Wane glanced over at him. "Go after him, of course. What else would we do?"

"I don't know. But...how? Are we just going to go in and capture him?"

"That's the idea. I doubt it will be that easy, though."

James frowned. "Why is this our responsibility?"

"I already told you. He knows everything about your parents: their powers, their weaknesses. He doesn't know your powers yet. You are the only ones that could fight him. And the five of you will become the leaders soon. Protecting the city is your responsibility now."

James nodded. He studied the ground as he walked.

Wane sighed. "I think you would be involved eventually. He's not concerned with your parents anymore. You're the future leaders, therefore, his new targets."

"What if we don't want to be the leaders?" James asked.

Wane studied him. "We're not going to force you into it. And no one would blame you if you stepped down. It's your decision."

James glanced away. He slowed, allowing Wane to walk ahead of him. He had never considered backing out. It had never seemed that he had a choice. But now, it was all he could think about. He blew out a gust of air.

Wane turned to look at James. "You don't have to decide right now."

James cracked a smile. "It's a lot to think about."

"I know. We've contradicted many things you thought you knew about yourself."

"Pretty much everything."

"Just where you were born," Wane said. "You're still the same person."

James sighed. "I want to help. It would help if I knew more about why, though."

Wane nodded. He thought for a moment. "I know, but some things you just aren't ready to know yet. For now, just know that you're fighting for your family. And your home."

"A home I've never been to."

Wane chuckled. "Details."

By that time, Wane and James had arrived at the opening to the lab. They descended the stairs to find the other four slumped in their chairs, looking like balloons without air.

Wane raised an eyebrow. "Nothing?"

"Not one freakin' thing," Griffin muttered. He slumped farther into his chair.

Brigid shook her head. "I don't know what else to do."

"You're doing fine. I know it's a lot, but all we can do is keep trying. Redo searches you've already done if you have to," Wane said. "We'll find him."

* * *

"Grab some buckets from the closet. We're going to need them," Wane said.

It was the next morning, and Luke and Wane were on their way out of the lab to train.

Luke stared at him. "Why...?"

"You're going to be playing with fire," Wane said, a grin spreading across his face.

Luke returned the smile and rubbed his hands together. "Sounds good to me."

Wane chuckled and took Luke outside, close to the edge of the lake. "You need to learn to control your powers," he said.

Luke smirked. "I can't even get it to work correctly half the time."

"And we're going to fix that," Wane said.

Wane pointed to the grass beneath their feet. "Set the grass on fire."

Luke nodded. He squinted his eyes at the ground and furrowed his eyebrows. Finally, a small flame appeared. The fire crackled, then burned out. Luke sighed.

"Frustration helps no one. Especially not you," Wane said.

Luke chuckled. "Good to know."

"Try again."

Luke stared at the ground again, and the same thing happened. He clenched his teeth and tried again without pausing. Again, the same thing happened.

Luke continued to make small flames. After several attempts, Luke focused on the ground again. Wane watched patiently. This time, a huge flame erupted.

Both Wane and Luke jumped back. Luke's eyes were wide. The fire started to spread, showing no signs of burning out like the others.

"Get the water!" Wane exclaimed. They rushed to the lake, grabbed the buckets, and started throwing water at the fire. After several minutes, the flame grew small enough for Luke to stomp it out.

Luke looked up at Wane. He shook his head in disbelief. "I didn't even know I could do that."

Wane smiled. "See? The more we work on it, the better it will get."

Luke nodded.

"Try and burn just a single blade of grass. Without disrupting the blades around it," Wane said.

Luke raised his eyebrows. "Is that even possible?"

"This morning, you thought what you just did was impossible."

Luke smiled. "True."

He chose a blade and focused on it. He made several small fires, but never singled out the one blade of grass. Luke blew out a gust of air.

"We'll work on it later," Wane said. "It will come eventually."

Luke said nothing. He looked to Wane for his next instructions.

"Now we need to make it easier. So you don't have to concentrate so hard to make fires."

Wane and Luke worked for several hours, going back and forth between making it easier and burning single blades of grass.

Finally, late into the afternoon, Luke stared at the ground, his face relaxed. All of a sudden, the grass beneath him started to burn.

"Good!" Wane exclaimed. "Next?"

Luke nodded and looked down again. His face was still controlled. A small flame appeared, like the flames on matches, and a single blade of grass caught fire. It burned, and then was gone.

Wane's smile spread across his entire face. He clapped Luke on the back. "That's awesome," he said.

Luke returned the smile. "Thanks."

"Ready to be done for the day?"

"Yes," Luke said, laughing.

"Let's go then," Wane said. He led Luke back down the staircase and into the computer lab. Marah, James, Brigid, and Griffin were spread out around the room. Brigid was still at her computer, Marah was seated beside her, and James and Griffin were sprawled out on the beanbag chairs in the corner.

Wane raised an eyebrow at James and Griffin. "Have you been working at all?"

"Yes!" Griffin exclaimed.

"We were just taking a break," James said.

Wane smiled. "Sure you were." He turned his attention to Marah and Brigid. "Find anything?"

Brigid turned around. Her shoulders drooped as she shook her head. "Do you even have to ask?"

Wane sighed. "That's alright."

* * *

The computer screen was harsh on their tired eyes. Brigid blinked slowly. She glanced over at Marah. "What does he think we're going to find that we didn't yesterday?"

Marah shook her head. "I have no idea."

"Marah, your turn," Wane said. Marah turned around and nodded. Brigid looked over at James, Griffin, and Luke, who had already retired to the beanbags. She watched Wane and Marah until they had almost made it out the door.

"What do you expect us to do?" she called out.

Wane turned around. "Keep looking."

"I have been looking. For three days straight," Brigid said. She shook her head. "There's nothing to find."

Wane sighed, his frown deepening. "He's out there somewhere. We just have to keep looking."

Brigid nodded slightly and turned around. She closed her eyes, a deep sigh escaping from her lips. When she turned around, Wane and Marah were gone and James had come up behind her.

"He doesn't understand. I've tried everything a million times," Brigid said.

James nodded. "I know. But there's nothing else we can do. We have to find him somehow."

Brigid sank down into the chair. She stared blankly at the computer. "I don't know what I'm doing wrong."

"Nothing. This guy is just really well hidden."

"Apparently."

James chuckled. "If it was easy, we wouldn't be here."

Marah followed Wane down the pathway and out onto the archery field. He handed her a bow, and she smiled.

"We're not going to work this for long. I already know you never miss."

Marah grinned. "It's still hard to believe."

"And it will be. But you'll get used to it, eventually."

Marah nodded thoughtfully. She looked up at Wane. "Do you really think we'll be able to find him?"

Wane said nothing for a moment. Finally, he nodded.

"Yes. At some point, he'll get too confident and he'll make a mistake."

"That could be years from now."

"It could. But I don't think it will be. And there's still the possibility that we can find him without him slipping up."

"She's tried everything," Marah said. "What else is there for us to do?"

"Wait. Keep trying. It's all we can do," Wane said. "But for now, we can train."

Marah grinned. She lifted her bow and shot the arrow straight at the target, without taking her eyes off of Wane.

Wane chuckled. "Impressive."

Marah bowed playfully. "Why thank you."

"I figured we wouldn't need to work on this. Let's focus on looking into the future."

Marah nodded. "Are there restrictions with that ability?"

"You never know. You could have different restrictions...there could be different things you could do with it. You just have to learn as you go," Wane said.

"Different things I could do with it?"

"Yes...sometimes, with skills like that, there are other ways you can do it." He paused. "Like, for example, Brigid's mother. She can read people's emotions, but if she's touching them, she can actually read their mind."

Marah raised her eyebrows. "Wow."

"You just have to try different things and see what you can do with it."

Marah nodded. "Where would you start with that?"

"There's a lot you can do. But, we can't focus on all of that right now. We'll probably just look for restrictions today."

Marah nodded.

"Let's see," Wane said. "We'll see if you can choose what you see first."

"Choose what part of the future I look at?" Marah asked.

"Yes. I don't know if you can do that or not. Try and look at...what you'll be doing tomorrow morning."

"Alright," Marah said. She closed her eyes. Wane watched her closely, watching for any sign of what she was seeing.

A few moments later, Marah opened her eyes. She sighed and shook her head.

"It didn't work?" Wane asked.

"No. I tried to look at tomorrow morning, but I only saw this conversation."

"The one we're having right now?"

"Yes. That's why I knew you were going to ask that. And I know that you're about to say that maybe I can only see a few minutes into the future."

Wane raised his eyebrows. He chuckled. "That's exactly what I was going to say. And that's probably what it is."

Marah frowned. "But when I saw the future in my dreams, it didn't actually happen until much later the next day."

Wane pursed his lips. "It might be extended when you sleep. Because you have so much more concentration than when you're awake."

Marah nodded. "Could be."

"And that's why we try these things," Wane said. "Now, I want you to try something else. While you're seeing the future, try and tell me what you're seeing."

Marah frowned. "I don't know if I can-"

"Can't hurt to try."

Marah nodded. She closed her eyes. A moment later, she opened her mouth to speak. "Con-" was all that came out. She opened her eyes.

"I started to tell you, then it blurred, then went away completely."

Wane nodded. "We can keep working on it. If you can do it, it definitely won't come quickly. There are some restrictions that you can overcome with a lot of practice."

Marah cocked her head. "Really?"

Wane chuckled. "Yes. Want to try it again?"

"Sure," Marah said. She paused. "What happens when we find him?"

Wane frowned, surprised by the question. "Marah, don't worry about that right now. I know it's hard, but try and focus on your training. That's what's most important. And I promise, when we find him, you will be ready. But don't focus on it right now."

Marah nodded and closed her eyes again. She started to open her mouth, but then said nothing. By the expression on her face, Wane could tell that she was in deep concentration. What she was seeing was obviously more than a simple conversation.

Finally, Marah opened her eyes. She stared at Wane, a strange expression on her face. Wane stepped towards her, the concern written clearly on his face. "What is it?" he asked.

Marah shook her head in disbelief. "They found him."

17

"What?"

"They found him," Marah repeated.

Wane's eyes were wide. "This soon?"

Marah studied him carefully. Then she shook her head, ever so slightly. "No."

"They didn't?" Wane asked, looking down at her in shock.

"No."

"Then why did you tell me that they did?"

"I wanted to see what you would say," Marah said. "Wane. What are we going to do when we find him?"

Wane sighed. "We go after him."

Marah nodded and glanced away. "Oh."

"Marah...you don't need to worry. What's wrong?" Wane asked, his gaze softening.

She met his eyes again.

"It's...it's nothing," she whispered.

Wane nodded, seeming to read her thoughts. "You don't need to be afraid, Marah."

"Don't I?"

Wane looked at her curiously.

"We're going into this, with only two—maybe three weeks—of experience. How can this possibly work?"

"You're not finished training yet," Wane said. "Not nearly. Believe me, if you had a reason to be afraid, I'd be the first to tell you. I want you to succeed more than anyone. But I don't think you need to be afraid. Not yet, anyway."

Marah nodded, considering this.

"That doesn't help much, does it?"

"No," Marah said. She smiled then. "But that doesn't mean I'm not going to do it."

* * *

The next morning, even though they had all completed individual training, the five of them repeated the ritual from the past few days. They went straight to the lab after breakfast, planning to search on the computers until Wane arrived.

But, this morning was different. By the time they had made it to the lab underneath the lake, Wane was already there waiting for them.

Griffin stared down at the nonexistent watch on his wrist. "Are we late?"

Wane smiled. "Not at all. But it's time we move on. We've finished individual training. Now, we see how well you work together."

"Cool," Griffin said, nodding. "And what does that mean exactly?"

"Instead of training one at a time, we're doing two at a time," Wane said. "We'll look for him in the mornings and train in the afternoon."

Brigid smiled. "Sounds good to me."

"Good," Wane said, returning the smile. "We're going to go straight to training today, though."

Wane started up the steps and they followed him out into the sunshine. He led them around to the edge of the lake before turning back to face them.

"We're going to start here today," he said. "First to train will be Griffin and Luke."

Griffin's face fell before he could stop himself. He and Luke met each other's eyes, their expressions identical looks of disgust.

Luke shook his head. "There is no way."

"The five of you are a team," Wane said. He sighed. "And you all need to be able to work together. Especially you two."

"Fine," Griffin grumbled.

"Good." Wane pulled out his remote and studied it. After a moment, he pointed it towards the lake and pressed a button.

The five of them watched the lake curiously, but nothing happened at first. Then, slowly, something began to rise out of the water.

The water fell away from the metal platform until they could see it in its entirety. It was a perfect circle, positioned in the center of the lake. And it was plenty big enough for Griffin and Luke to move around on.

Wane nodded in satisfaction. He glanced over at Brigid. "Could you please take them over to the platform?"

"Sure," Brigid said. She held out both hands and turned to Griffin and Luke, who looked much less eager.

"I don't—" Luke began.

"Are you sure—" Griffin said, at exactly the same time.

Wane stopped both of them with a wave of his hand. "You will train together, whether you like it or not. Now go."

Luke took Brigid's hand first and rolled his eyes. Griffin took his time, however, grumbling the whole way. Finally, the three of them made it to the platform and Brigid returned quickly to the shore.

Luke and Griffin glanced warily at each other, then turned to Wane.

"Figure out a way to get back to the shore," Wane called to them.

Luke furrowed his eyebrows, glanced down at the water, and then returned his stare to Wane. "Couldn't we just...swim?"

Wane smiled. "No, you can't. I don't think you want to find out what lives in there." He shook his head. "Be a tad more creative than that."

James, Marah, and Brigid watched in amusement as Griffin and Luke peered over the edge at the water. Then, they set their sights on each other.

"So what's the plan?" Luke asked.

Griffin shrugged. "I don't know. Why don't you just burn us a path out?"

Luke rolled his eyes. "Cause that'll work."

"Do you have any better ideas?"

"Probably."

Griffin sighed. "Then by all means. Do share."

"I might."

On the shore, Marah glanced at Wane's irritated expression, then turned back to James. "There's no way they're going to get off that thing."

James smirked. "Not a chance."

Luke sat down on the metal platform, rested his cheeks in his hands, and glanced testily up at Griffin.

"What?" Griffin asked.

"Let's just freakin' swim."

"You can test the waters first, then."

Luke stood up and walked over to Griffin's side of the platform. "No way. You jump in, and if nothing gets you, I'll come next."

Griffin sighed and shoved Luke's shoulder. He hadn't meant much by it, but there was no going back. Before Wane or any of the others could react, Luke and Griffin were in a full-blown fist fight.

Wane sighed heavily and rubbed his temples before pulling the remote back out. He pressed a button, and the platform disappeared—dropping Luke and Griffin straight into the lake.

Griffin surfaced first, spewing lake water out of his mouth. Luke was not far behind. They both swam, as fast as they could, back to the shore.

They stood up next to James, Marah, and Brigid, water dripping from every stitch of clothing on them. They glared at Wane through the wet hair that hung in both of their eyes.

"What was that for?" Griffin demanded.

"I said you had to learn to work together," Wane said. "Not against each other!"

"You just dropped us in a lake with who knows what!" Griffin exclaimed, spraying water all over the rest of them with his elaborate hand motions.

Wane shrugged. "There's nothing in that lake."

Griffin started to protest, but Wane stopped him.

"That's beside the point. You all need to take this seriously. We're training for a reason, and you need to be ready. Next time, there might actually be something in the lake and I might not be here to get you out. You have to work together," Wane said. He took a deep breath. "Go get some lunch and meet me back here."

Griffin raised his eyebrows as Wane walked away. "Well he's cranky today."

James had to smile at that. "He has a point, you know."

"Yeah I know," Griffin said. "But he didn't have to drop me in lake water to prove it."

Brigid giggled and started down the pathway. "Let's go."

* * *

As soon as they finished lunch, the five of them returned to the lake. Wane had not yet arrived, so they settled down to wait. Marah sat on the edge of the dock and pulled her toes through the water. James and Brigid skipped rocks they had found along the edge of the lake. Luke walked the line of trees, setting fire to one leaf at a time. And Griffin dug the toe of his shoe in the mud along the water line.

"I don't think I like the idea of joint training anymore," Griffin muttered.

Marah smiled. "Tired of it already?"

Griffin glanced back at Luke, then lowered his voice so only the others could hear him. "Only because I had to start with him," he said, grimacing at the memory.

"He's not that bad," Brigid said. She tossed another pebble gracefully across the surface of the water and laughed at Griffin's expression. "He's not!"

"If you say so," Griffin said.

"Can't you two get along? Even at all?" James asked.

"No, we can't. We just don't..." Griffin paused. "See eye to eye."

Brigid laughed and looked up at Griffin, who was nearly an entire foot taller than her. "Not many people do."

Griffin rolled his eyes, trying hard to suppress a smile. "You're hilarious, Brigid."

"I know," Brigid said, her eyes sparkling.

At that moment, Wane appeared at the break in the trees, signaling the end of their conversation. "Ready for more training?"

Griffin frowned. "Always."

"Good to hear," Wane said, raising his eyebrows questioningly. "Follow me."

He turned and led them back down the pathway, towards the front of the camp. After a little ways, they turned to the right and followed the path to the baseball field, where the obstacle course had made a reappearance.

The five of them stared up at it, not nearly as confident as they had been a moment before.

Wane cleared his throat. "Alright, next is Marah and Griffin."

"What?" Marah shrieked, looking as if Wane had just signed her death warrant.

Griffin's face fell. "But I just went!"

"I know that," Wane said. "Think of it this way: you get most of your training done in one day. Then you can relax for the next few times."

Griffin sighed. "Fine."

Marah and Griffin started towards the course, their footsteps dragging through the grass.

"Wait!" Wane called out. They turned, their eyebrows furrowed.

"If your talent requires certain objects, you can use them."

Marah smiled, and Wane tossed her a bow and a quiver of arrows. Marah placed the arrows on her back, and admired the sleek, wooden bow. Then, she noticed the small hole in the wood, shaped as a crescent moon. She raised the bow and peered through the hole. *Perfect*, she thought.

"And I haven't told you what you have to do yet," Wane continued.

Marah and Griffin exchanged glances but remained silent, listening.

"All you have to do is figure out how both of you can get up onto one of the rocks."

Griffin glanced back at the silver starting platform. "Can't we just—"

"No, you can't use the platform. You have to start from below the rocks."

Marah nodded. Griffin only shook his head as they made their way towards the rocks, which loomed easily 100 feet overhead.

Finally, they arrived at the edge of the net.

"Should we climb in?" Griffin asked.

Marah shook her head. "Underneath."

The net was high enough for the two of them to walk underneath without a problem. Once they were directly beneath one of the rocks, Griffin met Marah's eyes.

"Got a plan?"

Marah nodded. "Throw me," she whispered.

"No way," Griffin said, his eyes wide.

"We have to. We'll pull a hole in the net and you can throw me up."

"What if I throw you too high? Or not high enough?"

"Then I'll fall in the net," Marah said. "I can look though, if you want me to."

"Look? Oh...yeah, that'd be nice."

Marah smiled and closed her eyes. A moment later, she reopened them and looked up. "Yep. I made it."

"Well that's good," Griffin said, laughing. He reached up and easily pulled the ropes apart to form a hole, just big enough for the both of them.

"Ready?" he asked, peering through the new hole.

Marah nodded. "As I'll ever be."

Griffin smiled. He looked up at the rock, then back down at Marah, deep in thought. "I'm not sure which way would be the best to throw you," he finally said.

Marah raised her eyebrows and nodded, but said nothing. Griffin pursed his lips, still thinking. Then, he smiled.

"Here," he said. Griffin made a small circle with his finger, and Marah turned around. He grabbed her waist and tossed her up, catching her feet with his hands and resting them on his shoulders. She peered down at him, and he smiled up at her.

"Sure you're ready?" he asked.

"Toss away."

Griffin bent his legs and pushed her upwards. Before she knew it, Marah was nearly eye level with the rock. She reached out and grabbed the edge before gravity caught up and tried to pull her back down.

"Got it?" Griffin called from the ground.

Marah clung to the edge of the rock, trying to catch her breath. Finally, she was able to let go with one hand and reach out farther. She found another groove in the rock and secured her hand inside. Then she pulled as hard as she could, until her entire body was on top. She spun around on her stomach and looked down at Griffin. They both smiled.

"Coming?" she shouted down to him.

He grinned back at her. "Nah, I thought I'd wait down here."

"If you say so," she said, rolling her eyes.

Marah watched in confusion as Griffin started pulling at the rope net above him. He pulled apart the knots until he had a single coil of rope in his hand. Then, he looked up at her and tossed it up in the air.

If anyone else had thrown it, the rope would not have come close to Marah's rock. But, since it was Griffin, the rope not only reached the rock, but kept going. Until finally, several feet above Marah's head, it started its descent back down to Earth. She stood up and caught it easily, then looked down at Griffin.

"Send one end down," Griffin said. "I'll climb up."

Marah secured the rope around a jut in the rock, dropped the opposite end to Griffin, and clung to the knot to make sure it would stay tied. She felt the rope pull taut and braced herself, putting all of her weight into keeping the rope secure. It rubbed against her hands uncomfortably all throughout Griffin's climb, making it worse the longer she waited.

After what felt like an eternity, Griffin's head appeared above the rock. He pulled himself up, then pulled the rest of the rope behind him. He untied the rope, circled it around his arm and smiled at Marah.

"What now?"

She shrugged. "No idea."

They heard Wane's booming voice almost immediately. "Good job, you two. Now come back down, without just jumping into the net."

Griffin sighed. "Got to make everything complicated."

Marah chuckled. "Always."

Griffin peered down at the net below them, which was of no use anymore. Because of the rope he had removed, there were gaping holes all throughout that area of the net.

"Guess we couldn't have used that anyway," Marah remarked.

Griffin smirked and nodded.

They both stared at the ground, deep in thought. Marah pulled her bow through her hands mindlessly, trying to think of some way to get down safely. After a moment, she noticed the bow fully. She stared at it, then the ground, switching back and forth until she smiled, having thought of the perfect plan.

"I have an idea."

Griffin raised an eyebrow. "Well, that was fast."

"Can I use the rope?"

"Of course," Griffin said. He handed her the rope and watched in amazement as she pulled one of her arrows out, tied the rope around it, and loaded it into the bow. She handed him the other end of the rope and he held it.

Marah raised the bow up slowly, seeing the ground with a renewed determination. Finally, she released. The arrow flew through the air—taking the rope with it—until it wedged itself into the ground, forming a perfect diagonal from the grass to Griffin's hand.

Griffin shook his head and laughed. "Dang."

"It's kind of like a zip line," Marah said, laughing along with Griffin. She pulled out another arrow, and he looked at it closer. "Some of them are metal," she said. She tried to bend it, but there wasn't even a small amount of give.

"Sweet," Griffin said. "Here, I'll tie the rope around the rock again."

He took his end of the rope and knelt down on the opposite side of the rock that Marah had shot off of. He peered over the edge, then threw the rope so hard that it wrapped around the rock several times before coming to a stop. He secured the knot, stood back up, and smiled at Marah.

"Let's go," he said.

Marah nodded and smiled nervously at Griffin. She placed the arrow on top of the rope and leaned over it. She held on to the end closest to her, then reached her arm under the rope to grab the other end. She turned and glanced at Griffin.

"Here goes nothing." And then her feet slid off the rock.

It felt like flying, with the exception of the arrow above her head—which she was clinging to like her life depended on it. Thinking about it, it probably did.

The ground was approaching quickly. Marah lifted one foot and pressed it to the rope, hoping it would slow her down. Thankfully, it worked and she was able to slow herself enough to land her feet lightly on the ground.

When she looked up, she saw James, Luke, Brigid, and Wane were all grinning at her.

"Can I go next?" Brigid asked, laughing. Her laugh was slight and twinkling, the kind of laugh that made you feel like all was right with the world. It almost made Marah forget the reason they were training, the reason they were even there.

Griffin's voice brought her quickly to the present.

"You didn't leave me an arrow!" he shouted.

Marah turned back towards him, saw him raising an eyebrow at her so far up in the air.

"Sorry!" she called, pulling a metal arrow from her quiver. She loaded it into the bow and looked up at Griffin. "Ready?"

He nodded, and she released the arrow. It was moving so fast that it was nearly invisible, but Griffin pulled it from the air without hesitation. He smiled, held it up for her to see, and then started down the rope, flying even faster than Marah had.

Once Griffin was near the ground, his legs straightened and he landed in an instant, perfectly still. Marah guessed that had something to do with his reflexes. Griffin returned the arrow to her, and they stood together, waiting.

Wane smiled. "Very good," he said. "This is what you have to do. Work together, play to each other's strengths."

Marah and Griffin nodded, smiling and breathless.

"It will get easier as we practice. Being able to work together like this will be very helpful later."

They followed him out of the baseball field, talking in hushed tones as they made their way down the path. He stopped at the entrance to the dining hall and turned back to them.

"We'll search for him in the morning, and then do some more training after lunch," he said.

"You're not going to eat with us?" Brigid asked.

"No. That is your time together. A big part of working well together is knowing each other," Wane said, waving them inside. "So get to know each other."

"We know each other!" Griffin said, stalling in the doorframe. He and Wane exchanged a smile, and Wane gave an exasperated shake of his head.

"I'm sure you don't know everything," Wane said. Then he disappeared behind the door, leaving the five of them alone inside.

They filled their plates with food from the enormous buffet. The first half of the buffet was filled with regular American food: chicken fingers, burgers, and hot dogs. The second half was filled with an ethnic food that changed every day. Today it was Mexican.

Griffin smiled and rubbed his hands together. "My favorite."

They sat down to eat, the conversation changing course completely every few minutes. At some point, Brigid tried to explain what exactly they would be doing on the computers to find Marcus, but it was so foreign to the rest of them that she eventually gave up.

"I can just do it," she sighed. "And I'll tell you what to do if I need you."

"Sounds good to me. Take all the time you need..." Griffin said, trailing off.

Everyone knew what he meant, and no one finished the statement. They all agreed without having to voice it.

Griffin nodded to himself, then quickly changed the subject. "So, Luke. Got any siblings?"

Luke raised an eyebrow at him. "No."

"Oh," Griffin said. "Does anyone?"

They all shook their heads.

"Do you?" Marah asked, looking at Griffin.

He shook his head. "No."

"I guess there's only supposed to be one kid in the family," James said. "That way they know who to give the necklace to. And the powers."

Luke nodded. "Makes sense."

"What if there was more than one?" Brigid asked.

James shrugged. "I don't know. First born gets the powers, maybe?"

Griffin laid his head back on the chair and closed his eyes. He sighed. "Who knows. Oh wait...they do," he chuckled bitterly to himself. "We'll just have to add that to the list of things they need to tell us."

"We at least deserve an explanation. Or more details," Marah said. "We're the ones going after him."

"That would be nice," Brigid sighed.

"But apparently it doesn't work that way," Luke said.

James shrugged. "They're going to have to tell us sometime."

"But right now, we forget about it. Focus on what we know and what we need to do," Marah said.

James nodded. "Right."

18

The morning was covered with fog, and the clouds overhead kept James' cabin in prolonged darkness. He peered through the window and saw Marah across the circle of cabins, her head out of her window as well. The wind whipped at his face, and he yelled over it.

"Has it ever been like this?" he asked.

Marah shook her head, looking worried. "Never. It's been sunny every day since we got here."

She disappeared from the window, then came out her door a moment later. The wind whipped at her hair, threatening to undo the small braid she had used as a headband every day since they'd arrived. James watched her for a moment before exiting his cabin as well.

Griffin, Luke, and Brigid were not far behind.

"What is this?" Griffin shouted, staring up at the sky.

"Didn't Wane say that the sky was an illusion?" Brigid asked.

James nodded. "Yeah. They must control the weather somehow."

"Then why in the world would they send a storm in?" Luke asked.

At that moment, Wane stepped into the clearing. Seeing their perplexed stares, he too turned to the sky. He smiled and stepped closer so they could hear him.

"We have people in Jericho that control the weather, both for the city and this camp. Occasionally, they get bored and send in some...interesting weather," he said.

As if on cue, snow started to fall from the sky, lightly dusting the grass and their hair. Then, just as quickly as it had come, it was gone—the white hats on their heads the only trace remaining.

"See what I mean?" Wane asked. "But I asked them for this weather."

"And...*why* would you do that?" Griffin asked.

Wane chuckled. "Because the real world isn't always sunny."

And with that, he turned and disappeared back into the trees, seeming to blend with the shadows.

Griffin sighed. "Fantastic."

The five of them followed Wane down the path, the wind growing stronger by the minute. Leaves were being ripped from the trees, and they pelted them as they walked, making it impossible to see any more than a few feet in front of their faces. The trip to the lake was silent, except for an occasional outburst from Griffin, who was behind the rest of them.

"What the heck was that?!"

"Ow!"

They laughed to themselves each time his voice pierced the air, and even Luke couldn't help but smile.

"How much farther?!"

"That was my eye!"

Finally, they made it out of the trees and to the lake, whose waters looked just as dangerous. The door to the lab was already open, so they clambered down the steps to warmth.

Griffin came down the stairs last. "Tell them to turn off the weather!" he exclaimed.

James turned to look at him and burst out laughing. Griffin's hair was sticking a million different ways, and a leaf was caught in the mess of it all, sticking straight out of the side of his head.

Griffin turned his glare on James. "What?" he demanded.

Brigid, Marah, and Luke had turned by now, and they too joined in the laughter. None of them were able to tell Griffin what was so funny, until finally, James walked over and pulled the leaf out of his hair. He held it in front of Griffin's face.

Griffin pursed his lips, trying desperately to hold onto his glare. But James could see the smile pushing through. Griffin gave in after only a moment, and the grin broke out across his face. He took the leaf from James and shook his head, at a loss for words. Finally, he sighed and laughed along with the rest of them.

By that time, the large screen in the middle of the room had come to life. Wane stood beside it, waiting for them to join him. Once they had gathered behind him, he began.

Wane pulled a document from the corner of the screen and enlarged it. "We have access to government databases—search engines that most people don't even know exist. There's a record of everything. When people move, where they move to, where they came from, what they look like...what they do on a regular basis. If he's out there, we will find him. We just have to be patient. There's a lot of information to sift through."

Brigid nodded, seeming to understand everything Wane had said. The others merely stared at the screen, mesmerized.

"You can start by looking at everyone who has moved out of where we found him last," Wane said.

"That's what we've been doing," Brigid said, sighing. "There's nothing to find."

"Then cross-reference all recent moves with his appearance."

"Doesn't he change his hair color almost every time?"

"Yes, but he can't change his height and weight."

Brigid nodded. "True. We'll get started."

Wane turned to the other four, and they nodded along with Brigid. "Good luck. I'll be back after lunch."

"Where are you going?" Luke asked.

Wane raised an eyebrow and looked down at Luke. He started to speak, but Luke interrupted him.

"We have a right to know."

Wane nodded. "You're right, you do. And I'm sorry. I'm going back up to Jericho to help your parents with their search."

"Our parents are looking too?" Marah asked.

"Yes. We're doing all we can," Wane said. "You're not alone in this."

* * *

Five hours later, James felt very much alone. He stood on a branch, one that he barely trusted to hold his weight for long, watching Brigid climb the tree with ease, growing farther away from him by the minute. She jumped gracefully from branch to branch, never stopping long enough to question any particular branch's commitment to holding her in the air. The footholds she had used barely had even bent with her weight. On the other hand, nearly every branch James had stepped on had squealed in protest, screaming at him to step away.

James stared up at Brigid, watched her climb the tree as if she were floating. For a moment, she seemed to him like some small and delicate creature—a butterfly, maybe—and he feared that if he moved, she would disappear and never be seen again.

Brigid stopped and looked down at James, actually seeming to have weight for the first time since she had begun her ascent up the tree. She cocked her head at him, obviously wondering why James hadn't moved.

Her stare pulled him from his thoughts, brought their task to the forefront of his mind. He glanced at Griffin, Luke, Marah, and Wane, who were standing beside the archery targets and struggling against the still blowing winds.

He focused his gaze on Marah, allowed himself a smile, then quickly turned it to a frown. She hadn't spoken to him since that day on the dock, when she had run from him without explanation. He wanted to ask, wanted to help her, but it seemed impossible. He tried to meet her eyes, but her gaze was focused carefully on Brigid. He couldn't figure out why her silence upset him so much; he had only just met her. And he had never had much interest in the girls he'd known before. But somehow, for some reason even he didn't know, she was different. But, then again, what if it was nothing? What if it was everything new, all of the stress, tricking him into thinking there was something there?

James shook his head, chastised himself for being ridiculous. He was supposed to be focused on training. And what did it matter if Marah wouldn't speak to him? What did it matter if there was something between them or not? If he wasn't well trained enough to keep her and the others alive, nothing would matter.

He started up the tree again and did the thing he did best—wiped his mind of all thoughts and only allowed himself to think about what was right in front of him. He reached for the next branch, and the farthest his mind traveled was to the next one. It was working, not that he was surprised. It had always seemed to work.

Brigid stopped near the top of the tree. She peered through the leaves, across the field to the other line of trees. Wane had said that they had to find a way across. But how? She glanced down at James again and realized that she would have plenty of time to plan.

Somehow, her teleporting had to come into play.

What else? she thought. His materializing? What could he possibly materialize?

She paused, smiled.

A bridge.

Brigid stared down through the branches and saw his dark hair making its way steadily upwards.

"James!" she called, and she saw his face.

"Yeah?"

"Hurry up!"

He smiled. "Getting bored up there?"

"Yes, actually," she called back.

He chuckled and returned his focus to the climb. She turned away and looked back across the field. This was impossible. Why were they being forced to do this? Train and fight a man they'd never known? Ripped from home...probably never to return? And the worst of all: why had their parents never told them?

Brigid sighed and glanced back down at James. She sank down on the branch and leaned her head back against the trunk to wait. The wind pulled harshly against her face, and she was glad for the French braid she kept in her hair. She pulled the braid forward, running her fingers through the end of it.

For the first time in a while, she allowed her thoughts to wander.

Sure, she missed home, but not as much as she had thought she would. There really was nothing to go back to if she was honest with herself. She had had plenty of friends, but for some reason, she had never been nearly as close to them as she was already to the four with her. She couldn't figure out why—maybe it was the fact that they had known each other as children. Maybe.

And, she knew that her friends from home would forget about her as quickly as she had forgotten about them.

James was growing closer; he would reach her in a matter of minutes. When she looked down at him, he met her eyes and smiled. And that simple smile gave her the answer. Immediately, she knew why she didn't miss home.

Because she couldn't imagine going back to a place where she wouldn't see them again. Now that she had found them again, she realized that a life without Marah, James, Griffin, and Luke wasn't worth going back to.

With that realization, she thought of her parents. They had lived without their teammates—without their best friends—for fourteen years. And just to keep them safe. Her respect for her parents swelled, and she regretted doubting their judgment. If they had done all that just to keep her safe...they had to have had a reason to keep this from her.

Brigid smiled to herself, and James' voice broke the silence.

"Enjoying your stay?" he asked, grinning at her.

She returned the smile, her spirits lifted. "I thought I was going to be here for days, you were going so slow."

"Ha, ha. Very funny," James said. He followed her gaze, and they both stared at the expanse they were expected to cross.

"Think of a plan while you were up here?" James asked.

"Actually, yes," Brigid said. "Can you materialize a bridge?"

James laughed. "I can try. But something tells me that would be too easy."

Brigid shrugged. "I thought so too. But maybe that's what the wind is for."

"True," James said. "I'll try."

James pulled himself farther down the branch, getting as close to the edge as he could. He stared across the field, willing a bridge to appear. But nothing happened. He tried again. Again, nothing.

He turned and looked at Brigid. "It's not working."

Then, he held out his arm and a coil of rope appeared. He furrowed his eyebrows at it. "I guess I have to make it in pieces."

"Makes sense," Brigid said. "One thing at a time."

James moved to be next to Brigid. He held up the rope. "Let's tie it to the tree, then you can transport it over to the other side."

Brigid nodded.

James secured a knot around the strongest part of the branch, then handed the other end to Brigid. "Can you make it over there?"

"I think so," Brigid said. "I can pretty much tell where the branches are over there. And if anything goes wrong, I'll just transport back to here, or to the ground."

"Okay. Be careful," James said.

"I will."

Brigid tightened her grip on the rope, then disappeared. James studied the trees across from them, waiting for a trace of her.

Finally, her blonde hair appeared in the leaves. She turned and waved, and he waved back. After only a moment, she was back. She smiled at him. "That wasn't too bad."

He laughed. "Good. Ready for the next one?"

"Of course."

He materialized another coil of rope and tied it to the branch next to the first one. He handed the opposite end to her, and she disappeared again. Her reappearance in their tree was even faster this time.

"Is it secure?"

"Yes, James. I can tie knots," Brigid said.

He laughed. "Just making sure. But if I fall, it's your fault."

"Don't be a baby."

"I'm making the boards now."

"You do that."

James laughed to himself and scooted out to edge of the branches. He studied the ropes and concentrated as hard as he could on what he wanted to appear. Then, small wooden boards began to fall, seemingly from thin air, one after the other until the ropes were covered. Each end of every board rested on one of the ropes, straddling them so that James and Brigid could walk across.

"Is it secure?" Brigid asked.

James laughed aloud. "Don't be a baby."

Brigid couldn't help but smile. "Very original."

"Ready to go?" James asked.

Brigid nodded and started across the branch to the first board. She placed her toe on it tentatively, then pressed more weight on the board. It didn't budge. She turned and smiled at James. "Very nice."

"Told you so," James said.

Brigid put both feet on the board and stood there for a moment. Then, she disappeared. James jumped in surprise. Nearly a second later, though, she appeared only a few boards after the first. She continued to do this—disappearing and reappearing every few boards—until she had made it all the way across.

James shook his head. "Unfair!" he shouted.

Brigid shrugged. "What good is a talent if you don't use it?"

James shook his head and started onto the bridge. The boards seemed to hold his weight as well, so he moved across—with as much caution as possible.

Everything was going well, until about halfway across, one of the boards gave more than it should have. Before James could react, the board snapped in two and he was falling. The first thing he heard was Marah screaming.

He had only a moment of complete terror—of the awful feeling of your body at the mercy of gravity—before his hand caught the rope. He slammed to a stop and rocked back and forth a few times. He steadied himself and held onto the rope with both hands.

He heard Griffin's voice. "Get him off of there!"

But, there was only silence from below him.

All of a sudden, Brigid was above him. She smiled down at him and offered her hand.

"Thanks," James breathed. He took her hand. Before she moved though, she raised one eyebrow.

"Why'd you make yourself a rotten board?" she asked.

James coughed out a laugh. "We'll discuss that when I'm on solid ground."

"Fine with me," Brigid said. She smiled. "Close your eyes."

When he reopened his eyes, he was still on the bridge. He stood beside Brigid, on a good board this time. She released his hand. "We still have to make it across."

"Right," James said. He followed her over the remaining boards and gave a sigh of relief once they were standing on the tree branches.

"Made it," James whispered.

Brigid smiled. "Yes we did." She held out her hand again. "And we're going down the easy way."

"Sounds good to me."

They appeared next to the others and Wane smiled widely at them.

"Very nice job," he said.

"What was with the rotten board?" Griffin asked. "Didn't you make them yourself?"

James sighed. "I don't know."

"Focus," Wane said. "Things like that can happen, even if your focus falters for only a moment."

James nodded. "Oh."

"That's why I asked for the wind," Wane said. "It's distracting, isn't it?"

Brigid laughed. "Very."

"This is why we're training this way. You have to learn to work together; learn the ways your abilities can complement each other," Wane said.

"Complement each other?" Griffin asked.

"Exactly," Wane said.

Griffin raised one eyebrow, then turned to Luke. "I like the way you can blow stuff up. It's very...cool."

"Not that kind of compliment," Marah said, laughing.

Realizing what Griffin had thought, Wane laughed as well. "Not literally compliment each other, Griffin. I mean that you have to learn how your powers go together."

Griffin nodded, still looking slightly confused. "Gotcha."

19

After several hours of fruitless searching the next morning, the five of them sat at the lunch table, nearly finished but in no hurry to move.

"Do you think we'll ever find him?" Griffin asked Brigid.

Brigid shrugged hopelessly. "I don't know. Seems impossible right now. He's like a ghost."

"Who is he anyway?" Marah asked.

"Some guy that used to be friends with our parents, I guess," James said.

"What was his name again?" Griffin asked. "His real name, at least."

"Marcus," Luke muttered.

"Marcus," Griffin repeated, seeming to taste the word. "Wonder what he did."

"Who knows," Brigid said.

"We might not want to," Marah said.

Griffin laughed bitterly. "You're probably right about that one."

Before they could discuss Marcus any further, Wane pulled open the door.

"Are you coming?" he called inside.

The five of them stood and hurriedly put their plates away. Once they had followed him out into the sunshine, Wane began to speak.

"Today is Luke and James," he paused. They both groaned before he could finish his thought. He held up a finger. "And Marah and Brigid."

Marah and Brigid wore equal masks of shock.

"What?" Brigid exclaimed.

"You heard me correctly."

Griffin smiled and followed, while the others dropped grudgingly behind.

"Why all four of us?" James asked.

"Why leave just Griffin out?" Marah asked.

"Why are we still joint training?" Luke asked.

"Why *me?*" Brigid demanded.

The other three smiled at her question, and the mood immediately lightened.

"Well, it can't be that bad," Marah said.

"The more people, the more powers we have to work with," James reasoned.

"Two training days in a row aren't *that* terrible," Brigid said.

"Maybe we're almost done," Luke sighed.

When they finally looked up from their conversation, Wane had led them all the way back to their cabins.

"What're we doing here?" Luke asked.

"I'm about to tell you," Wane said. He motioned for them to follow as he passed through their circle of cabins and kept going, all the way to the line of forest at the back of the circular clearing. He stopped, turned to them, and cleared his throat.

"You will be working in teams, and—for the first and last time in training—against each other."

The four groaned simultaneously, as he had expected.

"Marah and Brigid—you will work together, and Luke and James—you two will be together. The goal is to find what I have hidden in the forest before the other team does."

They kept their groans to themselves this time.

"What have you hidden?" Luke asked.

"You will know it when you see it."

"Not even a hint?" Brigid asked.

Wane smiled. "No, you will know."

"You need to go ahead and get started—it may take a while," Wane continued. He pointed to one tree. "Luke and James, you will start here." Then, he pointed to another tree, only a few feet away. "Marah and Brigid, you will start there."

The two pairs positioned themselves, ready for Wane's signal to move.

"One more thing," Wane said. "If you are in need of any assistance...look to the trees. You may go."

The four of them stared at Wane, their mouths slightly open. They had not even registered his final sentence. Wane met their eyes, smiled. "I said, you may go," he said, snapping them out of their surprise. They stumbled for a moment, then were enveloped in the dark woods.

Griffin smiled after them, pleased with his good fortune. Maybe training two days in a row had turned out well after all. He turned to Wane as he pulled the same, small silver remote from his pocket.

"Do you go anywhere without that thing?" Griffin asked.

Wane laughed. "Yes, it only works in here. Makes things much easier, having one remote."

Griffin nodded, then a thought occurred to him—one he couldn't believe he hadn't thought of until now. "Did you design this place?"

"Yes, I did," Wane said.

"Impressive."

Wane pressed a button on the remote. He slipped it back into his pocket, but it didn't look like anything had happened.

Griffin raised one eyebrow. "What'd that do?"

"Made the forest bigger, more complicated. Added some obstacles."

"You are cruel."

Wane shook his head. "No. Most lessons aren't fun, though."

Griffin nodded. They stood in silence a moment before he spoke again. "Did you ever live on Earth?"

"On Earth? No."

Griffin grew silent again.

"Did you like it?" Wane asked.

"Earth?" Griffin asked. He shrugged. "I don't really have anything to compare it to," he said, staring at Wane.

Wane smiled. "You'll see Jericho soon enough."

* * *

The sunlight filtered through the leaves, giving them shade and plenty of light to see by at the same time. James scanned the trees to the right of them as they walked, Luke scanned the left.

"You would think we'd have run into them by now," James said. "They were only a few trees away."

Luke shrugged. "Who knows what happened to them. Maybe they're lost already."

James rolled his eyes, but said nothing.

"We need to focus on this thing we're supposed to find," Luke continued.

"What do you think it is?" James asked.

"No idea," Luke said. "You would think Wane could have at least told us what it was. But of course not."

"He said we'd know."

"Like that helps," Luke said. He scooped up a pinecone from the forest floor and held it up. "I could say that I know this is it. And we could be done."

"That's not it."

"Well, no duh. But it could be, with all the hints we have."

James smiled. "I think we're looking for something slightly more unusual than a pinecone."

"Let's hope."

Almost a mile away, Marah watched as Brigid scaled the tallest tree they had found so far. Brigid's head broke into the sunlight and she studied their surroundings before returning to the ground.

She shook her head in disbelief. "We've only been walking for a few minutes, and I can't even see the end of the forest. In either direction."

"How is that even possible?" Marah asked.

Brigid shrugged. "I don't know."

"Probably another one of Wane's tricks," Marah said.

"You're probably right," Brigid said. "We need to figure out how to find this thing. I want to get out of here as soon as possible."

Marah nodded. "We need to figure out what he meant by 'look to the trees' too."

"'If you need help, look to the trees'...what does that even mean?" Brigid asked.

Marah shrugged, and they kept walking.

Almost an hour passed, with nothing but walking for either pair. The woods were silent, and as far as they walked, the trees continued to look exactly the same.

"This is ridiculous," Luke muttered. "How long are we going to just walk through the forest?"

James stopped abruptly, turned, and glanced behind him.

"What?" Luke asked, dropping his voice down almost to a whisper.

"Did you hear that?" James asked.

"I didn't hear—"

Then, the leaves in the bush behind them rustled. James and Luke stared, not even daring to take a breath. After a moment, bright yellow eyes appeared between the leaves.

"What is that?" James asked, his voice as hollow as his insides felt.

The nose that belonged to the yellow eyes poked out of the bush, followed by the rest of its head. It looked like a dog, except with a much longer and thinner head. Then it opened its mouth.

The teeth were razor sharp, too sharp for any normal dog. Liquid, the exact bright yellow of its eyes, dropped from the sharpest two teeth into its mouth.

"Run," Luke breathed.

The two of them turned and took off running, going as fast as they could in the thin spaces between the trees. James risked a glance behind them as they ran.

"There's more, maybe three."

Luke said nothing, just grit his teeth and kept running.

After a few minutes and several attempts to turn and lose the dogs, they had made no progress. Their bodies were tiring, but the dogs were still close behind and gaining ground fast.

"James," Luke breathed. "What's the biggest thing you can materialize?"

"I've done a bookshelf."

"Do it, I'll blow it up," Luke said.

James nodded. He glanced behind them, tried to focus on the bookshelf instead of the dogs. He focused, pictured it, and it was there.

"Go," he said.

Luke nodded. He turned, and James heard the explosion behind them. He heard the dog's squeal, heard the leaves around the bookshelf crackling into dust.

"It won't hold them for long," Luke said. "Make another one. And whatever you do, don't stop running."

Making the bookshelf was easier this time. He turned back to Luke after only a second. "Your turn."

Luke only had to glance before James heard the explosion.

They continued like this for at least three bookshelves, each appearing and exploding faster than the one before it. Finally, Luke's breath began to grow heavy. "We need to stop...we'll lose...energy."

James only nodded. They slowed to a jog and made a few more turns to make certain they had lost the dogs. When they could only hear their footsteps against the ground—no dogs, and no crackling flames, they returned to a walk.

"What the heck was that?" Luke asked.

"I have no idea. Nothing normal."

"Have you ever seen a dog drool yellow?"

James chuckled. "Never. And I'm never sleeping in this camp again, knowing what's in the woods."

Marah and Brigid had settled into a comfortable walk when the sounds of James and Luke's explosions reached them.

"What's that?" Brigid asked.

Marah shrugged. "Check from the tree again?"

Brigid nodded and started up the closest one. She jumped from branch to branch, making it easily to the top. She peered over the top branches, and saw—not too far away—flames coiling up from the trees. She made her way to the ground.

"I think we found Luke and James," she said.

"Should we go?" Marah asked.

"Aren't we against each other?" Brigid countered.

Marah sighed. "Yes. But they might be in trouble."

"Alright."

They turned, heading straight towards where Brigid had seen the fire.

After only a step, a pile of leaves fell from the trees, landing right in front of them.

"Um..." Brigid began.

There was a small pop, and Marah and Brigid exchanged glances. Then, the pile of leaves burst into flames.

Brigid gripped Marah's arm, and they both turned and ran in the opposite direction.

"We have to go around it!" Marah shouted over the flames. "We need to find them!"

Brigid nodded, and they turned back to the fire, following along the edge of it until they reached the end. They circled around the flames, heading in the direction they hoped James and Luke would be in. However, the fire was spreading, and fast. They ran, seeming to be in the clear.

But, the fire was catching up.

They heard the crashing and stopped just in time. The tree beside them broke in half and toppled to the ground, engulfed in flames. Marah let out a scream and they immediately turned and ran the opposite way.

"We can't get to them!" Brigid yelled, pulling Marah along with her.

"But—"

"We can't help them if we die trying!"

Marah didn't respond, but she kept pace with Brigid. They both ran without slowing until they were a good half-mile away from the fire.

Brigid stopped to catch her breath, stole a glance behind her.

"It's gone."

Marah nodded. She stood up and circled the area, pacing with her hands on her hips, seemingly deep in thought. Brigid stayed where she was, taking in air as if she hadn't tasted it in days.

Marah ran her hand across one of the trees, then stopped abruptly. She leaned in for a closer look. "No way..." she whispered.

"What?"

"We might have found what he meant by look to the trees."

Brigid, curious, waited for her to continue.

"There's a little circular indentation in the wood. And it's too perfect to be natural," Marah said. She grasped her necklace in her hand, pulled it up to look at it.

"Think it'll fit?" Marah asked.

Brigid shrugged. "Can't hurt to try."

Marah nodded and pressed her charm into the bark. The outline of a small rectangle appeared around the circle, the lines glowing bright blue. Marah and Brigid exchanged glances of amazement as the rectangle slid out, forming a small drawer. The inside still glowed a brilliant blue and a small circle floated out. It didn't seem to be solid, but Marah didn't dare touch it. As she looked closer, she saw that it was an exact replica of the necklace she had just placed into the indentation. The crescent moon glowed brightly, illuminating both their faces, before floating upwards and disappearing into the sky.

"Well that was weird," Brigid murmured.

"Brigid, look at this." Marah was staring back into the small drawer, whose lights had faded to match those of the forest around it. Brigid followed her gaze, saw the apples piled inside.

Brigid shook her head in disbelief. "I guess there are supplies in the trees."

Not as far away as Marah and Brigid might have thought, Griffin and Wane stood, watching the cloud shaped as a crescent moon dissipate. As soon as that had disappeared, another took its place—this one in the shape of an apple.

"What is that?" Griffin asked. It was almost amusing now, all the tricks that Wane had at his disposal.

"Apparently Marah found the first tree with supplies inside."

"You are just full of surprises, aren't you," Griffin muttered.

Wane smirked. "This is all just to prepare you."

"Prepare us for what? To fight some dude that made you mad?" Griffin asked, his smile disappearing.

"Griffin, he didn't just 'make us mad'," Wane said. He stared into the trees, his expression growing somber. Wane's face broke Griffin's resolve a little, but not much.

"Then what did he do? How can you expect us to fight him, when you won't even tell us what he did?"

"There are things you're better off not knowing. At least, not now."

"Why can't we know?" Griffin demanded. "Wouldn't you want to know the reason you were fighting, especially if you or your friends might not make it out? Wouldn't you?!"

"Griffin," Wane pleaded. "I know you deserve to know. But it's not the right time. I don't want you to have to do this anymore than you do. But there is no other way."

"No other way?! How can you say that? There's no other way but to send in a bunch of kids? You never thought to try?"

"We've tried everything."

"Well, you can't blame me for not believing you. You can't even give me a viable reason to go after this guy," Griffin said.

"He stole your home from you! Forced you to live here and hide for fourteen years!" Wane shouted. He quieted again. "That has to be enough for right now, I'm sorry."

"That is not enough!" Griffin shouted, the anger he had stored since his arrival at camp exploding out. "My time here hasn't been all that bad, but the rest of them?" Griffin stopped, took a breath. Images of his friends scrolled through his mind as he spoke, fueling his anger. Brigid, when she pulled away from him—for reasons he could only guess at. Luke, his face when Wane had refused to tell him where his father was. James, the sadness in his eyes when he told Luke that his father was dead. Marah, with the quiet, unassuming smile that hid so many secrets. Griffin stopped the images and swallowed the sob that threatened to escape his throat. "And you want to put us through more to fix it?!"

Wane closed his eyes, and Griffin simmered down—not much, but enough not to scream in his face. He thought he saw a tear escape, but Wane opened his eyes before he could be sure.

"This is not how I wanted any of this to happen. This is not how I wanted you to find out about your past. And I certainly don't want you going into this fight. But there is no other way. If there was, we would have found it, I promise you that."

Wane paused and took a breath. "Would you consider James and Luke your friends?"

He barely gave Griffin the chance to nod before continuing.

"He's the reason they don't have fathers."

20

"What?" Griffin asked, the anger rushing out in a tidal wave, replaced only by sadness and confusion. "What do you mean?"

Wane clapped a hand over his mouth, trying to desperately to bring back the words he had let tumble out. He shook his head, his eyes slowly closing.

Griffin watched him in shock. He stared into the woods. Luke and James were in there somewhere, completely unaware. He had to tell them.

As soon as his mind was made up, Wane removed his hand from his mouth and met Griffin's eyes. "You cannot tell them."

"What? Of course I have to tell them!" Griffin exclaimed.

"No," Wane said. "They can't know. Not yet. It's too complicated, more complicated than you know right now. And it would only be a burden for them to know now."

"They deserve to know."

"I know they do. But let them focus on training, let them live without that knowledge for just a little bit longer," Wane said. "We will tell them. Soon enough."

"They deserve to know," Griffin repeated.

"And they will. Soon. But with everything else going on, do you want to add that?"

Griffin sighed. "No."

He would go along with what Wane wanted for now. And in a way, he was right. But what he didn't realize was that Griffin was going to have to live with the secret. And if his friends ever figured out that he had known...they would never forgive him.

Marah pushed the small drawer of wood back into the tree, still studying it closely.

"Now what?" Brigid asked, interrupting her thoughts.

"Look for more of these," Marah said, running her finger over the circle. "It's the only lead we have right now."

"But what if they only have food?"

"What if what we're supposed to find is in one of them?" Marah countered.

Brigid nodded. "True."

They took opposite sides of the path, examining each tree as they walked slowly past.

It wasn't the fastest method, but for the first time since they'd run into the woods, they had a tangible goal. They walked in silence for a while, occupied in the search and their own thoughts.

"What do you think Griffin's doing?" Brigid asked.

"I don't know...hadn't thought about it. Though I'm sure we'd rather be doing what he's doing," Marah said.

Brigid chuckled. "Probably."

They fell back into a comfortable silence, even the sound of their footsteps fading as the grass grew softer. Finally, it was shattered again by Brigid, who shrieked with delight.

Marah jumped and turned on her heel to see her. "What?"

"I found one!" Brigid exclaimed. Marah hurried over to her, stared down at the little indentation, and smiled.

"Your turn," Marah said.

Brigid grinned and pressed her necklace into the tree. The bluish glow lit their faces again, and this time, the half-moon floated from the opening.

Once the light had faded, they saw a light blue blanket folded into the small compartment.

"They really like the color blue, don't they?" Marah remarked.

Brigid smiled. "Apparently."

They pulled the blanket out and pressed the drawer closed. Brigid glanced upwards.

"It's getting dark," Brigid said.

Marah sighed. "Are we going to have to sleep out here?"

"I guess so," Brigid said. She looked back down at the blanket, which had turned out to be a lot bigger than they had thought. "We need to set up somewhere to sleep."

Brigid smiled. "And I bet I know who has rope."

Marah returned the smile, seeming to read her thoughts. "How are we supposed to find them?"

"Well the fire was in that direction," Brigid said, pointing west. "And my guess is that they ran straight." She turned, facing northwest. "So we go this way."

Marah nodded. "Sounds right."

They started in that direction, leaving their path and weaving through the trees. After several minutes, Brigid glanced at Marah. "Could you look into the future and see if we're coming up on them? Maybe every now and then?"

Marah smiled. "I was hoping I'd get to use my abilities today."

Brigid laughed, and Marah slowed, closing her eyes for a moment.

"Not yet," she said. "Just lots of trees."

They continued through the forest, Marah closing her eyes every few minutes.

Finally, after what felt like hours, Marah stopped. She grabbed Brigid's arm, pulled her back beside her, and held a finger to her lips. She pointed in front of them, through a thick patch of bushes. Brigid grinned, nodded. They crept forward and knelt behind the bushes.

Marah peered through the leaves. For some reason, the insides of the bushes were somewhat hollow, leaving plenty of room for the two of them to sit inside. She tapped Brigid on the shoulder and pointed inside. Brigid nodded, and they crawled in one at a time.

The ground was comfortable enough, and the bushes gave them the ability to see James and Luke clearly without being seen themselves. The two of them settled down to watch, waiting for the perfect opportunity.

"This is stupid," Luke muttered. "There is nothing to find."

James sighed. "And it looks like we're spending the night."

Luke glanced upwards, saw the sky growing darker. "Like I said. Stupid."

"We're going to have to find somewhere to sleep," James continued.

"Luckily for us, we've got you. Why don't you just materialize us a house or something?"

"Not unless you want to put it together," James said.

Luke sighed. "Oh yeah. You're a one board at a time kind of guy."

"That's it," James muttered.

"Why don't we just make a tent or something?" James asked. "I'll make a rope and a blanket and we'll be good."

Brigid smiled and got up onto her knees.

"Works for me," Luke said, and Brigid steadied herself. She kept her focus on James, who had his back to the girls at the moment. She rocked back and forth slightly, waiting.

Marah watched Brigid out of one corner of her eye and kept Luke in the other, making sure that they had not been seen. She turned her full focus to Brigid, and it all seemed to happen at once. If she hadn't been watching closely, she probably would have guessed that it did.

A coil of rope appeared in James' hand, Brigid disappeared from beside her, and the rope was gone just as quickly as it had come.

James looked down at his hand. "What the..."

"What'd you do with it?" Luke asked.

"Nothing! I materialized it and then it disappeared again!"

The sound of branch snapping pierced through the air, much louder than it should have been.

Luke glanced at James. "Brigid."

James shook his head, putting it together as well.

Luke smiled. "Let's go get our rope."

"I can make another—" James started.

Luke rolled his eyes. "Come on."

As soon as they disappeared into the trees, Brigid reappeared beside Marah. She smiled, breathless, and held up the rope. "Mission accomplished."

* * *

Marah and Brigid set up their tent nearby, tying the rope between two trees. An hour or two later, James and Luke gave up their search and set up camp as well. The night was uneventful at best. Not even a slight breeze interrupted them.

As soon as the sun poked through the blanket, Marah sat up, wide awake. She stretched, groaning with the effort.

"Sleep well?" Brigid asked, sitting up as well.

"Not at all. The ground is not as comfortable as you would think."

"You can say that again," Brigid said. She laughed. "Let's find this thing and get out of here."

"Please. You think James and Luke found it yet?"

"Doubtful. We'd know. And they're probably still looking for me."

Marah laughed. "True."

The two of them disassembled their camp quickly. Marah folded the blanket and laid the coil of rope neatly on top.

"What do you want to do with it?" Marah asked.

"I guess we leave it here. We're not really going to need it, are we?"

"What if we spend another night here?"

"We better not," Brigid said. "We'll leave it here. Not having a tent will be motivation to find it faster."

Marah laughed. "Works for me."

James awoke to the sound of Luke groaning. He stared up at the blanket above him, waiting to see if he would have to be the first to get up. Luke had insisted on sleeping separately, so they each had their own tent made of ropes and blankets. James rolled onto his side, then onto his other side. Finally, he gave up and disassembled his tent around him. He stood and made a not-so-neat pile of his supplies. He glanced over at Luke's tent and saw his shadow still lying inside.

He smiled and yanked the blanket that created the top of his tent off of the tree. The sunlight hit Luke in the face and he jumped. He rolled over onto his stomach, grumbling the whole way. James couldn't tell what he was saying, but he guessed it wasn't anything pleasant.

"Rise and shine," James said.

Luke grumbled again. "I hate you."

James nodded and wandered away. "I know."

After several more minutes, and a lot more cursing (James was sure of it now) under his breath, Luke stood up. His blonde hair stuck out in various directions, and his glare was menacing. James kept his distance.

"I thought you were a morning person," James said. He couldn't help it; it was just so much fun to provoke him.

Luke rolled his eyes and his glare grew deeper. "When I sleep in an actual bed. Not the ground."

"Oh. Well let's get going."

"Hang on, sunshine," Luke muttered. "I'm not ready yet."

James frowned and Luke proceeded to disassemble his own tent, leaving it in the same type of pile that James had left his in.

"Ready now?" James asked.

"Just about—"

James stopped him. "You call me sunshine again..."

Luke raised one eyebrow. "Touchy."

"Let's go."

The two set off down the path, the space between them somehow more silent than when they had been sleeping.

"Are we still looking for the supply trees?" Marah asked.

Brigid followed close behind her, glancing at the trees on both sides of the path as they walked. "I guess so. We don't really have anything else to do."

"And if it's not in a tree, we can still find it eventually. We're walking around either way," Marah said.

"Right. So this is our best bet."

"Right."

They continued, now studying every tree they passed and the areas around them. After a while, they came across two trees, right next to each other. Both trees had the circular mark in the center.

Marah stared at both of them. "Aren't they usually more spread out than this?" she asked.

Brigid nodded. "I don't know if this is good or bad."

"Well, we have to try both, don't we?"

"Yes."

"I have a bad feeling about this," Marah said.

Brigid bit her lip. "Me too."

"Here goes nothing," Marah sighed.

Brigid nodded and placed her necklace into the tree. The drawer opened, the half-moon floated out, and the bright blue light faded just like each time before. Brigid took half a step back, her eyes on the opening.

"Is there anything in there?" Marah whispered.

"I don't know," Brigid said. Just as she finished speaking, another type of smoke, this one thicker and more of a yellowish tint, floated out of the drawer.

"What is—" Brigid stopped.

Marah turned to look at her, saw her falling. Before she saw Brigid hit the ground, her own knees buckled and the world slipped away.

The forest all looked the same. James passed tree after tree, tried to keep track of where they'd been and where they were going. But there was nothing to distinguish one part of the forest from another. Absolutely nothing. For all he knew, they were walking in circles.

"We are never going to find this thing," Luke muttered. "There's nothing out here."

"How big is this forest anyway?" James asked.

"Who knows? Who really cares at this point?" Luke asked.

His question was met with silence, but that was really the only answer he needed.

They continued walking, following the path aimlessly. James made a few hopeless turns, taking each one on a whim.

"You got a plan here or something?" Luke asked, after the first couple of turns.

"Not at all."

"Just making sure."

Their steps were rhythmic, accidently matching each other after so many hours of walking. The silence was finally comfortable, and their breathing was even, accustomed to the movement.

All of this was interrupted, however, when James stopped abruptly. He stared in front of him, and Luke almost ran into his back. Curious, he followed James' gaze.

Brigid and Marah were lying on the ground ahead of them. Asleep, or unconscious, or....James stopped himself from considering the worst. Asleep or unconscious.

"What happened to them? Still asleep?" Luke asked.

"They wouldn't still be asleep. And they took our rope, remember? They wouldn't have slept in the open like this after going to all that trouble."

"Then what in the world happened?"

James shook his head. "I don't know."

He hurried forward now, knelt down next to Marah. He shook her gently, but she didn't wake. Luke shook Brigid and got the same response.

"This doesn't look good," Luke said.

James didn't take his eyes from Marah. "What happened to them?"

Luke looked up and studied the trees around them. Then, he noticed the opening in the tree. He pointed to it and James looked up. "Looks like that had something to do with it."

"That's what Wane was talking about," James said. "If you need help, look to the trees."

"It was a trick?"

"I don't know."

James and Luke met each other's eyes, and James shook his head in frustration.

Before he could speak, the opening—as if finally realizing that it hadn't been fully emptied—let out one last spurt of yellow gas.

Brigid sat up, her limbs groaning like old unused doors and her head throbbing so badly that she was sure there was actual movement. She remembered the awful yellow gas—especially its immediate effects. She glanced around; saw Marah on the ground beside her. And...James and Luke? She blinked, tried to make sure she was seeing correctly. How had James and Luke found them? Luckily, they hadn't gotten ahead. They, too, were out cold.

After a moment, Marah roused as well. She stared at James and Luke in confusion, then met Brigid's eyes.

"Guess we need to hurry up and get out of here," Marah said.

Brigid nodded. "They found us at the worst possible time."

Marah smirked in agreement.

"Shall we check the other tree?" Brigid asked.

"Do we really want to go there?" Marah asked, her gaze skeptical.

"Might as well. If there's one good and one bad, we've already gone through the bad."

"What if there's two bad?"

"We risk it," Brigid said. "If we don't, we start from scratch again."

Marah frowned. "Let's open it."

Brigid turned and pressed her necklace into the circle. She and Marah jumped backwards, as far away as possible from the tree while still being able to see if anything came out of the small opening. Finally, it opened and the blue light faded. They waited, held their breath, but there was no yellow smoke.

"Think it's safe?" Brigid asked.

Marah shook her head. "No idea."

Brigid took a hesitant step forward. She stared at the small opening in the bark, then glanced down at James and Luke and back behind her at Marah. Marah nodded her forward, and she closed the gap quickly.

Marah held her breath as Brigid glanced down into the small drawer of wood. Brigid turned around, her smile wide. She held up a small piece of paper.

"We win."

21

"We win?" Marah asked.

"Yes we do," Brigid said. She laughed.

"Why?"

Brigid held up the piece of paper. "It's a map."

"No way."

Brigid laughed. "Yep!"

"Well let's go, before those two wake up!"

Marah and Brigid took off down the path, hurriedly finding their spot on the small map.

"It's not that far away," Marah shouted as they ran.

Brigid nodded. "We should get there soon."

They continued running, taking turns when the map indicated. Finally, they came across a small clearing. Brigid stared down at the map, then back at the grass.

"This is where it's supposed to be," Brigid said.

"Then where is it?"

Brigid shrugged, staring back down at the map. She frowned, then glanced back up at Marah. Marah followed her gaze down to the paper as she pointed.

"See those two trees at the back of the clearing?" Brigid asked.

Marah peered down at the paper, squinted her eyes in attempt to see it clearly. "Is that a one?"

Brigid nodded. The two stenciled trees each had a small one in the center. Marah looked up at the real-life trees. The part of the map that they were studying brought to life in front of them.

Marah crossed the small patch of grass. She looked at the two trees from the drawing and saw the exact same circular indentations that the two of them had seen all morning.

"Brigid," she called distractedly. "You might want to look at this."

Brigid met her at the trees and frowned at the circles. "More drawers?"

"I think we have to do it at the same time. One at each tree," Marah said.

Brigid's eyes brightened and she nodded excitedly. "That's it. That has to be it."

"Want to try it?" Marah asked.

"Now or never," Brigid breathed.

They both lifted their necklaces and met each other's eyes. Brigid nodded softly, and they placed the necklaces in at the same time.

The wind, which had been nonexistent until now, picked up dramatically. Marah felt herself being lifted off the ground, and time seemed to slow. She knew the wind was whipping around them, but she could no longer feel it. She knew that Brigid was still beside her, but she was afraid to look, much less move. All at once, the forest and its trees disappeared. The wind still circled her, trapping her in a translucent cyclone, even though she could not feel it. Then, she felt solid ground, knew she was sitting and felt the solid surface beneath her. She peered through the cyclone as it slowed and allowed her to see more clearly.

She did not recognize the place, though for some reason, she felt that she should. It felt barely, vaguely familiar. But it was impossible to place. She looked down at the bench beneath her and at the street in front of her.

The street was long and winding, and the businesses that lined it were quaint. The sky was a brilliant blue, and there were people milling about, though somehow she knew that they couldn't see her. She scanned the scene, trying to find some way to identify the place. But there was nothing.

And then it was all gone. The beautiful city was gone just as quickly as it had come. Where had the winds taken her? As she puzzled over what she had seen, the camp solidified around her. The cyclone—still there, but seeming to tire of her presence—dumped her onto the ground and was gone as quickly as it had come. Marah glanced around and saw Brigid beside her, looking as disoriented as she felt. She looked up and saw Wane and Griffin's faces above hers.

"How'd it go?" Griffin asked.

Marah rubbed her forehead and groaned. "What was that?"

"You didn't recognize it?" Wane asked.

And suddenly, it all fell into place. She knew why she had recognized the place. She only wished she had realized it sooner.

Marah jumped to her feet, too quickly. She stumbled and Griffin grabbed her arm.

"Careful," he said.

Wane only smiled. "'You know."

Marah nodded. "Why couldn't we have stayed longer?"

Brigid was standing as well, following the conversation with her eyes. Now, she spoke, seeming to come to the same realization as Marah had.

"Was it really?" Brigid asked softly.

Wane nodded, and Griffin finally put the pieces together.

"They got to go to Jericho?" he pouted.

Wane smiled. "They deserved it." He turned to Marah and Brigid. "Very impressive, girls. Good job."

"Thank you," Marah and Brigid echoed each other.

"You made wonderful time," Wane said. He laughed. "When your parents tested this out, it took them nearly three days."

Brigid laughed. "We're smarter than we look."

At her words, James and Luke were dumped onto the ground just as Marah and Brigid had been moments earlier.

Luke stared up at them. "What the heck?"

Brigid smiled. "We won."

"No you didn't."

"Yes we did. I don't think you found anything?" Brigid taunted.

Luke frowned. "That's not fair. We didn't even have time to look. The wind started right when we woke up!"

James only laughed. He stood and brushed the grass off of himself. "They won, fair and square. Just be thankful that we're out of there."

22

After a quiet lunch, Wane convinced a very uneager, exhausted group of five to return to the lab.

Luke complained as they made their way down the path.

"We just got out of the forest. *Why* are we going straight to the lab?" Luke asked.

Brigid shrugged. "I just want to sleep."

They continued in silence, their footsteps dragging across the worn path.

Wane was waiting for them at the entrance to the lab. He smiled enthusiastically at their aggravated expressions. "I could have kept the schedule and made you train this afternoon. But I didn't."

"You could have let us sleep. But you didn't," Luke muttered.

Wane ignored him. He motioned to the lab behind him. "Searching on the computer doesn't take that much energy. You'll just search today, get plenty of sleep tonight, and then we'll start up with training again tomorrow. James and Griffin are going next."

James and Griffin frowned. Brigid allowed a slight smile, while Marah remained indifferent and Luke kept his infuriated grimace.

Wane led them down the steps and into the all too familiar circle of computers. No longer in need of assistance from Wane, Brigid started up the computers and the main screen on the back wall on her own. She pulled up the remains from the search they had done the day before—had it only been one day?—and turned back to Wane.

"Start where we left off?" Brigid asked.

Wane nodded. "Just keep trying."

Wane started up the steps, promising to return by dinnertime. Luke and Griffin sank into the beanbags immediately, on the only side of the room where computers weren't placed. Brigid settled down in front of one of the desktops, and Marah stood in front of the main screen, waiting for whatever Brigid might need. James looked longingly at the beanbags, then finally decided to stand behind Brigid's chair.

"What can I do?" James asked.

Brigid turned to look at him and smiled. His eyes were drooping closed even as he spoke to her. "You have to train tomorrow. Just rest right now. I'll tell you if we need help."

James looked to the empty beanbag beside Griffin. It was tempting, but he knew he shouldn't. He shook his head. "No. You can't do it all."

He sat at the desktop beside her, shook his head again to wake himself up. "Just tell me what to do."

Brigid smiled. "Thank you."

"No problem," James said.

Brigid motioned for Marah to come over. She left her post by the main screen and leaned on the desk that held Brigid's computer. She peered across the tables at James, but looked away as soon as he met her eyes. "Yes?"

"I told you how to pull up the search," Brigid said. "And where to start. Can you show James so I can keep looking?"

"Sure."

Marah moved to stand behind James' chair. She reached over him for the mouse, her arm brushing his as she did so.

Brigid's excited shriek broke the silence, and Griffin jumped, rolling loudly onto the floor.

Marah pulled away from James, stood up much too quickly. He sighed. He knew she should not be his focus, especially not with everything else they had to worry about. But as much as he tried to deny it, it was Marah that filled his thoughts when he wasn't worrying about his responsibilities as a leader. When he wasn't worried about finding Marcus, fighting Marcus, training to be ready. All he did was worry. And think about Marah.

Brigid's exclamations and Griffin's accusations pulled James from his thoughts.

"What are you screaming about, Brigid?" Griffin asked.

"I found him!" Brigid exclaimed.

Luke and Griffin both jumped to their feet.

"What?!" Luke asked.

James pushed his chair away from the desk, almost slamming into Marah in the process. "What? You found him?"

Brigid nodded. She jumped out of her seat and hurried over to the main screen. She pulled up a document from the bottom of the screen and enlarged it. "This is him. All of his information."

Marah shook her head, her expression a mix of disbelief and something else that James couldn't even begin to decipher. "We have to tell Wane," she said.

"Right," Brigid said. "I'll be right back." And then she disappeared.

Only a moment later, Brigid reappeared with Wane in tow.

"We found him," Brigid said, without giving Wane a chance to even take a breath.

"You did what?" Wane asked.

Luke smirked. "I guess you transported him without telling him why?"

Brigid smiled. "Of course I did."

"You found him?" Wane asked again.

"Yes," Brigid said. She took a deep breath and pointed Wane towards the main screen. "All of his information."

Then she pulled up the picture of a driver's license. "And him." She turned to Wane excitedly. "That's him, right?"

Wane's face was pale. "That's him. How did you find him?"

Brigid shook her head. "I have no idea. I was redoing a search I'd already done several times. And he just...popped up. I can't believe I missed him before."

Wane shook his head in amazement. "I can't believe you found him so quickly." He turned to Brigid. "Wonderful job, by the way."

Brigid beamed. "Thank you."

"Where is he?" Marah asked.

"The Black Stone Desert," Brigid said. She scrolled down the document. "In...Nevada."

"Sounds like a lovely place, don't you think?" Griffin asked.

Marah stared at the screen, her eyes wide. "Wonderful."

"So...what?" Luke asked. "Are we going after him?"

Wane nodded. "Tomorrow morning. We can't waste any time."

"Tomorrow morning?" Griffin asked, incredulous. "That soon?"

"If we don't move quickly, we could lose him again," Wane said.

"How are we going to get there?" James asked.

Wane shrugged. "I don't know. Bus, train, car. We'll figure it out. But we need to get ready. You each get one bag."

Then he turned and strode out the door. The five of them stared after him.

"I guess he needs to get ready, too?" Griffin said.

"We only get one bag?" Brigid asked.

James chuckled. "I guess so."

They stared at each other for a moment. Griffin shook his head. "This is too weird," he said.

Brigid nodded. "I didn't think we would actually find him."

"Certainly not this soon," Marah said. She stared at the picture on the screen. "What are we going to do when we get there?"

Brigid shook her head slowly. "I have no idea."

Luke stuffed his hands in his pockets. He, too, stared at the man's face on the wall. "Are we even ready for this?"

Griffin let out a shaky breath. "We're about to find out."

Brigid took one more look at the picture and then powered the computers off. The lights faded, leaving the five of them standing in the darkness. No one said anything. Brigid started up the staircase, and the others followed slowly behind her.

They stepped out into the sunshine just as Wane was returning. He motioned for them to hurry. "Go ahead and have some dinner. Then you need to pack."

They nodded and followed him down the pathway to the dining hall. Wane pushed the door open and walked quickly to the buffet. He filled his plate first and took off. On his way out the door, he called back to them. "Eat quickly!"

Griffin nodded to him. "Will do."

The five of them filled their plates and sat down at their normal table.

"This might be the last time we sit here together," Griffin said.

James raised an eyebrow. "You don't think we're coming back?"

"Who knows where we're going," Griffin said.

Luke nodded. "They could be sending us to another place we don't know about. They don't tell us much, you know."

James smirked. "I know."

Griffin nodded. "And there's always the option that we don't make it out of our little expedition alive."

"Griffin!" Brigid exclaimed.

"What?" Griffin asked. "It's the truth!"

"It's possible," James said. He shook his head at Griffin. "But we'll be fine. Right, Griffin?"

Griffin shrugged. He smiled playfully. "It's possible."

Marah rested her forehead in her hands. She sighed heavily. "This just keeps getting worse."

"You can say that again," Brigid said.

Griffin smiled. "Sorry about that."

"We can't look at this in a bad way. We found him. And the rest will work out somehow," James said.

"Let's hope so," Luke said.

"But we don't know what this guy can do," Marah said. "We don't even know who he is!"

Griffin nodded. He glanced at James. "She's got a point."

"I know. But...but we have to trust that Wane has told us everything we need to know."

"He couldn't possibly have prepared us for every possible scenario," Marah argued.

James shrugged. "I don't know. But I don't think he would send us into a situation where we were certain to fail."

Marah nodded and sat back in her chair.

"Wane's going to come with us, right?" Brigid asked.

"I would think so," James said.

Griffin chuckled weakly. "I would hope so."

A few minutes later, they cleared their plates and left the dining hall. James led the way down the pathway and to their cabins.

"What are we supposed to bring?" Griffin asked.

James shrugged. "Necessities. Whatever fits in one bag, I guess."

Brigid sighed. "And I was just getting used to camp life."

"I hope we come back," Griffin said. "This place is growing on me."

Marah pushed the door to her cabin open and leaned against the doorframe. She smiled. "Slowly."

The five of them disappeared into their respective cabins. A wind swept through the trees. The leaves whispered nervously to each other as if they, too, knew of the events to come.

Sometime later, James placed his full backpack on the floor next to the door. He glanced around the room and sighed. It looked just like it had the day he had found it. The few possessions he had were either packed in his bag for the journey or set aside in the closet.

James sat down at his desk and stared out the window. Only part of him was watching the outside; the other part of him was still wondering. Wondering if he would be able to come back to his little cabin. Wondering if he would ever go back home. Wondering if he would be able to stay with his new friends. And most importantly, wondering what would happen tomorrow.

Movement outside James' window caught his attention. His thoughts stopped for a moment as he tried to figure out what it was. But, there was nothing there.

James shook his head. He must be going crazy.

Then, Griffin's face popped up right next to the window. James jumped in surprise, and his chair clattered to the ground. Griffin grinned and laughed, though James couldn't hear him through the glass. Griffin disappeared then came through the doorway a moment later.

"Gotcha," he said.

James shook his head. "Not cool."

Griffin chuckled. "Dude. I scared the snot out of you!" He laughed again, clearly enjoying the moment.

"Alright, alright. Have your victory."

"Oh, I will."

"Just wait. I'll get you back," James said.

Griffin rolled his eyes. "Whatever."

"I will."

"No, you won't."

"You'll see," James said. "I'll get you back when you least expect it."

Griffin laughed. "I'll believe it when I see it."

James lifted his eyebrows. He shrugged. "You just wait." He lifted his pack off the floor and unzipped the top. "I feel like I'm forgetting something."

Griffin smiled. "Me too. I always feel like that, though. I guess we'll figure out what it is when we're too far away to come back."

James chuckled. "That's usually how it works."

Griffin nodded. "Like I knew I had forgotten something when I packed for camp. But I didn't remember until we got on the bus that I only had one pair of underwear."

James' mouth dropped open. "You've been wearing one pair of underwear this whole—"

"No!" Griffin interrupted him. "Of course not! I washed them in the lake. I'm not disgusting."

James chuckled. "You're insane."

"I will take that as a compliment."

James laughed and pushed the door open. "You should."

The sunlight was fading as James and Griffin made their way to Marah's cabin. Griffin raised his fist to knock, but before he could, Marah had already opened the door. She smiled at their bewildered looks.

"Saw you coming," she said.

Griffin stepped inside and shook his head. "Unfair advantage."

"If you say so," Marah said. "Finished packing already?"

"Yes," Griffin said. "Aren't you?"

"Yes. I think I've rearranged this room at least eight times."

"Nervous?" James asked.

Marah smiled. "How'd you know?"

Griffin dropped down onto Marah's bed. He picked up one of the pillows, fluffed it, then placed it underneath his head. His eyelids fluttered closed and he sighed in contentment.

Marah rolled her eyes. She looked over at James. "He's sleeping at a time like this?"

"I think he could sleep anywhere, anytime," James said.

"He's ridiculous."

"Popped up in my window before we came here," James said. "Nearly scared me to death."

Marah raised her eyebrows. "He did that to you, too?"

"He snuck up on you?"

"Tried to," Marah said. She grinned. "Happened to be looking out the window when he tried to sneak up. That's why I saw both of you coming. I was making sure he wasn't going to try it again."

James chuckled. "He would. Think he tried it on the other two?"

"Wouldn't be surprised."

James glanced over at Griffin, who was now snoring loudly. "Why don't we go find out? He won't miss us."

Marah grinned. "Let's go."

The two of them left the cabin together and walked the short distance to Luke's. James was the first to notice that the front window had been shattered. He peered through the shards of glass at Luke, who was seated at his desk.

"What happened to your window?" James asked.

Luke looked up in surprise. He looked at the window and snickered. "Griffin."

"Tried to scare you, too?" Marah asked.

Luke raised an eyebrow. "Oh, so he tried it on everyone?" He shook his head. "That dimwit thought he could sneak up on me. Soon as he popped up, I made the glass explode. Ran away screaming like a little girl."

James couldn't help but laugh.

Marah peered through the window. "Finished packing?"

Luke nodded. "Ages ago. Just trying to find something to pass the time."

"Us too," James said. "We're going to see how Brigid's doing. Surely Wane will be back soon."

"Where did he go?" Luke asked.

"Who knows," Marah said.

"Getting ready for tomorrow, most likely. I'm sure he'll want to check in on us again before he leaves for the night," James said.

Luke nodded. "We'll see."

James and Marah walked over to Brigid's cabin and knocked on the door. A moment later, the door opened only a crack. Brigid peered through. Then, her eyes brightened and she opened it wider.

"Oh," she said. "It's just you two."

James smiled and stepped inside. "Let me guess. Expecting Griffin?"

"He tried scaring you, too?"

"Of course."

"Didn't work on me, though," Brigid said proudly. "Saw his reflection through the mirror." She motioned towards a small, handheld mirror on her desk. "Right before he popped up, I transported so that my face was right against the window. So *I* scared *him* to death."

James chuckled. "Looks like I'm the only one it worked on."

"Well, the poor guy had to scare *someone*," Brigid said.

Marah nodded. "Probably a good thing. Or we'd never hear the end of it."

"True," James said. "My ability doesn't really help with that kind of thing anyway."

Brigid shrugged. "Sure will help on our trip, though. You could go without packing at all and still be fine."

"Wish I had thought of that before I packed," James said, shaking his head.

Their conversation was interrupted by a loud knocking on the door. James opened it and grinned. Griffin was standing there, frowning at him. "Fall asleep for only a minute and you've ditched me already!"

Before James could reply, Wane had entered the clearing. "Everyone finished?" he called out.

Luke came out of his cabin, and James, Marah, and Brigid filed out of Brigid's cabin. They congregated around the fire pit, as was their usual, unspoken custom.

"I think so," Brigid said. "But, seeing as we don't exactly know what's going on, packing was difficult."

"I'm sure you have everything you'll need. The trip, I've discovered, will take about two days," Wane said.

Griffin gawked. Wane ignored him.

"What happens when we get there?" James asked.

"That's the part I'm not sure about," Wane said ruefully. "All we know is general location; I don't know where in that area he is exactly, or what the place will be like."

"How are we supposed to know where he is?" Marah asked.

"Oh, that part won't be difficult. Hardly anyone lives in that desert."

"So, the part we should be worried about?" Griffin asked.

"What awaits you when you do find him. There's no way I can find out."

They stared at him, their eyes wide with fear.

Wane grimaced. "But you probably didn't want to hear that."

"Probably not," Brigid squeaked.

"It will be fine. You've learned more than enough here. You're ready."

"But—" Marah began.

"No buts," Wane said. "You are ready."

Marah sighed. The rest of them looked about as convinced as she did.

"You will be fine. I promise," Wane said. "Have faith in yourselves."

Brigid gulped. They nodded.

Wane stepped up onto one of the tree stumps and pulled the dust out of his pocket. "See you in the morning," he said as he threw it into the fire pit. And then he was gone.

"That was a terrible pep talk," Griffin said.

Marah groaned. "I don't want to do this."

The five of them exchanged glances, their fear growing stronger and their frowns growing deeper by the minute.

James took a breath, trying to calm himself. A voice echoed through his mind. It was the same voice, saying the same thing that he had heard over and over the past week.

You are their leader.

It was the position he hadn't asked for. The position he, oftentimes, would rather have given to anyone else. What was so special about him that he had to lead them? Why him, when he knew as little as they did?

James sighed. He wanted answers, but he knew better than to ask these questions now. He knew that, for now, he needed to swallow his fear and act like a leader. Even though he felt like the farthest thing from one.

"He's right," James finally said. "We have to have faith in ourselves."

Luke raised a skeptic eyebrow. "How are we supposed to do that when we don't know what we're walking into?"

James frowned. "I don't know. Expect the best instead of the worst."

Marah nodded. She turned her sad eyes towards James. She looked as if she knew something that the rest of them didn't, but James was too afraid to ask.

"I know we should be optimistic, but...I don't know...we've had our powers for just a little over a month. How are we prepared for this?" Marah asked.

James opened his mouth to reply, but Brigid spoke up before he could. "She's right, you know. We just found out about all this. It feels like one thing after another. We don't know anything about this guy we're going after," she said.

"We don't know half the things we should about what we're fighting for," Griffin agreed.

James sighed again. "I know."

"I think I'd rather still be looking for him," Luke said.

"Me too," Marah said. She laughed softly.

No one said anything for a while after that. They looked at each other hopelessly, waiting for some ounce of courage or inspiration. But none came.

Griffin sighed. "I guess this is going to be like training. We have to do it, so we might as well have a good attitude about it."

"Training wasn't life-threatening," Brigid said.

James cracked a smile.

"Well, true," Griffin said. "But, it might not be *that* bad."

"But, then again, it could be *very* bad," Luke said.

Griffin frowned at him. "You are not helping."

Luke shrugged.

Night had fallen. The sun was no longer visible, but the full moon gave plenty of light to see by. Marah shivered. Luke glanced towards the fire pit and flames erupted from it.

Marah smiled. "Thanks."

Griffin raised an eyebrow. "Where did that come from?"

Luke smiled. "Lots of practice."

"See?" James said. "We've all had lots of practice. We're better off than we think."

The rest of them considered this.

Brigid nodded slowly. "I guess you're right."

"I am. We can do this," James said.

Marah smiled. "Maybe we can."

They stayed out talking well into the night. Luke kept the fire going; it was the only light they had to see each other by. It flickered, crackled, and bounced against each of their faces. It danced, seeming to take on a life of its own.

When it was nearly midnight, James pushed himself slowly off of his tree stump.

"We need to get some sleep," he said.

Griffin nodded and stood up. The others stood as well, struggling to even hold their eyes open. They mumbled their good nights and wandered off to their own cabins. The doors fell closed one at a time, and the camp was left in silence, except for the crackling of the fire.

It popped and crackled alone in the darkness, until finally fading away into nothing.

23

"Morning!" Wane called.

James woke with a start. He sat up and looked through the window. The sunlight burned his eyes, stunning him for a moment. He heard a loud groan that sounded like Griffin.

He smiled, until he remembered what today was. Today, they were leaving.

James fell back onto his pillow and closed his eyes. He did not feel nearly as optimistic as he had the night before. With a sigh, he swung his legs over the side of the bed and stood up. He stretched and looked around sadly at the spotless room.

After only a few minutes, he was ready to go. He picked up his backpack, and left the cabin without looking back. The more he thought about it, the worse it was. So he tried not to think about it.

Wane had disappeared already, so James went straight to Marah's cabin and knocked on the door. She opened the door and smiled at him. He stepped inside and looked around. Her cabin looked exactly like his, except for her name above the window. Instead of Anningan, hers said *Artemis: Greek goddess of the crescent moon.*

James looked at Marah. She was sitting on the edge of her bed, staring down at her hands. She felt his eyes on her and looked up. She stood and met James in the middle of the room.

"Are you ready?" James asked softly.

She swallowed hard. "No."

James paused, searching for words. He didn't want to ask about what he had seen in her eyes the night before, but he knew he had to. Hesitantly, he asked, "Last night, why did you look so...sad?"

Marah glanced away. She turned, but James grabbed her hand and pulled her back. "What did you see?" he asked.

Marah sighed. She closed her eyes, then opened them again. She met James' gaze. "Nothing. I can't see that far into the future."

"Then, what—"

"I just have a bad feeling about this."

"Don't," James whispered. He took her other hand; now he held both of her hands in his. He searched her face.

"I only just met you. All of you," Marah said. Her voice broke. "I can't lose you now."

"You won't lose us," James said. "I promise."

Marah smiled. "If only I could believe that."

A single tear dropped onto her cheek. James brushed it away with his fingertip.

"Believe it," James said. "Everything will be okay."

Marah smiled. Then, she frowned and started to pull away, just like she had at the lake, the last time they had been alone.

James tightened his grip on her hands. "What's wrong?" he asked. And when she didn't answer, "Please don't do this to me again."

Marah looked up at him, her eyes filled with regret. "I'm sorry."

"What is it?" James asked.

"Nothing."

"You can tell me, Marah," James whispered.

She shook her head sadly, pulling her gaze from his. "Not yet."

The moment was interrupted by a loud banging outside. Then Griffin's loud voice. "James! Get up!"

James sighed, but there was a hint of a smile on his lips.

"Every time," he muttered. Then he opened Marah's door and leaned outside. "I'm over here," he called over to Griffin.

Griffin turned around and grinned. "Oh," he said, dragging the word out. He winked at James. "I see."

James rolled his eyes. "I came over to see if she was ready to go," he said.

"Whatever you say," Griffin said.

James walked outside and met Griffin beside the fire pit. Marah followed a few minutes later.

The three of them sat down on the tree stumps. Before they could say anything, Luke's door swung open. He stepped outside and nodded at them.

"Sleep well?" Griffin asked.

Luke only laughed.

He sat down on one of the open stumps, and a moment later, Brigid appeared on the one next to him. Luke jumped. Griffin frowned at her. "Can we trade?" Griffin asked.

Brigid smiled and shook her head. "Definitely not."

The five of them sat in silence, trying to suppress their yawns.

"Did anyone sleep at all?" James asked.

"Off and on," Marah said.

"Barely," Brigid said.

"Not really," Luke said with a sigh.

"Pretty well, actually," Griffin said.

James raised an eyebrow at him.

Griffin sighed. "No."

"Well, this should be fun," Luke said. He smirked. "Remind me why we decided to do this?"

"Because we have to find this guy we've never heard of and protect this place we've never been to," Griffin said.

"It sounds awful when you put it that way," Marah said.

"What other way can you put it?" Griffin asked.

No one seemed to know what to say to that.

"Well," James said. "Our parents seem to think we should do it. So I guess we have to go along with it until we know more."

"And when will that be?" Brigid asked.

James didn't have an answer for that, but he was saved from trying to find one by Wane's approach. Wane stepped into the clearing and smiled at the group of them.

"Good," he said. "You're all up."

They smiled weakly at him.

"Are you sure about this?" Griffin asked.

Wane looked over at him. "I'm sure, Griffin. I know you don't want to do this—I'd be worried if you did. But it has to be done."

"We might not be ready," Brigid said.

Wane sighed. "You're ready. You just don't think you are. So this is the perfect opportunity to show you that."

"If you say so," Luke muttered.

Wane nodded encouragingly. "You're ready."

They still weren't completely convinced, but their smiles had grown stronger. James stood up. "What's the plan, then?" he asked.

Wane smiled. "Leaving as soon as possible. Are you all packed?"

They nodded in unison.

"Good. Get your stuff, then, and follow me."

The five of them retrieved their bags and returned quickly to Wane. "One bag each?" he asked, surveying what they had brought. "Good."

They looked up at him nervously. James swung his bag onto his back and the others did the same. Wane turned and led the way down the well-worn path.

They walked in silence all the way down the path, out of the trees, and to the dining hall. Wane did not stop there, though. With a bit of confusion, they followed him down to the field where the bus had been parked when they first arrived at camp. They passed the camp sign and kept going down the road.

"Shouldn't be too long now," Wane called back to them.

Griffin frowned, realizing something. "Me and James never got to train together!" he exclaimed.

Wane turned. "That's alright. We have to leave today, and you two were always close when you were kids. I'm not worried about your ability to work together."

Griffin nodded, then smiled at James. "Fair enough."

A few moments later, Wane stopped abruptly. Marah, James, Griffin, Brigid, and Luke looked around in confusion. They had stopped in the middle of the road, and it didn't look like there was anything around them for miles. Wane held up his hand in what looked like thin air.

All of a sudden, the air in front of them began to ripple, like a small wave, and a large wooden door appeared. Griffin glanced back at James, then at the door, then back at James. James shook his head in disbelief.

The five of them crowded around Wane and the doorway, watching intently to see what he would do next. And what was behind the door.

Wane turned to face them. "There are a few things you need to know before you go," he said.

The doorway was instantly forgotten.

They glanced at each other wildly. "You're not coming?" Brigid gasped.

Wane shook his head. "No."

"Then...what...how—" Griffin stuttered.

Wane raised his hand to stop him. "You'll be fine."

"We were barely convinced of that before," Brigid protested. "And that's when we still thought you were coming."

"How are we supposed to get there?" James asked.

Wane shrugged, a teasing glint in his eyes. "I guess you're going to have to figure that out."

Marah stared at him. She shook her head, unable to say anything.

"I have complete confidence that you can do this. Now go do it," Wane said. He turned around and turned the knob of the wooden door. It swung open to reveal a field that stretched on for miles—so far that they were unable to see the end of it.

James raised an eyebrow. The others stared through the doorway with grim expressions.

"Um," Griffin began.

Wane turned back to them and smiled. "Think of it as character building."

The five of them stared at him as if he had just grown a second head.

"Character building," Luke repeated.

"Precisely," Wane said. "Now, there is something I need to talk to you about before you go."

They looked at him expectantly, curious as to what he would say. James and Griffin exchanged puzzled looks. Marah and Brigid exchanged looks of sheer terror. Luke kept the same stoic expression he had had since they'd arrived at the wooden door.

"First of all," Wane said. He glanced over at James. "I realize that none of you chose to be here. And I realize that all of this has been thrown on you rather unexpectedly."

James furrowed his eyebrows. He had no clue where this was going.

"That being said," Wane continued, "You can decide whether or not you want to continue. It is entirely your decision whether or not you take up your positions as leaders in our city. So, once you leave here, you can make your choice. You can either head home, or you can go to Nevada and find this man."

Wane paused for a moment. He met each of their eyes before continuing. "I will not blame any of you if you choose not to continue. And I will never bother you again. But I must say, if you choose to stay, the journey will be long and at times, it will be difficult. But it will be worth it, that I can promise."

His statement was met with silence. They stood, contemplating what he had said, for what felt like hours.

Finally, Griffin broke the silence. "Intense," he whispered.

James grinned. The rest of them chuckled softly. Wane smiled. "Well then, I guess you should get going."

Wane ushered the five of them out the doorway. The world outside was bright and sunny, with a crisp fall breeze blowing across the grass. They looked around in amazement. All this time, the field had been right outside their camp—and they had never known it.

Wane leaned towards them, his expression growing more solemn. He held one hand on the door and the other on the invisible doorframe. "Good luck."

They nodded in response. "Thanks," James said.

"Oh!" Wane exclaimed. "I almost forgot."

James looked at him curiously. Wane let go of the door, holding it open with his foot instead. He held out one hand, palm up, and pulled up his shirt sleeve. He tilted his wrist towards them and they leaned in to see. Right in the middle of his wrist, Wane had a small, circular tattoo.

They stared at the mark in confusion.

"What is it?" Brigid asked.

Wane smiled, as if it should be obvious. "The moon."

The five of them nodded to themselves—the tattoo instantly made much more sense.

"Everyone living in Jericho has one," Wane continued. "And our most trusted friends...allies, you could say, that live on Earth also have one. While you are on Earth, look for this symbol. That is the only way you can know whether or not to trust someone."

"Wow," Marah murmured.

"Isn't that easy to fake?" Luke asked.

"You would think," Wane said, grinning as if he had been waiting for the question. "But it cannot be replicated."

From the seemingly never-ending supply of moonstone dust in his pocket, Wane pulled out a pinch and sprinkled it over his wrist. A moment later, a small, blindingly bright light pierced through the dust. Then another, and another. James counted seven lights in all.

Wane shook the dust off and showed them his wrist. Seven glowing letters lined the top curve of the moon. *Jericho.*

"Sweet," Griffin whispered.

Wane chuckled. "Yes. So, not as easy to fake. And anyone with the true mark will know to show you the letters first."

"Alright," Wane said. He cleared his throat. "I guess you should get going."

He paused. "Believe me; I know that the five of you can do this. I wouldn't be sending you if I didn't believe it. I may not have shown it lately, but it's only because I had to be hard on you. I've waited a very long fourteen years to see you again, and you're the closest thing to family that I have. I wouldn't be doing any of this if I didn't care."

James smiled. "Thank you." The other four smiled as well.

Wane swallowed, his eyes saddened. "Go on, then," he said. "Good luck."

They nodded.

Griffin glanced around. "Can you at least tell us where we are?" he asked.

Wane smiled at that. "On a farm," he said.

And with that, he closed the door and he and the camp were gone.

24

They stared at the place where the door had just been. It looked as if the camp had never been there. It was only grass and trees, for miles and miles, in all directions.

James turned around and noticed something that he hadn't seen before. Far off to the right, there was what looked like a small house. He pointed it out to the others.

"I guess we should head over there," James said. "Whoever lives there can tell us where we are."

"And give us directions home," Luke said.

James turned and stared at him. Marah, Brigid, and Griffin also looked shocked.

"What?" James asked.

Luke raised an eyebrow. "We're going home aren't we?"

His question was met with silence. He gave an exasperated sigh.

"He said we could leave. None of you wanted to do this in the first place anyway. What? Now that we're actually allowed to leave you want to stay?"

James sighed. "I don't know what to do."

"We might as well go to that house and then decide," Marah said. "We have to go there either way."

Luke nodded. "Alright."

"We'll decide as soon as we leave," James agreed.

They started off in the direction of the small house— picking their way over rows and rows of plants. They passed by strawberries, pumpkins, and everything in between. The house grew bigger the closer they got to it.

When they were about halfway there, Griffin tripped over an abnormally large strawberry. He stumbled and caught himself, saving his face from a very unpleasant meeting with the dirt. He cut his eyes at James.

"How long is this going to take?" Griffin asked.

James tried to suppress a laugh. "Looks like we're almost there."

"Just watch out for the strawberries," Luke said. He smirked.

Griffin looked dangerously close to punching Luke square in the face.

Marah stepped in between them as quickly as she could. She nodded as if nothing had happened. "So," she began. "Should we be looking for that moon symbol on whoever lives here?"

"Probably," James said.

"Oh yeah, already forgot about that," Griffin said. "Probably would be a good idea. That way we know they won't kill us."

Brigid grimaced. "What are we supposed to do? Demand to see it before we walk in the door?"

"Shouldn't we just wait for them to show it? Wane said they would know to," Marah said.

James shrugged. "I guess we'll have to wait and see."

They came up closer to the house. It was small, and looked as if had been there for hundreds of years. They had come to a road; there was a mailbox on the edge of the road and a dirt path leading to the house. No one was coming down the road and it looked as if no one had in a long time. As far as they could see, the house they were standing at was the only one around.

"Let's look at the mailbox first," Griffin suggested. "It might have a name on it."

They turned and headed for the mailbox. The mailbox looked as old as the house that it was in front of. The deep blue box on the top was supported by a wooden stake that had been wedged into the dirt. The red flag hung limp—useless.

It didn't look like there was anything extra on the mailbox—until they were right up next to it. James was the first to notice the small circular shape carved in the bottom corner of the mailbox. He traced it with his finger. "The moon," he murmured.

"Looks like we're safe," Brigid said.

"Still could be a fake," Luke said. "We need to see the tattoo."

With bated breath, they headed down the dirt pathway to the house. James stepped hesitantly onto the wooden porch. The board creaked dangerously, but stayed where it was. He released a breath and moved closer to the door. He turned around and looked curiously at the others. None of them had made a move towards the porch.

"Coming?" James asked.

Griffin stared warily at the rotting wood. "We'll wait. You can tell us if they have a tattoo or not." He paused, a grin sneaking slowly onto his face. "And if they don't, we can run."

"So they can grab me...but you'll have time to run?" James asked, his eyebrows furrowed in disbelief.

The grin spread across Griffin's face. "Exactly."

James shook his head and turned around. He knocked softly on the door, then, gaining more confidence, he knocked harder. He held his breath and waited.

They could hear someone moving through the house. There was a crash, more scuffling, and then the door swung open.

The man in the doorway grinned at them. He looked to be in his thirties or forties, and he had sandy brown hair. His hazel eyes sparkled with excitement.

"It's really you, isn't it?" he asked, grinning from ear to ear. "Fantastic," he whispered, mostly to himself.

For a moment, he stood there, studying them. His smile never faded. "Oh, I'm sorry! Do come in," he said.

James shuffled his feet. He had no idea how to approach the tattoo delicately enough so as not to dampen the man's obvious excitement at the sight of them. Why it was so 'fantastic' to see them, though, was beyond him.

Thankfully, the man seemed to realize he had missed something when the five of them remained where they were standing. His eyes widened, and he started muttering to himself, most likely berating himself for forgetting to show his tattoo. He held up a finger and disappeared into the house, returning only seconds later with dust in between his thumb and index finger. He showed them his wrist, and sure enough, there was the small black circle. Then, he sprinkled the dust onto it. The letters glowed clearly. *Jericho.*

James smiled and stepped into the house. The other four followed closely behind him. The house was dark at first, but his eyes quickly adjusted. Directly to the left of the front door, there was another door that opened to reveal a long, dark staircase. The man led them down the stairs, to the right, and down a long hallway, switching on lamps that were positioned at certain intervals down the hall as he passed them.

"What's your name?" James called out to him as they made their way down the hall.

"Henry Knight."

"Nice to meet you, Mr. Knight."

"You can call me Henry," he said, with a smile in his voice.

Finally, they arrived at a small, box-shaped room. There was a circular table in the middle, with a lamp hanging above it. Henry switched on that lamp and the others—there was one attached to the wall in each corner of the room. On the back wall, there was a refrigerator, sink, and cupboards. On the left wall, there was a long, navy blue sofa.

"Sit down, sit down," Henry said, motioning towards the table. They sat, and he walked over to the back wall. He opened one of the cupboards and pulled a box out. He carried it over to the table and layed it in the middle.

"Moon pies," he said, smiling. "Only thing down here that reminds me of home. Not exactly moon food, but its close enough."

The five of them returned the smile and each took one.

"You lived there? Jericho?" James asked.

"All my life," Henry said. "Offered to come down here when the trouble started."

"Do you miss it?" Brigid asked.

"Oh, yes." He smiled wistfully. "I loved it up there."

The five of them had stopped nibbling on the snacks; Henry had their full attention.

He raised his eyebrows. "Oh! That's right. I keep forgetting you kids have never been there. Funny, how that is. Legends in a place you've never even been to."

Griffin choked on his pie. "Legends?"

The rest of them had similar looks of shock.

"Well, of course you're legends! How could you not be? You're practically royalty!"

"How are we royalty?" Marah asked.

"Your parents are the leaders of the city. Kings and queens, really, but we don't call them that. You will be too, and on top of that, you're going to save the city! You're legends, alright."

They glanced away, feeling guilty. Griffin gulped, and Luke nibbled nervously on his moon pie. Henry didn't seem to notice their discomfort.

He smiled at them again. "It has been so long. Too long," Henry said. He chuckled softly. "Still remember the day each of you were born. Mighty exciting day, it was. Been looking forward to this day ever since you left."

They didn't know what to say. They'd never received this much attention, or been treated like this—like they were celebrities, or something.

"Well, thanks," Griffin said.

Henry nodded happily. "Anything I can help you with?"

"Actually, there is," James said. "First of all, could you tell us where we are?"

Henry stared at them in surprise. "Wane didn't even tell you where you were?" He chuckled. "Man of strange tactics, that one."

Griffin nodded in agreement. James kicked him under the table.

"We're in the lovely, very empty state of Nebraska. And you're headed to?"

"Nevada. Black Rock Desert, to be exact," Marah said.

"Right, right. Wane had me get your tickets last night," Henry said. He stood up and pulled five slips of paper off the countertop. "Got them right here."

He handed one to each of them. "The bus leaves shortly. You can stay here until then."

"Thanks," they replied together.

Henry smiled so wide, he looked as if he had won the lottery. "Oh, don't mention it."

Luke glanced around the room. "Why are we so far down in the basement, anyway?" he asked.

"Safety precaution. You never know. Can't have the five heirs to the throne of Jericho out in broad daylight! Not when Marcus could have friends anywhere."

Marah looked at Henry curiously. She opened her mouth to speak, but hesitated. Finally, she said, "Did you know him? Marcus?"

Henry scowled for the first time since they'd met him. "I knew him, alright. Liked him pretty well, too, until....well, you know." Henry's frown grew deeper. "You catch him, alright? Catch the scoundrel and put him in his place. He doesn't deserve to be free. Not after what he did."

They nodded solemnly. Marah stared down at her hands. Griffin reached for another moon pie.

"But let's not talk about him, not today," Henry said. His smile returned. "My old friend, Wane. How is he?"

James smiled back. "He's good. Been busy helping us train."

"Good man, that one. Prepare you well?"

Griffin snickered. "We hope so."

"You will be brilliant," Henry said.

Marah smiled. "Thank you."

Henry returned the smile. He glanced down at his watch and sighed. "I believe it is time for you all to be on your way."

"Already?" Griffin asked.

Henry smiled at Griffin, then nodded sadly. "It is."

He led them back to the front door and held the door open. He followed them outside, pulling the door closed behind him. He pointed down the road. "Take this road. When you come to the fork, turn right. Follow that for a little ways. Take the next left turn and you'll find yourself at the bus station."

"Thank you," James said. The five of them waved goodbye and started off down the road.

"Best of luck to you!" Henry exclaimed. He stood on the porch and watched the road until the five of them were no longer visible.

25

A few minutes later, Luke glanced behind him.

Griffin followed his gaze. "What are you looking for?"

"Making sure Henry couldn't see us anymore," Luke said. Then he turned on James. "You were supposed to ask for directions home, too."

James stared at him. "How was I supposed to ask him that? You heard him, he's been waiting his entire life. To meet *us*. And you want me to ask him for directions home?"

Luke sighed. "I guess not. But we still need to know."

"After all that, you still want to go home?" Marah asked.

Luke stopped walking. He met each of their eyes. "Just because our parents are the leaders, everyone thinks that we're going to do it, too. Everyone thinks we're so great just because our parents were." He paused. "What if we're not cut out for this?"

"But what if we are?" James asked.

Luke furrowed his eyebrows. "What?"

"We'll never know if we don't try," James said.

"He's right, you know," Brigid said. "And who's going to do it if we don't?"

Luke snorted. "Wane."

"Yeah, right." Griffin muttered.

"I think we should go," Marah said. "So what if we've never actually been to the moon? These people really care about us. Maybe, right now, we should just do it for them."

The three guys frowned and glanced at each other.

"I hate it when she's right," Griffin said.

"I'm going," Brigid said. Marah smiled at her in appreciation.

"That's two," Marah said. "Anyone else?"

James sighed. "Three."

"I will not give in to peer pressure," Griffin said, crossing his arms.

James raised an eyebrow at him. It was all he needed to do.

Griffin let out an exasperated sigh. "Just this once."

Marah smiled. Then she looked at Luke. "Luke?" she prodded.

Luke stared at the rest of them. Then he glanced down the street. "I'm sure the four of you would be perfectly capable on your own."

"Luke..." Marah began.

"Fine," Luke muttered.

Brigid smiled. "It's settled then. We're all going."

Luke muttered under his breath.

"What was that?" Brigid asked.

"Oh, nothing."

"Good."

James chuckled. "Ready to go?"

"Lead the way," Marah said.

The five of them started down the road again. Because it was obvious that no cars would be coming, they were able to walk down the middle of the street.

A few minutes down the road, Griffin asked, "What happens if a car does come?"

"The road is completely straight and the ground is flat. We'll see them coming with plenty of time," James said.

"Just making sure."

They continued down the road. They watched carefully for any oncoming cars, but none ever came.

Several minutes later, Griffin spoke again. "How long do you think it's going to take?"

"It's only been ten minutes, Griffin," Luke said.

"I know that, thank you very much. But how much *longer*?"

"Who knows. But, since we haven't gotten to the first turn yet, I'm thinking it'll be awhile," James said.

Griffin sighed. "Awesome."

When only about five minutes had passed, Griffin spoke up. Again.

"Well, this is fun," Griffin said.

"Every five minutes," Luke muttered. Griffin ignored him.

"Maybe we should sing a song. Pass the time," Griffin said. He took a deep breath, and was about to start singing, when Luke interrupted him.

"Griffin."

"Yes?"

"Don't you dare."

"Kill joy," Griffin muttered under his breath.

Another five minutes passed.

"How about twenty questions?" Griffin asked.

Luke glared at him.

"What?" James asked.

Griffin smiled triumphantly. "Twenty questions. I ask a question, and we all give an answer."

"And why would we do that?" Luke asked.

Griffin frowned at him. "Well, we decided not to go home. And Wane said that if we chose to do this, it would be a long and difficult journey. Did he not?"

"Your point?" Luke asked.

"Well, it would be nice to know each other better. Because we'll be together for the long and difficult stuff."

"I think it's a good idea," Brigid said.

"Thank you, Brigid," Griffin said. He sent a smug smile in Luke's direction.

Luke grumbled. "Whatever."

"Okay. What's your favorite color?" Griffin asked, grinning.

Luke groaned. "You have got to be kidding me." He looked over at James. "Is he serious?"

James smiled. He glanced at Griffin. "Perfectly."

Luke rubbed his temples and sighed. "Of all the people to be stuck with."

James chuckled.

Griffin cleared his throat. "I said, what's your favorite color?"

"Pink," Brigid said. She smiled up at Griffin.

He smiled back. "Thank you."

"Silver," Marah said.

Griffin grinned. "Mine's green."

"Blue," James said.

Luke sighed. He glanced over at Griffin. "Black."

Griffin's eyes widened slightly. "Well, that's...great." He coughed. "Next question. Um, your favorite...ice cream flavor."

Luke rolled his eyes. Brigid answered first again. "Strawberry."

Marah thought for a moment. "Cookie dough, probably."

"Rocky road," Griffin said, glancing over at James.

"With every topping imaginable," James said.

Griffin laughed and patted his stomach.

"Mine's chocolate," James said.

Luke smiled to himself. "I'm lactose intolerant."

Griffin glanced over at Luke in surprise. Luke stared back at him. Griffin closed his mouth. "Right. Well, okay then."

When Griffin had turned away, Luke smirked. James only shook his head.

"Next question," Griffin said. "What's your favorite...fruit?"

"These are the most ridiculous questions I've ever heard," Luke whispered to James. James stifled a laugh.

"Give him a break," James said. "He's trying."

"And I'm trying not to smack him across the face."

"Just answer the question."

James and Luke turned to the others. Griffin was looking at them expectantly.

"We've already answered," Griffin said.

"Oh, well, I guess we missed that," James said.

"Please do tell us again," Luke muttered.

Griffin sighed. "I said that my favorite fruit is an apple."

"Mine is peaches," Brigid said.

"And mine is grapes," Marah said.

"Well, that's just wonderful," Luke whispered. James elbowed him in the side.

"I guess mine would be oranges," James said.

Luke nodded. "I would have to say...poisonous apples."

Griffin stared at him.

"Or strawberries," Luke added.

Now, Griffin was glaring. "Are you *trying* to annoy me?"

"Yes."

"Would you *like* to walk in silence?" Griffin demanded.

"Yes."

"I didn't think so!" Griffin shouted at him. "Next question!"

Luke looked like he was trying to decide whether to hurt Griffin or laugh at him.

"Fine," Luke said. "My favorite color is red. My favorite ice cream flavor is vanilla. And I actually do like strawberries. Happy?"

"Very."

"Good."

"Next question," Griffin said. "And your actual answers please."

He thought for a moment. "What's your biggest fear?"

Luke stared at him. "How did we get from our favorite color to our biggest fear?"

"I will ask the questions," Griffin said.

"Fine then. My biggest fear is that I'll be stuck with you people for the rest of my life."

"That this road will never end," Griffin said.

"That I'll be old and alone...with a bunch of cats," Brigid said. She tried to suppress her smile.

"That we're all going to die," Marah said.

James disguised his laugh with an over exaggerated cough.

"Marah!" Brigid exclaimed.

"What? It's a realistic fear!" Marah replied.

Griffin nodded. "She has a point. But we're all going to die eventually. Me? I'd like to kick the bucket at eighty-eight."

"Eighty-eight," James repeated.

"And why do you want to die at eighty-eight?" Luke asked.

"Seems like a good number," Griffin said. "Very nice, long life."

Luke snickered and shook his head. "If you say so."

Griffin seemed to be the only one to notice that James hadn't given an answer. But with one look at his face, he decided not to push it. The others may not have noticed, but he knew what James was thinking.

"Alright," Griffin said. "Next question. Let's see...what's your favorite type of plant?"

"You know...my biggest fear is actually that someone will punch you in the face and I'll miss it," Luke said.

Brigid laughed. Griffin glared down at her. She closed her mouth. "Sorry."

"Moving on," Griffin said.

"Just ten minutes. Can you please *shut up* for ten minutes?" Luke asked.

Griffin's shoulders drooped. He sighed and stared down at the ground.

They continued down the road in complete silence.

26

Some time later, they came to the bend in the road that Henry had described. Griffin sighed in relief. "Finally."

"Which way are we supposed to turn again?" Griffin asked.

"After all that, you don't remember which way we're supposed to turn?!" Luke demanded.

"Of course I remember. It's left."

"It's right," James said.

"Oh...well, we would have gotten there eventually."

Luke snickered. "Right. And then your biggest fear really would have come true."

"So would yours," Griffin said.

"I wouldn't have followed you," Luke said, as if it was the last thing he would ever do.

Griffin glared at Luke. "Well, it's a good thing James remembered."

They turned onto the next road. The farther they walked down it, the more it looked like an actual town. There were a few buildings, rather than the flat fields they had seen on the way, and a few cars actually passed them. They stepped up onto the sidewalk, out of the way of oncoming traffic.

"So there is life in Nebraska," Luke said.

James laughed. "I guess we finally found it."

"Don't we take the first left?" Marah asked.

James nodded. This road was much shorter than the one they had been on before, so they reached the turn quickly. They turned left, followed that road for only a minute, and then arrived at the bus station. There was no one in sight, and only one bus was parked out front.

"I guess that's our bus," Brigid said hesitantly.

They looked around. The station was a small white building, with its name written across the top being its only decoration. They walked over to the single bus and peered through the door. The driver was already seated in the bus. He had hair the color of dark chocolate and eyes the color of emeralds. When he saw them looking at him, he was clearly annoyed. He pushed the door open.

"Look, kids. I know I'm the first bus of the day and I know I'm already here. But I can't let you on right—" He paused and stared down at them. He furrowed his eyebrows in concentration. Then, his eyes widened. "Oh."

James, Luke, Griffin, Marah, and Brigid glanced at each other.

"What?" Griffin asked.

"Wow," the man whispered to himself. Then, louder, "It's really you."

The five of them were still slightly confused.

"Wane sent you, right?"

"Oh!" Marah exclaimed. "Yes."

The man finally seemed to realize the reason for their confusion. "Oh, my apologies," he said. Then, he pulled down his sleeve and showed them the tattoo on his wrist.

James raised an eyebrow and waited.

The man sighed, pulled some dust from his pocket, and sprinkled it onto his wrist. The letters glowed clearly.

James smiled. "Nice to meet you."

The man chuckled. "Wane taught you well. I'm Stephen Bradley." He held out his hand, and James shook it.

"I'm James."

"Please. Of course I know who you are," Mr. Bradley said. He shook his head in disbelief. "James Wood, as I live and breathe."

He smiled at the others. "All of you. Wonderful to finally see you again."

"You know our parents?" Marah asked.

"Of course. Lived in Jericho myself. Came down here when they needed the help."

"Like Henry?" Brigid asked.

"Ah, you met Henry?" Mr. Bradley smiled. "Yes, we came down together. Don't get to see him much anymore, though."

"Thank you," Marah said. "For doing this."

He smiled at her. "For giving you a ride? Not a problem at all. My pleasure, actually. Henry and I can now say we were the first to see you again," he said, grinning.

Marah returned the smile.

"Well, you kids need to get your seats. I'll take your tickets," Mr. Bradley said. He took their tickets, smiling at each of them as he did so. They smiled back at him, then made their way to the back of the bus. In the very last row, they found two sets of seats facing each other, with a table in between them that had been attached to the wall.

"Perfect," Brigid said, smiling. She slid into the seat facing the back. Marah slid into the seat facing Brigid, James and Griffin sat beside Marah, and Luke sat down beside Brigid. They piled their bags into the rack above their seats and then settled back down. Brigid crossed her arms and rested them on the table. She looked around at the other four.

"Ready to be stuck here for twenty four hours?" Brigid asked.

Luke groaned.

"A whole day?" Griffin asked.

"More than that," James said. "Didn't Wane say the trip would take about two days?"

Marah sighed. "Yes."

"And I thought the road was bad," Luke grumbled.

Brigid frowned at him. "It won't be bad."

"You think sitting in a bus for two straight days is going to be *fun*?" Luke asked.

"For once, I'm with Luke," Griffin said, not looking particularly happy about it.

"Griffin," Marah said, "You're the one always saying that we have to do it, so we might as well have a good attitude about it."

James swallowed a laugh at Griffin's expression. Griffin shot a look at James, then turned back to Marah. He sighed. "You are not supposed to use my words against me."

Marah shrugged, a smile creeping onto her face. "I'm just repeating what you said."

Their conversation was interrupted by a commotion at the front of the bus. They glanced over the edge of the seats. Mr. Bradley caught their gazes and winked at them. Other passengers had just begun boarding.

The passengers boarded quickly, and after only a few minutes, the bus was completely full. James scanned the new faces. Most of the people he saw weren't very unusual. There was a young woman with blonde hair pulled back so tight it looked like she had glued her hair to the top of her head. Another young woman with hair the color of dirt, though James thought there might actually be some dirt in it. She had two small children with her, a boy and girl, who also looked as if they hadn't washed their faces in days. There was a very well-groomed man with a black briefcase. There was an old man, with a contented smile on his face, holding a duffel bag that looked like it had been made out of old curtains.

The last person that James noticed made his insides form into a knot tighter than the blonde woman's ponytail. The man sat in the center of the bus. He had shaggy, jet black hair that came past his ears. His eyes were the same color as his hair. Similar to the color of coal, James thought. The man was wearing a long black overcoat. Seeming to sense James' eyes on him, the man turned and stared back at him. His gaze was cold, and the sneer on his face made James turn away as fast as possible.

James leaned towards Marah. "Don't look right now, but there's a man in the middle of the bus. He's wearing a dark coat."

Marah glanced around at the different people. Then, her eyes widened. "I see him."

"You weren't supposed to look!"

"He didn't see me looking, calm down."

Brigid raised an eyebrow at them. "What?" she whispered.

Brigid's question piqued the interest of Luke and Griffin, so they leaned in as well.

"What's going on?" Griffin asked.

James sighed. "There's a man in the middle of the bus with a dark coat on. I was looking around and he stared back at me. I might be paranoid...but he doesn't look right."

"What do you mean, he doesn't look right?" Luke asked.

"I mean, he doesn't look like a normal bus passenger," James said.

Griffin raised his head slightly and looked around. His eyes widened after a few moments, and James knew he had found the man. "Oh," Griffin whispered.

"Yeah."

"Well, now I have to see him," Luke said.

"Be discreet about it, please," Marah whispered.

Luke nodded, slid out of his seat, and stood up. He stretched and scanned the bus. Then he slid back into his seat.

"Real discreet," Marah said, frowning.

Luke grinned. "I see what you mean," he said. "Think he's with Marcus?" Luke turned to Brigid. "That's his name, right? The guy we're after?"

Brigid nodded grimly.

"Maybe," James said. "I don't see how Marcus could know where we are, though."

Marah didn't look convinced. "You never know."

"What's the plan, anyway? When we get there?" Griffin asked. "Does anyone know?"

James sighed. "I have no idea. We don't even know where he is exactly."

"What are we going to do? Just come up with a plan really quick, right before we walk into it?" Luke asked.

"I don't think we really have a choice," Brigid said.

"Wonderful," Griffin muttered.

Finally, they heard the bus doors creak closed and the engine rumble to a start. They pulled out of the station's parking lot and began the long trip to Nevada.

Brigid peered out the window. "No turning back now."

The others smiled weakly.

Griffin turned to James. "Want to materialize us some snacks?"

"You're hungry already?" James asked.

"Before getting on this bus, we walked down a deserted road for almost an hour. Of course I'm hungry!"

James chuckled. "Alright. But make sure no one's looking."

Griffin glanced over at the people seated in the row across from them. They were already sound asleep. Griffin snorted. "I think we're good," he said, pointing at them. "No one else can see us."

"What do you want then?" James asked.

"Hmm...how about some steak?" Griffin suggested.

"I thought you wanted a snack!" Brigid exclaimed.

Griffin sighed. "Fine. How about...some pretzels?"

"That's better," James said, laughing. "Anyone else?"

Marah and Brigid shook their heads.

"I'm good right now," Luke said. He leaned his head back onto the seat. "Only forty-eight hours to go."

27

Several hours later, after each of them had agreed to a snack, Marah announced that she was going to try and get some sleep. She used her bag as a pillow, leaned against the window, and was sound asleep in a matter of seconds.

"Well, that was fast," Griffin said.

James smiled. "It's been a long day."

Luke studied Marah across the table. "Think she's seeing the future?"

Griffin raised an eyebrow. "Maybe. I wonder if she can see what's going to happen tomorrow."

"I don't think I want to know," James said.

"That could help us, though," Luke said. "If she could see what the place is before we get there."

James glanced over at her. "Depends how far into the future she can see."

Brigid leaned her head on the seat and looked out the window. The sun was setting, and the sky was a beautiful mixture of reds, oranges, and yellows. She smiled to herself, hoping that she would be able to see many more of those. Though she would never admit it to the others, she was terrified of what would happen in the next few days. What if something went wrong? What if one of them, even all of them, didn't make it out alive? All of the responsibility of finding this man had been put on her, and now she regretted finding him. How could she ever forgive herself if someone got hurt? Or...worse?

Brigid closed her eyes and tried to close out the guys' conversation. She wanted to fall asleep, but her thoughts would not slow. Though she had only just met the four people sitting with her, she felt as if she had known them much longer than that. She had always gotten attached to people quickly, caring for them after only a short time. But how could she not care for these people? After spending every waking moment of the last few weeks with them? She felt closer to this group of friends than anyone else she had ever met. Their situation had brought them together, and whether they liked it or not, it had bound them for a lifetime. Like she had said, there was no turning back. Not now, and not ever.

* * *

"Is she asleep?" Griffin whispered, motioning towards Brigid.

Luke looked over at her. "I think so."

Night had fallen, and it was getting harder to see one another in the dark interior of the bus. Griffin stretched his arms over his head and then leaned back onto the seat. After only a few moments, he was snoring loudly. James shoved him, and the snores subsided for a moment.

Luke smirked. "How are we supposed to sleep now?"

"There's no way," James said.

They sat in silence for a moment. James frowned, battling with himself. He couldn't decide whether or not to say something. In the end, he decided to try.

"Luke?"

"Yeah?" Luke whispered back.

"Still awake?"

"Obviously."

James smiled. "Just making sure. I wanted to say..." he paused.

"Yeah?" Luke asked.

"I'm sorry. About blowing up at you that day. After the obstacle course."

Luke remained quiet for a moment.

"It's alright. You had good reason to be mad."

"I had no reason to say those things."

"Maybe not," Luke said. James could hear the smile in his voice. "But like I said, you had good reason to. And I'm glad you did."

"Glad?"

"Yeah. I was mad at my parents, not you. And whatever my dad did has nothing to do with any of you. But I needed to get that out of my system. When I see my mom again, I'll ask her about him. And I'll deal with whatever it is. But for now, it's not important. And we need to focus on what we're doing."

"Good luck, when you do find out. And I'm glad you got it out of your system."

Luke chuckled. "Thanks." He paused for a moment. "And I'm sorry about your dad."

"Thanks," James said quietly.

"I mean it. You had every reason to be mad at me. I was upset about my dad. That's no big deal. He did something to my mom, who knows what. I'll find out later. But you..."

"It's nothing. I didn't know him, anyway."

"It isn't nothing, James. And I'm sorry."

"I'm sorry, too."

"So we're good?"

James laughed. "Yeah, we're good."

Luke smiled and rested his head on the seat. James did the same. After a few minutes of silence, Luke's breathing slowed. James lifted his head.

"Luke?" James whispered.

As he had expected, there was no answer. He was the only one left awake, but he knew that he would not be able to sleep. He settled into his seat and let his mind wander.

Not knowing what would happen, even what they were walking into exactly, was driving him crazy. And what would happen when they found him? And what if...he stopped, not wanting to go there. He couldn't think that way. Not now.

James stared through the darkness at Marah, Griffin, Luke, and Brigid. He couldn't see their faces, only their shadow. But it was enough. Of all the people to go through all of this with, he thought, these were the people he wanted to be with. Even though he had just met them. And how could he bear to lose any of them?

No.

He would not let himself think that way.

Instead, he thought about what Luke had said. He wondered what Luke's dad had done. Wondered what life would be like if his own dad were still alive.

James slid his hand into his pants pocket and sighed in relief. It was still there. He pulled the paper out and unfolded it carefully. It was too dark to see the picture, but he had every inch of it memorized.

It was his father. Sitting on a sofa, he didn't know where. Smiling up at the camera. He was wearing a royal blue sweater and around his neck, the full moon. The same full moon that James was wearing now.

He slid the picture back into his pocket, where it had always been. He didn't need it to know what his father looked like. The many hours he had spent staring at the picture had etched the image of his father into his mind. He could never forget, and he didn't want to.

James had his father's dark hair and his bright blue eyes. And his smile, his mother had always said. He and his mother had sat and talked about him for a long time the day before James had left. The same day she had given him the necklace.

He remembered every word of that conversation. And he wondered when, if ever, he would get to talk to her again. Her voice echoed through his mind.

You have his smile. His laugh, his eyes. His determination. His spirit. His strength...He loved you so much, James. And he would have been so proud.

Would he have been? Proud? And, James wondered, had he been the leader, too?

More than ever, James wished his father could be there. Wished that he could be there to help him, tell him how to lead. Because he had no idea how to do it. How to give his friends hope, when he had none of his own. How to lead them into this without letting them down. And, if his father had been the leader before, how to live up to his memory.

Jonathan Wood. The father he had never known.

Luke was right.

It wasn't nothing.

28

"Excuse me?"

James glanced around. It was still nighttime; he must have fallen asleep for only a moment.

"Excuse me?" the voice asked again.

"Who's there?" James said, looking for the source of the voice.

"Are you James?"

James' eyes widened in alarm. How did this person know his name?

Finally, he found where the voice was coming from. There was a person standing at the end of their table, holding it for support. James squinted through the darkness at them.

"Who are you?" James asked.

The man sighed. He sounded eager to return to his seat. "I'm sitting a few seats ahead of you. The driver wants to talk to some kid named James that's sitting in the back of the bus. Are you him?"

"Oh, yes," James said. "Thank you."

The man grunted in response and returned to his seat.

James ignored him, his focus on getting out of his seat. He was blocked in by Griffin, who was sound asleep. He nudged him in the arm. Griffin didn't respond, so James nudged him a little bit harder. Again, nothing. James shoved him. Griffin jumped awake and glanced around.

"What? Are we there already?" Griffin asked, his voice thick with sleep.

"No, Griffin. I just need you to let me out. Then you can go back to sleep."

"Oh. Good," Griffin said, and then his snoring resumed.

James sighed. "Well, there goes that idea," he whispered to himself.

With no other option, James pulled his legs up and stood up on the seat. The bus ran over an especially large bump at just that moment, almost sending him flying across the table. But, just in time, James grabbed the wall and steadied himself. He took a deep breath and waited for a moment. Then, going as fast as he could, James stepped over Griffin and jumped into the aisle. He brushed his hands together and smiled. Then he walked to the front of the bus.

Mr. Bradley greeted James with a bright smile. "Sorry to interrupt your sleep," he said.

"Not a problem," James said. "When do you get to sleep?"

"Oh, I'm fine at the moment. You get used to driving through the night. I'll catch up on some sleep when we stop in the morning."

"Is that our stop?"

"No, sorry. We'll stop in the morning, then again around noon. Then I'll drive through the next night. The stop that morning is where you get off."

"Long drive," James said.

"Very. But it'll give you time to rest. Before..." He stopped there. But he didn't need to finish. James knew what he meant.

"What do you need?" James asked.

"Thought it would be best to talk to you when no one can see," Mr. Bradley said. "I've got some messages from Wane."

"Oh, good."

"But first, there's a towel right on the seat right behind me. You can use that and put it on the floor beside me, make yourself comfortable."

James smiled and did as he was told.

"Sorry I don't have something better for you," Mr. Bradley said.

"Not a problem at all, sir."

"Oh, you don't need to call me sir. Just Stephen is fine."

"Alright then, Stephen. What did Wane have to say?"

Stephen smiled. "Right, right. Well, he told me to let him know if you kids showed up here. Said he'd told you that you could go home if you wanted." He chuckled to himself. "I knew you'd come."

James smiled. He was grateful that they had decided to come. Stephen continued. "So I told Wane that you were here. And he told me to give this to you."

Stephen pulled a small device from a compartment beside his seat. "He gave me this the day before you came. You place it in your ear. You'll be able to hear him while you're in the desert and he'll be able to hear you."

James nodded and took the small earpiece from him. He positioned in it his ear until he was sure that it would not fall off.

"Thank you," James whispered.

"My pleasure. Oh, and one more thing."

"What's that?"

"Good luck."

James smiled. "Thank you. We're going to need it."

"I don't think you will," Stephen said. "But good luck, nonetheless. I know you will succeed."

"I hope so," James whispered.

"I know so," Stephen said. He smiled at James. "Now go get some sleep."

James nodded. "Thanks again."

Before James could walk away, he heard Wane's voice in his ear. He smiled at the sound.

"James?" Wane asked.

"I'm here," James said.

Stephen looked up at him in confusion, then seemed to realize who he was talking to. He smiled and returned his attention to the road.

James could hear the smile in Wane's voice. "Everything going well?" Wane asked.

"So far, so good."

"Great. I'll check back in tomorrow."

"Talk to you then."

James smiled and looked over at Stephen. "Goodnight," he whispered. Then he returned to the back of the bus. When he had reached his seat, he sighed. Griffin was still slumped over, fast asleep.

James wedged his foot onto the seat next to Griffin and stepped over him. He slid down onto the hard seat and tried to get comfortable.

He could feel the earpiece in his right ear. He smiled to himself. It had given him hope. Hope that the next few days would go better than he had expected.

"Goodnight Wane," James whispered. Then he drifted off to sleep.

* * *

James' peaceful, dreamless sleep was stopped short by a hard shove. He opened one eye.

"What?"

"We need you to materialize some breakfast," Griffin said.

James closed his eyes again. He raised an eyebrow. "Didn't you pack food?"

"Well, yes. But yours tastes better."

James laughed. He sighed and sat up. "Fine," he said, opening his eyes slowly. "What do you want?"

"Um, pancakes would be nice. Maybe some bacon...eggs...hashbrowns..."

A plate of pancakes appeared in front of Griffin. "That's all you're getting," James said.

Griffin breathed in their scent. He sighed happily. "Thanks, man."

James chuckled. "No problem." He looked around at the rest of them. "Everyone else?"

They made their 'orders' and James materialized a plate of food for each of them. Several minutes later, they had all finished...and Griffin had licked his plate clean.

Griffin smiled. "That's almost as good as camp food."

Luke glanced out the window. "Are we getting close?"

"Not really. Mr. Bradley said we have another day. Our stop is in the morning," James said.

Luke groaned.

"When did he tell you that?" Marah asked.

"Last night," James said.

Griffin stared at James, confused. "When did that happen?"

"After everyone had gone to sleep. He sent someone back to tell me he wanted to talk to me."

"And?" Griffin asked.

James pulled the small device out of his ear. The others leaned in to look at it.

"What is it?" Brigid asked.

"It's from Wane. Some type of earpiece. But I can hear him and he can hear me," James said.

"Cool," Griffin said. Then he frowned. "How come you're the only one that got one?"

James shrugged. "I guess he only had one."

"James is the leader, remember?" Luke said. He grinned. "It comes with its perks."

James smiled. "Not many."

"So Wane can talk to us?" Brigid asked. "When we find Marcus?"

James nodded.

"That'll be good," Brigid said.

"Hopefully it'll help us," Griffin said.

"Hopefully," James agreed.

"So let me get this straight," Griffin said. "We're stuck on this bus for another whole day?!"

James smiled. "That's right."

"I think I'd rather be there already," Griffin said, groaning.

Brigid gave a weak laugh. "Can't say I agree with that one."

"I don't know," Marah said. "Part of me never wants to get there. But part of me just wants to get it over with."

Griffin nodded. "Yeah, I want to get it over with. The suspense is killing me."

Luke smirked. "Better that than something else."

The rest of them tried to ignore Luke's comment, but they all agreed.

James put his earpiece back in. "Anyway," he said. "Wane is supposed to check in sometime today."

"Just let us know," Luke said.

James nodded. Only a moment later, he could hear Wane's voice. James smiled. *It's him*, he mouthed to the others.

"Morning, James," Wane said.

"Morning," James replied. Luke, Griffin, Marah, and Brigid were listening intently.

"Everyone awake?"

"Yes."

"Everyone doing okay?"

"Yes, we're all fine."

"Great. Just checking in. Let me know when you find him," Wane said.

"I will. Don't need to check in before then?" James asked.

"No. Not unless something goes wrong."

"Okay."

"Good luck," Wane said.

"Thank you."

James looked at the others. Griffin raised an eyebrow. "That was it?"

"He was just checking in," James said. "Making sure everything was going well."

"Oh. Well, okay."

James laughed. "Not much to it."

The five of them fell into a comfortable silence. Brigid pulled her knees into her chest and leaned against the window. Luke rested his cheek in his hand and picked at the peeling paint on the table. James and Griffin played tic-tac-toe on a piece of paper that James had materialized. Marah went through her bag for the second time that day.

After only a few minutes, Luke looked up from the table. He glanced over at Marah. "Did you see anything?" he asked. "Last night?"

Marah continued going through her bag, but when no one said anything, she realized that he had been talking to her. She looked up, a neatly folded t-shirt in her hand. "Me?"

"Yes," Luke said.

Marah look confused. "Last night?" And then it dawned on her. "Oh. You mean the future." She frowned. "No. I can't see that far into the future. I might see something tonight, since we're leaving in the morning."

"Do you think you will?" Brigid asked.

"I don't know. It depends."

"On what?" Griffin asked.

Marah shrugged. "I haven't figured that out yet. Sometimes I see things, sometimes I don't. I can't control what I see in my dreams."

"But you can control what you see when you're awake?" Luke asked.

"Yes. But I can only see a few minutes into the future then."

"That's inconvenient," Griffin muttered.

Marah smiled. "Not always."

"More than you can see," James said, laughing.

Griffin frowned and slumped in his seat.

At that moment, the bus lurched to a stop.

Mr. Bradley turned around and smiled. "Last stop of the day. Thank you for traveling with me." Then he opened the door and settled back into his seat.

Griffin held his forehead in his hand and sighed. "We're next."

"Don't remind me," Luke said.

James, however, wasn't listening. He was watching the strange man he had seen the day before. The man stood, straightened his coat, and retrieved his bag from above his seat. Then, he walked off the bus.

James turned hurriedly to the others. "He's getting off!" he exclaimed.

"Who?" Luke asked, alarmed.

"The guy in the trench coat that we saw yesterday...that might have been with Marcus!"

"The creepy one?" Griffin asked.

Brigid laughed at that. "Yes, Griffin. That one."

"We have to see where he's going," James said.

"Are you insane?" Griffin asked.

"He's gone. Why would you go after him now?" Marah asked.

"Just to see...what if he's taking a different way? Throwing us off his trail?"

"What if he's trying to get you off the bus?" Brigid asked.

"That's a chance I'm willing to take," James said. He stood up. "Anyone care to join me?"

Luke sighed. "I'll go."

Griffin stood as well. "Well, I can't be left out of this one."

James turned to Marah and Brigid. "Coming?"

Marah smiled. "I think I'll sit this one out."

"Me too," Brigid said. She grinned. "Good luck!"

James chuckled and led Luke and Griffin to the front of the bus. Mr. Bradley smiled when he saw them approaching.

"What are you three doing up here?" he asked.

"Thought we'd stretch our legs," James said. "Will we be stopped here for long?"

Mr. Bradley smiled. "Not too long. But you've got plenty of time to get some fresh air."

They smiled their thanks and started down the steps.

"Just make sure you're back in ten minutes!" Mr. Bradley called after them.

James stepped into the sunshine and turned back to him. "We will," he replied.

Luke and Griffin followed him down the path to the bus station. It looked exactly the same as the one they had left from the day before.

"Real clever," Luke said.

James raised an eyebrow. "What?"

"'Thought we'd stretch our legs,'" Luke mimicked James. "Wonder how many times you've used that one."

James frowned at him. "It was the best I could do on short notice."

"I'm just saying you should work on it."

"On my lying techniques?" James asked. He chuckled. "I'd rather not."

Luke shrugged. "Could be helpful."

Before James could reply, Griffin had slapped his arm.
"What?" James asked.

Griffin nodded his head to the right, attempting to be discreet. "There he is."

The man was standing at a vending machine, studying the snacks inside. James, Griffin, and Luke stopped at a vending machine a few feet away and pretended to be studying it as well. James watched the man out of the corner of his eye.

The man stood there for several minutes before finally pulling a few dollars out of his pocket. James continued to watch, while Griffin and Luke pretended to debate about what they should buy.

"Those crackers would be good," Griffin remarked.

"I'm allergic to peanut butter," Luke replied.

"Oh, well...how about that candy bar?"

"I don't like that kind...how about that one?"

"I don't like that one. Can't we each get our own?"

"We only have a dollar!"

And the argument continued, like that, for a good long while.

James, trying not to laugh at the other two, watched the man insert his money into the machine. He pressed a few buttons, and then reached down and pulled out a candy bar. Then, he turned and headed towards the street.

"He's moving," James whispered.

"I didn't want anything anyway," Griffin remarked, louder.

"I wasn't actually hungry," Luke said.

James smiled and started down the sidewalk. The three of them kept a good distance behind the man, watching to see where he would go.

The man stepped out onto the street and followed the edge of it. He kept glancing behind him, looking for someone. Or he knew that the three of them were following him. Either way, James, Luke, and Griffin kept on him.

He made it to a parking lot next to the bus station and strolled over to a blue convertible. James, Luke, and Griffin watched curiously. That was certainly not the car that they had expected him to go to.

Then, the man unlocked the car, slid into the seat, pulled out of the parking lot, and sped away.

29

"Nervous?" Marah asked.

Brigid tore her gaze away from the window. "That's a bit of an understatement."

"Terrified?"

Brigid smiled. "That's more like it."

"Me too," Marah whispered.

"What if—" Brigid began.

Marah shook her head. "That is not a safe question right now."

"I know," Brigid said. She sighed. "It would have been nice of our parents to at least tell us what we were getting into."

"Ignorance is bliss?" Marah guessed, making quotation marks with her fingers.

Brigid smiled wistfully. "Not this time."

"I don't understand why. But for some reason, they thought it was best for us not to know," Marah said.

"What's so terrible about knowing?"

Marah shrugged. "I would think it would help us rather than hurt us."

"Would have made the first few days of camp a lot easier."

"It certainly would have made more sense."

"I don't know," Brigid said. "But we know now. So I guess we can't worry about it anymore."

"I just wish we knew more about this Marcus guy."

"We may not want to know," Brigid said.

Marah frowned. "True."

The two of them grew silent. Marah stared out the window, and Brigid leaned her head back onto the seat and closed her eyes. They were so caught up in their own thoughts that they didn't hear Mr. Bradley's announcement.

"We're tight on time today, so we've got to get going. Everyone on?" he had asked.

There had been no answer, so Mr. Bradley had returned to his seat.

Marah heard the rumble of the engine starting up, but she didn't realize what was happening at first. Then, the bus station started to move in the opposite direction. Her heart nearly stopped.

"Brigid!" she exclaimed, trying hard not to scream. Brigid's eyes snapped open. She looked at the empty seats beside them and knew what Marah was going to say. Her face was drained of all color.

"No, no, no..." she muttered, stumbling out into the aisle as fast as she could. She and Marah ran to the front of the bus.

"Mr. Bradley," Marah breathed. He looked up, and his eyes widened in alarm when he saw their faces.

"What is it?"

"We left them at the bus station. James, Luke, and Griffin," Brigid said. She looked like she was about to cry. Or throw up.

His face turned just about as white as Brigid's. He cursed under his breath.

"I can't turn around," he said.

Marah stared at him. "Then what are you going to do?!"

Mr. Bradley pulled a walkie-talkie out of the compartment next to the steering wheel. He pressed the button, his hands shaking.

"Wane, its Stephen. I'm an idiot."

The device crackled. "What happened?" Wane asked, his voice strangely calm.

"I left James, Griffin, and Luke at the bus station."

"You left them. At the bus station," Wane stated, his voice still calm.

"Yes."

"Why did they get off the bus in the first place?" Wane demanded.

Mr. Bradley winced. "They said they were going to stretch their legs."

There was a pause. "You are an idiot."

Marah and Brigid would have laughed, had it been any other day, any other situation.

"I'm really sorry...I—" Mr. Bradley began.

Wane stopped him. "I'll take care of it. Do not turn around. They'll be there when you get there."

"I'm sorry."

"Just make sure you don't lose the other two."

* * *

"Well, he's gone," Griffin muttered.

"I guess he's not with Marcus." James sighed. "We should head back."

James turned around and stared. "Uh, guys..."

"What?" Luke asked. He tore his gaze from the road the strange man had taken. And then he saw it.

The bus was gone.

Griffin's mouth dropped open. "This cannot be happening," he said.

James ran to the street and glanced back and forth wildly. He shook his head. "They're gone."

"What are we supposed to do?" Luke demanded. "Marah and Brigid can't go after Marcus by themselves!"

"I know that," James said. "We just have to figure something out..." His voice faded as he tried to think of a solution. The three of them were silent, both from concentration and shock.

"Can't you ask Wane?" Griffin asked James. "You have that ear thing."

James nodded.

"Wane?" James said, holding his ear. "We're stuck at the bus station."

There was a snort, and then he heard Wane's voice. "Way to go. Went out to stretch your legs, did you?"

James eyes widened. Then he frowned. "How'd you know that?"

Wane chuckled. "I know everything I need to."

"What do you want us to do?"

"Stay put. I'm sending someone to pick you up. You'll catch up with the bus and be there when Marah and Brigid get there. Maybe even before."

"Thank you."

"Try not to get stranded this time."

James smiled. "We won't."

"What did he say?" Griffin asked.

"He's sending someone to pick us up. So we just have to wait here."

Luke nodded. "So we're supposed to just sit here?"

"Until our ride gets here," James said.

Griffin sat down onto a nearby bench. "Sounds good to me."

James sat beside Griffin, and Luke paced back and forth in front of them.

The three of them remained silent. After a few minutes, they heard the distant rumble of an approaching car. James and Griffin glanced at each other, then down the road. They couldn't see the car at first, but when they did, each of their mouths dropped open.

It was the same blue convertible that they had just watched leave.

"No way," Griffin muttered.

Luke turned and looked at James and Griffin. "He can't be our ride."

James shook his head in disbelief. He and Griffin stood up, but they were unable to move past that. The three of them were rooted to their spots until the car pulled up in front of them.

The man, the man with the shaggy hair and black trench coat, chuckled when he saw their faces. "Not what you were expecting, was I?" he asked.

"Um, no," Griffin said, holding his still-shaking hands together. James and Luke remained motionless.

The man smiled. "Well, come on. We've got a lot of ground to cover."

Luke raised an eyebrow.

The man mirrored Luke's expression. "What?" he asked.

Then, like all the others, he realized. "Oh, that," he said. "Mighty annoying, if you ask me. But of course, they didn't." He held out his wrist and sprinkled the dust over his tattoo. The letters glowed through the dust, and he shook it off.

"Satisfied?" he asked.

James, Luke, and Griffin nodded. They slid into the back seat of the car and the man took off.

A few miles down the road, James spoke up. "Thanks for the ride," he said.

The man smiled. "No problem."

"So, who are you?" Griffin asked.

"And why were you on our bus?" Luke added.

"Ah, I figured you'd ask that," the man said, chuckling. "Well, I'm Adam Scott. And I was on your bus to see how you'd react to me. See if you were observant."

"Guess we failed that test," Griffin muttered.

Adam laughed. "Not completely. You were right to see where I was going. You just didn't get back on the bus in time."

"Why did you want to know if we would follow you?" James asked.

"More training. That's one thing about Wane. No matter what you're doing or where you are, training is never over. Wane believes—and he is right, as usual—that there is always more you can learn. And he'll make sure you keep learning it."

Luke smiled. "This whole thing isn't a test, is it?"

Adam returned the smile, but then his face grew serious. "No, this is real. Unfortunately."

They fell into an uncomfortable silence.

After a few minutes, James cleared his throat. "You knew him, too?"

"Who, Marcus?" Adam asked. He shook his head, his disgust evident. "I knew him, alright. He's the reason most of us are down here and not up there."

"I'm sorry about that," James said.

"Not your fault. And there's certainly no need to be sorry for me," Adam said. He smiled. "It's an honor to be able to help you kids."

"Well, thanks," Griffin said.

James looked down. He still hadn't gotten used to it. The way people saw them as heroes. Or legends, as Henry had said. He didn't feel any more important than them. And he certainly hadn't done anything to deserve it.

Soon, night fell and conversation slowed. James saw Adam lift a phone to his ear. He talked softly, only loud enough for James to catch small parts of the conversation.

He leaned his head back and listened. The only thing he heard was, "They're fine. We'll be there soon." Then, his eyelids drooped and sleep overcame him.

* * *

The world outside the window was invisible, covered by the dark blanket of night. Marah leaned against the window, watching the outside without actually seeing it.

Instead, she saw snapshots of the future. Every few minutes, she tried again. But she could only see a few minutes past the present. It wasn't even late enough for her to see the morning.

"Marah?" Brigid's voice penetrated the silence.

"I'm awake."

"Me too. I think I fell asleep for a few minutes. Probably the most sleep I'm going to get."

"I'll probably get less than that."

Brigid paused. "Everything okay?"

Marah sighed. "No. But you already knew that."

"Anything else?"

Marah pursed her lips. She twirled a strand of her thick hair. "I'm afraid. Of what I might see."

"Don't be."

Marah frowned. "Why shouldn't I be? *If* I see something, I can see a lot farther into the future when I'm asleep."

"So you would see..." Brigid paused.

"Tomorrow," Marah finished.

"Wouldn't that be a good thing?"

"I don't think I want to know."

Brigid was silent.

"I feel like I owe it to all of you. You need to know what you're getting into. And I could see it."

"But?"

"What if something happens? What if I see it, but I can't prevent it?"

"We would have some warning. We'd have a better chance of preventing it than if we didn't know at all."

"But if we can't?"

"Then we can't. Marah, we can't think about what could go wrong right now. It'll drive us insane. We have to think about what could go right."

Marah sighed heavily. "I know. There are just so many things that could—"

"I know."

"Why? Why us?" Marah asked in a small voice.

"I don't know. But we have to help these people. We have to help our parents."

"And we need to put our new powers to good use," Brigid continued, a smile in her voice.

Marah smiled, even laughed. "Alright. But after this is all over, they're telling us everything."

"I agree."

"Hopefully they will."

Once Marah and Brigid fell asleep, morning came quickly. Too quickly, in their opinion.

Brigid opened one eye. She stared across the table at Marah, who had just awoken as well. They met each other's gazes, not saying a word. Neither knew what to do, what to say. They knew this day was coming. But when it came, it didn't feel real. It felt more like a nightmare.

"Did you..." Brigid asked, not wanting to finish the question.

Marah nodded, looking sick to her stomach. "Yes," she breathed.

Brigid's eyes widened. "What was it?"

Marah sat up straighter. She looked around, filling her lungs with the musty air of the bus. "Not much, really. We'll walk through a lot of desert to get there. The opening...the opening is a huge, bronze gate. I couldn't see it clearly, or what was behind it. It was too far away. And then the dream ended."

"At least we know what we're looking for," Brigid said. She smiled.

Marah returned the smile, the color returning to her face.

A few minutes later, the bus pulled to a stop. Brigid laughed and pointed out the window. Marah followed her gaze.

James, Luke, and Griffin were standing on the sidewalk, waving enthusiastically.

Marah grinned. "Guess they made it after all."

The doors swung open, and a few people filed out of the bus ahead of them. Marah and Brigid stopped next to Mr. Bradley.

"Thanks for everything," Brigid whispered.

Mr. Bradley smiled, though there was a sadness in his eyes. He stood and waved them out. "I'll see you off," he said softly.

The three of them climbed out of the bus and met James, Luke, and Griffin a few feet away. Mr. Bradley met each of their eyes. "It has been a pleasure—an honor—meeting each of you," he said. "Good luck. Make them all proud."

They all nodded. "We'll try," James said.

"Whatever happens, I will be. And they will be, too."

"Thank you," Marah whispered.

"We'll see you again?" Brigid asked.

Mr. Bradley nodded. He smiled the same sad smile. The one they had seen too many times lately. "Someday."

They watched him climb back into the bus, watched the doors slowly swing shut. Heard the engine start, the wheels roll across the gravel. Saw Mr. Bradley's wave as the bus drove out of sight.

And then they were truly alone.

30

A tumbleweed rolled past them. The wind blew the sand playfully around their ankles.

The five of them stared at the place where the bus had disappeared. Marah turned around and surveyed the vast amount of desert in front of them.

"Guess we should start walking," she whispered.

James met her eyes. He said nothing, but he didn't need to.

Griffin was the first to move. He kicked the sand with the toe of his shoe and started walking. He beckoned the others to do the same.

"Do we even know where we're going?" Luke asked.

"No," James said.

"Marah knows what it looks like," Brigid said.

Everyone turned to Marah expectantly. She blushed and glanced away. "I saw it in a dream last night. I don't know where it is, but it's a big bronze gate."

"A gate?" Luke asked incredulously.

Marah shrugged. "That's all I know."

"Did you see which way we went?" Griffin asked.

"I know we went this way," Marah said, pointing forward. "And then I think we just keep going straight. It's kind of hard to miss."

Luke snorted. "Sounds like it."

They started off in the direction that Marah had indicated, Griffin leading the way.

After a few minutes of walking, Marah broke the silence. "I knew it was a bad idea to go after that guy," she said, smiling.

James frowned playfully. "Fine. You were right."

"All I needed to hear," Marah said. She laughed.

"About that," Luke said, shaking his head. He was clearly still in shock. "The guy's not bad after all. He's *from Jericho*."

Brigid raised her eyebrows. "Seriously?"

"Then why'd he look so creepy?" Marah asked.

"Test from Wane," Griffin said. He grunted. "Didn't appreciate that one too much."

"A test?" Marah asked.

"If you can believe it," James said. "He told the guy to look suspicious. See if we'd go after him. He's the one that actually gave us the ride here."

Brigid chuckled. "Crazy."

"That's what I'm saying," Griffin muttered.

James laughed. "His name was Adam Scott. Guess we took a little too long following him."

"Just a little," Brigid said.

"Part of that was our fault. We didn't hear him announce we were leaving, or we would have said something," Marah said.

Griffin shrugged, a teasing smile on his face. "I knew it."

"Not a big deal. All that matters is that we all made it," James said.

"I think I'd rather be stuck at the bus station right now, though," Luke said.

James frowned, but said nothing.

The sand blew lightly in between them. They exchanged small, meaningless conversations as they walked. The longer they went without seeing anything, however, conversation became even more rare.

Finally, they walked in complete silence, each of them giving their complete attention to the scene in front of them. If the gate were to appear, they could not miss it.

"How far are we going to walk before we finally accept it's not out here?" Griffin asked. His question distracted the others from the search. They glanced at each other, no one giving Griffin an answer. Then, Marah sucked in a breath. They followed her gaze.

There it was.

The gate was enormous, just as Marah had said. If all five of them had stood on top of each other, the gate would be taller—if they had linked hands and stood in a straight line with their arms outstretched, the gate would be wider. The bronze gleamed almost golden, and the sunlight reflecting off of it stunned them.

As they grew closer, the design of the gate became clearer. The bronze of the gate was twisted to form the shape of the sun, with its arms outstretched in every direction.

Griffin shook his head. "Harsh."

"Yeah, wasn't this guy from the moon, too?" Luke asked.

James nodded. "Guess he doesn't care for it too much anymore."

Marah laughed nervously.

"I guess we finally found him," Brigid whispered.

Luke looked down at her. He gave a reassuring smile, though he looked just about as confident as she did. "Ready?"

"Not at all," Marah said.

"Do we have a plan?" Griffin asked.

James peered through the gate. The grounds were expansive, spreading farther than he could see. There was a forest of trees in the back, single trees placed sporadically throughout the grounds, and fields of the greenest grass he had ever seen. In the middle of it all was a spotless white house, with six columns flanking the front door. The only sand in sight was used to create the walkway to the house.

"Wow," Griffin breathed.

"Where did all that grass come from?" Luke asked.

James shook his head in disbelief. "I don't know. And I don't think there's a plan, other than head for the house. That's our best bet at the moment."

Griffin stared at the mansion warily. "If you say so."

"Well, we don't have anything better!"

"It'll work," Luke said. "We'll just see how it goes once we get inside."

"Don't forget about talking with the necklaces," Brigid said.

James nodded. "That'll help."

They turned and stared at the gate in silence. The desert was quiet; even the wind was still. It seemed as if everything was waiting for them to do something. To make the first move.

James looked at each one of them. "Whatever happens in there, this has been the best few weeks of my life. And I'm glad I got to meet all of you."

"Don't talk like that, man," Griffin said.

Luke gave a weak smile. "See you on the other side."

The gate swung open without a sound.

* * *

"Here goes nothing," Luke whispered. He started forward and the others followed him. As they walked, they spread into a straight line, growing farther apart from each other with each step. Luke on the far left, then Marah, then James, then Brigid, and then Griffin on the other end.

They moved as slowly as possible. Their footsteps didn't make a sound. The world they had just entered felt drastically different from the one they had left behind the gate. Nothing moved, and the wind was absent. Their eyes darted back and forth, meeting each other's gazes every now and then.

Suddenly, Luke stopped. He stood absolutely still. The others stopped as well, watching him. He held a finger to his lips. Then he turned and looked to his left.

There was a slight rumbling in the distance. Like a thunderstorm brewing miles and miles away. Their bodies tensed even more as they waited. A single tree stood to the left of Luke. It swayed only slightly, a movement undetectable to the five of them.

Then, a single, solitary leaf fell from its branches. It floated down, moving through the air like it was milk. The tip of the leaf touched the grass. And then, the rumbling grew louder.

An ear-splitting crack echoed through the desert. And, before any of them could react, the ground gave way, taking Luke with it.

Brigid screamed. James stared, his head shaking back and forth violently. This couldn't be happening. The world was no longer silent. It was anything but. Because of the chaos that ensued, the next soft rumbling was not heard.

But then it grew louder.

Just like the first time.

Marah glanced at the others. She knew what was coming. A look of terror descended upon her face in a matter of seconds. She started to run, but too late.

The ground beneath Marah gave way, and she was gone.

Brigid's scream turned into a sob. James fell to his knees.

He felt Griffin beside him, and looked up. Griffin pulled his eyes from the scene in front of them to meet James' gaze. He shook his head back and forth slowly.

"This wasn't supposed to happen," he murmured. "Not this soon. Not now. We need to get out of here."

"We need to find them. We can't leave," James said, standing up.

Griffin stepped away and wrung his hands together, shifting his balance like he was about to run away. "We lost them. Already." He sucked in a breath and started talking faster. "We shouldn't be here. We weren't ready for this."

"Yes we are. We can finish this on our own. We have to."

"It's over. We failed," Griffin whispered. "It's over."

"No it's not," James said. As he spoke, he heard the soft noise that warned of more disaster. "But it will be if you don't move and we fall through, too," James said. He pulled Griffin farther away from the gaping hole that had formed. "Don't give up on me now. This isn't over."

Griffin nodded. James took off running and Griffin followed, Brigid close behind. James swallowed hard. He placed his hand on his ear.

"Wane? Are you there? Wane?"

There was no answer.

"Wane!" James screamed. "They're gone!"

"Why won't he answer?" Griffin asked.

James shook his head. "I guess we're on our own right now."

James looked back to see if Brigid was still following. She was, small tears still rolling down her face. Once they were far enough away, the three of them turned to look at the place where Marah and Luke had been. Finally, they heard the third rumbling grow louder, and more of the ground started to fall away. The final hole was long and thin, stretching all the way from one side of the grounds to the other. There was only a small strip of grass in front of the gate, then the hole, and then the ground that James, Griffin, and Brigid were standing on.

"Do you think it will keep falling?" Brigid asked.

James shook his head. "I think it's finished."

Griffin stared at the gate. He sighed. "Well, there goes our way out."

They turned to the sound of something whistling through the air. James' eyes widened. Hundreds of arrows were flying straight at them. Brigid shrieked. They barely had enough time to drop to the ground before the arrows soared over their heads.

Griffin started to stand. "What the..." he began, but he dropped to the ground again before he could finish. Another group of arrows had flown at them. Griffin, Brigid, and James stayed on the ground for several minutes, waiting to see if any more arrows would come. But none did.

James stood up slowly. He brushed the grass off of his front side and glanced around. They were now off to the far right of the house, but were still not anywhere close. The house was placed right along the edge of the woods—farther away than he had originally thought. The three of them would have to cover a lot of ground to get there. And anything could be waiting for them along the way.

"What is this place?" Griffin asked.

James shook his head. "I have no idea."

31

His head throbbed.

He tried to open his eyes, but it felt like they were being held closed by some invisible force. He would not succumb to the darkness that threatened to overcome him.

Not again.

Slowly, the feeling returned to his body. He could feel the blood coursing through, awakening each part of him one at a time. First his toes, then his feet and his ankles. His legs, his arms. His wrists and fingers. His chest, neck, and head.

He tried to move, but quickly realized that he was unable. His wrists were bound together, and his ankles and stomach were bound to the chair he was sitting in. Finally, his eyes opened and the room in front of him solidified.

The room was small, and the plain, off-white walls reminded Luke of a jail cell. He turned his head. At the front of the room, there was a wooden door, and two television screens mounted to the wall on either side.

Where was he? And how had he gotten here?

Luke struggled to remember, but his memory felt as blank as the wall in front of him.

He tensed at the sound of a slight groan behind him. There was someone else in the room with him. Was this person bound like he was? Did he know this person?

"Who's there?" Luke said. He glanced around, but no matter how hard he tried, he could not see what was behind him.

There was no answer, so he tried again.

"Who's there?"

Another groan. "Luke?"

It sounded like a girl. And one he should know.

"Who are you?" Luke asked.

"Luke. It's Marah," she said. As soon as she said her name, Luke's memories came flooding back. Camp. His powers. Wane. The bus. The desert, the gate, and the ground opening beneath him. James. Griffin. Marah. Brigid.

"Marah," he said. "How did we get in here?"

"I don't know."

"More importantly, how do we get out?" Luke asked.

"Good question."

Luke struggled against the ropes that held him, but they would not budge. Whoever had tied them had done their job well.

Marah sighed. "We need to tell them we're okay. Let them know where we are."

"And where are we?"

"I think we're in the house. The big one we saw when we got here?"

Luke nodded. That would make sense. "How do you know?"

"Well, we can't be far. And there's nothing around here for miles."

"I guess you're right," Luke said. "But how could we tell them?"

"The necklaces."

"Uh, Marah, in case you hadn't noticed...our hands are tied. Literally."

"I know that," Marah said.

"Then what do you suggest we do?"

"I don't know! Figure out another way!"

"Why can't you?"

A sob caught in her throat. Luke immediately regretted his words. "Look, I'm sorry. We'll be okay."

"Luke. It's not you," she said through her tears. "They took my necklace. And we need to know if the others are okay."

He could hear the terror in her voice. "I'll find a way," Luke said. He looked down at his necklace. Thankfully, it was still there. But how could he press the stone without his hands?

"Any suggestions?" he asked.

"Use your chin."

Luke nodded. "Smart." He touched his chin to the edge of his collarbone, just missing the necklace. He tried again, moving farther down this time. He caught the top edge of the moon pendant, but missed the stone. He tried again.

Finally, his chin came in contact with the small, cold piece of moonstone on the necklace. He pressed it down.

He thought quickly, trying to remember everything he needed to tell them.

It's Luke, he said in his mind, hoping the others could hear him. *Marah and I are fine. They have us tied up, inside that house that we saw. We're stuck here, and they have her necklace, but other than that, fine. Everyone still okay out there?*

"Thank you," Marah whispered.

"You could hear me? Without your necklace?"

Marah nodded. "Yes. I guess once it's yours, it's yours. Whether you're wearing it or not."

"Until you pass it down," Luke said.

"Right."

Finally, they heard James' voice.

Glad to hear you're okay. We're all fine. At the moment. May take us awhile to get to you.

Marah gave a relieved sigh.

"Tell him that—" She stopped.

Luke raised an eyebrow.

"What?"

She said nothing. Luke turned to see what had silenced her. Then, he heard it too.

Footsteps, loud and precise, echoing through the building. They were coming closer. Marah sucked in a breath. Every muscle in Luke's body was tight, unmoving.

And then, ever so slightly, the doorknob turned.

* * *

"They're okay."

Griffin smiled at James. "I heard."

"And they're in that house," Brigid said.

James nodded. "That means we really need to get there now."

"Let's go," Griffin said.

They started walking towards the house, going as quickly as they dared. Brigid and Griffin glanced in both directions, watching for what would come at them next. James kept his gaze straight ahead, on the house.

Because of that, James was the last to notice the lasers.

"James!" Griffin shouted.

James stopped. He focused on the air in front of him. Red lasers crossed through the air, blocking their path.

Griffin raised an eyebrow at him. "Dude. Pay attention."

James took a breath. "Sorry. When did those get there?"

"Just now," Brigid said, shrugging. "Don't know where they came from."

"Like everything else in this place," Griffin muttered.

They stared at the bright red lines crossing in front of them. Griffin shook his head. "There's no way."

"But we have to get to the house," James protested. "Is there no other way?"

Brigid shook her head. "We have to pass through the lasers. No matter what."

Griffin groaned. James closed his eyes.

"Well..." Griffin began.

"We need to see what happens when you touch them," Brigid said.

Griffin raised an eyebrow. "Bright idea. Why don't you just walk through them first? Then you let us know what happens."

Brigid glared at him. "That's not what I meant."

"Stop it," James said. "Now is *not* the time to get into a fight."

Griffin crossed his arms and let out a breath. He glanced away. Brigid dug the toe of her shoe into the dirt.

James sighed. "Here." He held out his hand and a small pebble appeared in his palm. Brigid and Griffin returned their gazes to the lasers as James tossed the pebble into the maze of red lines.

The rock flew through the air, seeming to go in slow motion as they watched it. Finally, it came in contact with one of the lasers. There was a loud pop as the rock exploded and burst into flames. Then, a pile of ashes fell to the grass—the only part of the rock still remaining.

Brigid whimpered.

"We're going to die," Griffin said.

"No, we're not," James said firmly. Though he had a small feeling that Griffin was right.

* * *

The door swung open.

Time seemed to stop. Marah and Luke did not breathe. Whoever was there did not enter. Whatever was going on outside the house could not be heard from their small prison.

Their eyes were fixated on the doorway. They waited for someone to enter. For something to break the silence.

Finally, they heard another footstep.

And then a man entered the room. Marah and Luke studied him carefully. The man was not what they had expected. His frame fit easily inside the doorway—he looked to be about 5'9". He had dark blonde hair and a thin face. His blue eyes were so dark they were almost black. But the blue was still there—if only slightly. He looked normal enough, maybe even kind. But then he smiled and his whole appearance changed. One word came to Marah's mind when she saw him smile.

Evil.

His laugh was dark. Marah and Luke squirmed under his stare. The man took a step into the room. He started towards Luke first, studying him, that awful smile on his face. He circled, and did the same to Marah.

"What do you want with us?" Marah asked as he passed her.

The man only stared at her. Then he laughed.

"Marah. Artemis, am I right?"

Marah glared at him.

"William's daughter," he sneered. "Interesting name choice."

Marah said nothing.

"William was one of the few that never suspected me," he said. He laughed to himself. Then he turned to Luke. "But your father..."

Luke shook his head, his gaze piercing. Through gritted teeth, he said, "Don't even go there."

"You look just like him, you know," Marcus said, studying Luke.

"What do *you* know about my father?"

The man raised one eyebrow. He met each of their eyes, looking thoughtful.

"Do you know who I am?" he finally asked.

"Marcus," Luke spat.

Marcus met Luke's gaze easily. He stared at him for a moment, then his lip upturned into a slight smile. "They haven't told you, have they?"

Marah and Luke exchanged glances.

"What are you talking about?" Luke asked.

Marcus ignored him. He continued. "Doesn't surprise me. Wane's not the type."

"What?" Marah demanded.

Marcus looked at them. He smiled again. This time, though, his dark eyes sparkled with amusement. "Nothing. Nothing at all."

32

The blood red lines glared at them. They were so clear, so *still*, James could have sworn they were completely solid. But they all knew they weren't. And they knew if they touched the lines, they wouldn't be solid either. They'd be burned and reduced to dust.

James shuddered at the thought.

Brigid couldn't take her eyes away. "How in the world are we supposed to get through?"

Griffin glanced over at her. "It's easy for you. Just teleport over there."

Brigid nodded. "Right." She disappeared and reappeared on the other side. She peered through the lasers at the other two. "What about you?" she called.

James shook his head, a smirk on his face. "Why'd you leave without us?"

Brigid opened her mouth in protest. "I…" she laughed. "I don't know. I'm coming back."

Before she could return, her hair blew up towards her face. She turned in confusion. James and Griffin glanced at each other.

There was no wind.

Then, her hair blew again, the lasers faltered for only a moment, and something flew beside James' face. It was going too fast to even see what it was. He heard the wind rush by him as another passed. Griffin tensed, and James knew that he had heard one as well. Brigid stared across at them, her eyes wide.

A few more flew past, still invisible. James glanced back and forth, waiting for another. Griffin stared straight ahead, a look of intense concentration on his face. They waited.

Then, before James even knew what had happened, Griffin held one in his hand. Brigid's mouth dropped open.

James stared. "Dang."

Griffin smiled. He held up the small, silver star. It had six points, each so sharp that James didn't want to imagine what would happen if one were to come in contact with his skin. Griffin closed his eyes, his head shaking slowly.

"Ninja star," he breathed.

"What's a ninja star?" James asked.

Griffin held up the silver star. "This," he said. "Not something you want to get hit with."

James whistled. "This is not going to be good."

A few more whizzed by their heads. Brigid crouched down to a squat, glancing back and forth with nervous energy. "Where are they coming from?" she asked softly.

Griffin didn't take his eyes from the air in front of him. If another star were to pass him, he would not miss it. "Who knows," he said. "But at the moment, our biggest concern is where they're going."

James nodded. The three of them grew silent. Though silent was the last thing it felt like. James heard every sound, every rush of the wind, every breath. It was if his hearing had been amplified to notice the smallest of sounds.

They did not move. They did not breathe. If they moved, or shifted their focus for only a second, it could all be over. They could be dead.

In a matter of seconds.

James could not rid his mind of the image. The ninja stars were so small, so fast, so *sharp*. They could kill any one of them in an instant. He kept his focus right in front of him.

He couldn't catch them like Griffin, and he couldn't transport away like Brigid. But if he watched carefully enough, maybe he would have time to move away. Maybe.

The minutes stretched on, feeling more like hours. Hours of standing and watching. Waiting.

They stood completely still for several minutes, but no more stars, that they could see, came by.

James relaxed only slightly. "Are they gone?" he asked.

That was his first mistake.

Then, he turned and looked at Brigid.

That was his second.

At first, he felt no pain.

33

"Why are you doing this?" Marah asked.

Marcus did not answer for a moment. He just stared, studying the two of them. Marah glanced away. But, Luke did not—could not—take his eyes away. He stared back at Marcus, with almost as much concentration as Marcus stared at them.

Luke's mind raced. Who this man was. What he wanted. How they could get away. But he had no answers.

Finally, Marcus seemed to consider Marah's question.

"Why?" he asked. "The people of Jericho...their so called 'leaders'...they are weak. They are afraid of their own power."

Marah quickly returned her gaze to Marcus' face. She let out a breath, practically shaking with anger. "Our parents are not weak."

"They're stronger than you'll ever be," Luke said evenly.

Marcus shook his head, getting more aggravated by the minute. "You don't know what you're talking about. Strong? Your parents? They didn't tell you about Jericho or me until now. You call that strong?"

Marah sighed. Luke glanced away for the first time since Marcus had entered the room.

Marcus smiled. "Exactly. You cannot argue. They're weak and they're afraid. They are not fit to rule. When I return, I will defeat them and I will rule their city. I'll use their powers for their true purpose."

"Even if you were to defeat them, you wouldn't take the throne," Luke said.

"We would," Marah whispered.

"Don't you understand?" Marcus shouted at them. "You have walked into a trap! Your parents were too afraid to come after me themselves. So they sent you to your death!"

"They are not afraid of you," Marah said.

Marcus raised one eyebrow. "It was me against their entire city. And I still escaped. Of course they're afraid of me! Why else would they send their children, who just learned they even had powers?"

"Because they know what we're capable of," Luke said.

"And how could you possibly know that we just learned about you?" Marah asked.

Marcus' laugh was terrifying. "I know more about you than you do."

"You're lying," Luke said.

"But I'm not. Your parents are not as bright as they think."

"You're just jealous of them. They have powers and you don't," Marah said. Luke winced.

Marcus sucked in a breath. He glared at Marah. It looked as if he was struggling not to kill her on the spot.

"I'm jealous of them?" he screamed. He lowered his voice, his hands shaking with anger. "They haven't been able to find me for fourteen years! I could take their powers—I could kill all of them—anytime I wanted!"

Luke studied Marcus. He glanced at Marah. He wasn't sure how Marcus would react; he was already furious. No telling what he would do. But they had to keep him talking. Luke took a deep breath and said it anyway.

"Then why don't you?"

Marcus turned back to Luke. "What?"

"You said you could kill them anytime you wanted. So why don't you? Why'd you wait fourteen years?"

Marah looked at Luke, her eyes wide. Luke shook his head only slightly.

Marcus seemed confused. Maybe by the question, maybe by the fact that Luke was crazy enough to ask it. He snickered, seeming to look at Luke in a different way.

"You surprise me, boy. You're either very brave...or incredibly stupid."

"Probably both," Luke said quietly.

At that, Marcus actually smiled. A genuine smile that hinted at the person he used to be. But as quick as it had come, it was gone, the anger and hatred returning to his eyes.

"I am waiting. Because...because when I do return, I want to be sure. Sure that they will be defeated. Sure that they will suffer. Like they made me suffer."

Luke and Marah said nothing for a moment.

"Then what do you want with us?" Luke asked.

Marcus wet his lips. He glanced back and forth at the two of them. "Well, I do have something of yours. And you have something I want."

"What do you have of ours?" Marah asked.

"What do you want?" Luke asked.

"Of yours," Marcus said. He chuckled, lifting Marah's necklace out of his pocket. She gasped, and he slipped it back inside. "Not yet," he said.

"Give it back," Marah said.

"I said, not yet."

"What do you want it for?"

Marcus smiled evilly. "You will see soon enough."

"What do you want?" Luke asked again.

"Knowledge," Marcus said. "Tell me where your camp is and I'll let all of you out alive."

"Why do you want to know where our camp is?" Marah asked.

"That is none of your concern. But you do want to make it out of here alive, don't you?"

"It is our concern," Luke said.

"Not anymore. Do you want to survive, or don't you?"

"What about our friends?" Marah asked.

Marcus waved her off. "Probably already dead."

Marah choked back a sob. A few tears escaped, though, running down her cheek.

Luke glared at him. "We're not telling you anything."

* * *

Brigid clapped her hand over her mouth. Suddenly, the pain hit James, worse than anything he had felt before. He didn't want to look, but he knew he had to. He stared down at his right arm—at the gash that had formed.

The blood was seeping through his sleeve and down his arm. The pain was unbearable.

James clutched the side of his arm, stumbling backwards.

"James!" Brigid screamed.

His back hit one of the trees and he slid against it, down to a sitting position. His arm screamed at him. The pain consumed everything, his body, his thoughts. He could no longer see what was in front of him. He didn't hear Brigid's shrieks or Griffin yelling his name. He opened his mouth, but he didn't know if anything came out.

Griffin ran to James. He held his good arm, trying to get him to respond. "James!" he screamed in his face. "James!" But his face was still twisted in pain, his eyes still closed. Griffin ripped off the end of his shirt. He touched the hand that James was using to hold his wound. He needed him to let go, to respond. They needed to know how bad it really was.

Finally, James opened his eyes. "Griffin," he gasped.

Griffin was frantic. "It's okay, James. Please, just let go of your arm. I need to wrap it."

James shook his head.

"James, please."

He sighed and closed his eyes again. He slowly took his hand off of his arm and let it fall into his lap. His hand was sticky with fresh blood. Griffin swallowed hard. The gash looked deep. And there was so much blood...

He lifted James' arm as gently as he could. James winced.

"I'm sorry," Griffin whispered. He wrapped the cloth around his arm and tied it as tightly as possible.

"That should help."

James nodded slowly. "Thanks," he whispered.

The cloth turned red almost immediately. But it seemed to be helping—James' breathing slowly returned to normal.

"Better?" Griffin asked softly.

James took a few more breaths and nodded.

"James?" Brigid called.

Griffin turned and gave Brigid a small smile. "He's alright."

"Good."

Griffin nodded and returned his attention to James. "Think you can keep going?"

"Yeah, I'm fine," James said. He pushed off the ground with his good arm and stood up. He sucked in a breath. "Fine," he repeated.

Griffin raised an eyebrow. "You sure?"

"Sure. We have to keep going."

"Only if you're sure you can."

Brigid peered through the lasers. "Are you sure you're okay?" she asked.

James smiled. "I'll be alright. It's not too bad."

Brigid returned the smile, though she didn't look convinced.

"I think you're good to come back now," Griffin said.

Brigid nodded. "Let's try this again."

She took a step towards them, then stopped. All three of them heard it at the same time.

"What is that?" Brigid asked.

More rumbling, but it was different from the first time. It almost sounded like there was an animal underneath Brigid. And it was hungry.

"Is it going to cave in again?" Griffin asked hurriedly.

James shook his head. "This is different."

Brigid swallowed, her face white. She stared at the ground, waiting.

"What is it then—"

Her question was cut short. All of a sudden, something shot out of the ground. It looked at first to be a brown rope, but then Brigid realized that it was tree roots. She shrieked and tried to run away, but the root wrapped around her arm and pulled her back.

James and Griffin stared. Their mouths dropped open.

Another root shot out of the ground with surprising speed. It too wrapped around Brigid's arm. Brigid tried desperately to pull the roots off of her, but was unable to.

"Brigid!" Griffin screamed.

"We have to get over there," James said. He was still clutching his arm, but his voice had gained strength.

Griffin shook his head. "How?"

"Help!" Brigid screamed.

James and Griffin glanced around for some way to get over to her. But they were too late.

More roots shot up, one after another, wrapping around Brigid's arms and her stomach. Before she could scream, the ground beneath her had caved in and the roots had pulled her down into it.

Then, the hole sealed itself and it was quiet.

James could not bring himself to speak.

Griffin stared at where she had been, his face quickly draining of any color. "No," he whispered. "No, no, no."

"Not her, too," Griffin said. He looked over at James. "What are we going to do now?"

James shook his head. He opened his mouth to say something, but then stopped. He held up one finger and glanced around.

"What?" Griffin asked.

"Hang on," James whispered.

They both stood, listening. Finally, Griffin heard it too.

It was the same rumbling—growling—sound. It was coming towards them.

"Dude...we have to—" Griffin began.

Then the sound was right in front of them.

Below them.

And then it passed them.

"What the...?" Griffin muttered.

James turned around, following the sound with his eyes.

"It's gone, James."

James said nothing.

The sound grew louder.

"Maybe not..." Griffin whispered.

James cut his eyes at him.

"What?" Griffin asked.

"Shut up."

"Sorry."

The ground split open, and dirt and grass flew at them. James shielded his face, but kept his eyes on the opening. After a moment, Brigid flew out of the hole like she had been shot from a cannon. She hit the ground and rolled before sitting up. Her face and hair were streaked with dirt.

"Brigid?" Griffin asked, his mouth wide open.

Brigid tried to brush the dirt off of her arms. She glanced around. "Well that was fun," she finally said.

James smiled. "What just happened?"

"I have no idea. A way to make sure we don't make it past the lasers, I guess."

Griffin shook his head. "This place is unreal."

"You okay?" James asked.

Brigid nodded. "I'm fine. Just a little dirty." She paused. "I'm more worried about you."

James shrugged with one shoulder. "I'm fine."

Griffin looked at both of them nervously. "And I'm next."

"What?" James asked.

"Nothing, nevermind. Let's get going."

James nodded. He helped Brigid to her feet.

"You two are coming with me this time," Brigid said.

James chuckled. "I agree."

Brigid took James and Griffin's hands in hers and grasped them tightly. "Close your eyes," she whispered.

All three of them closed their eyes at the same time. They disappeared and reappeared on the other side of the lasers in only a moment. As soon as they were back on the ground, Brigid pulled them to keep going.

"I am not getting pulled under again," she said, dragging them further and further away.

They kept moving towards the house. The trees were growing more frequent, but they still weren't anywhere near the forest. They walked without interruption for a while, but to James, it felt like they weren't getting any closer to the house. Any closer to Marah and Luke.

His arm throbbed, but he tried to ignore the pain. He counted his steps, he counted the trees. Anything to distract him. Sometimes, he was successful. But other times, the pain was unbearable.

Soon, they came upon several boulders piled together. The pile looked to be five—maybe six—rocks high, but they were so large that the three of them were unable to see over them. The line of boulders stretched on in both directions, so far that going around would waste more time they didn't have.

Brigid looked up. With only a moment's hesitation, she began her ascent.

"I have a bad feeling about this," James said before following Brigid.

"So do I," Brigid said. "But there's no other way."

Griffin and James climbed to the top of the rocks, directly behind Brigid. They stood and looked around. From the top of the rocks, they could see just about everything. The house, the forest, the gate. Everything.

They were silent for a moment, taking in the view.

But, their silence was interrupted.

The rock started to shake. Brigid, James, and Griffin fell to their knees, grasping the surface of the rock for support. James tensed both of his arms to hold onto the rock, closing his eyes in agony at the pain.

"Another earthquake?!" Griffin exclaimed.

The rock continued to shake, then lifted into the air. It kept going until it was several feet above the tops of the trees nearby.

Brigid sighed. "You have got to be kidding."

"Really?" James asked, gritting his teeth.

But, Griffin smiled. "Hey! We're actually prepared for this!"

Brigid chuckled. "Wonderful."

The remaining rocks from the pile lifted up as well. They surrounded the rock that James, Griffin, and Brigid stood on.

Brigid stared at them. "What do you suggest we do?"

"Jump," Griffin said.

Brigid sighed. "Thank you for that bit of wisdom, Griffin. I meant which one."

"Well, be more specific next time."

James rolled his eyes. "Move towards the tree. We can jump onto it and get off of these."

Brigid nodded. She smiled at James gratefully, then turned towards the tree. Griffin glanced at James once Brigid's back was turned and gave an over exaggerated imitation of her. James only smiled.

Brigid jumped onto the closest rock. She steadied herself, then turned and looked over at the two of them. She smiled, and it almost seemed as if she knew exactly what Griffin had done behind her back. Knowing her, she probably did. "Are you coming or not?"

Griffin gave her a thumbs-up. "Working on it."

Brigid jumped to the next rock, and Griffin jumped to the one she had just left. Brigid jumped again, Griffin moved to the one she had left, and James jumped to the first rock. They continued like that until Brigid was standing in front of the tree. She motioned for James and Griffin to join her on the last rock.

Once they were all together on the rock, Griffin peered down at the tree. "Long jump," he murmured.

Brigid nodded. "It's our only choice."

"We have to," James said. He nodded to Brigid. "Go ahead."

Brigid looked down over the edge. She looked like she was going to be sick. "Are you sure..."

"It'll be fine, Brigid," James said. "Better than staying up here."

Brigid nodded. She stepped to the edge of the rock and took a deep breath.

As soon as she started to jump, the rock started to shake violently. She fell back onto the rock. James and Griffin fell to their knees.

"Brigid!" James screamed. "Go! Now!"

Brigid stood up haphazardly and leapt towards the tree. The rock continued to shake, Griffin and James holding onto it with all their might.

"Brigid?" Griffin called after a moment.

"I'm fine! Come on!" she yelled back.

James looked up. Griffin was closer to the edge than he was. "Go," he breathed.

Griffin glanced back at him. He frowned. "Are you sure?"

James nodded.

Griffin stood and jumped towards the tree, screaming, "Look out, Brigid!" as he fell. At that, James had to smile.

Griffin landed and looked back at the rock just in time to see it lurch and shake even more violently than before. James slid backwards, desperately trying to hold on. He gripped the rock with both hands, his left arm screaming in pain.

But, the rock lurched again, and it was too much.

Griffin watched James' body hit the ground and stay there, unmoving.

34

"You're not telling me anything. Trying to be the hero, are you?" Marcus asked.

Luke stayed silent.

"Don't waste your time, Lucas. Attempting to be the hero will only get you killed."

"Our friends," Marah repeated.

Marcus turned to look at Marah. He smirked. "You want to see your friends? Are you sure about that?"

"We're positive," Luke said.

Marcus shrugged. "If you insist. But don't say I didn't warn you."

He walked over to one of the television screens that were mounted on either side of the door. He slid his hand against the side of the screen and pressed a button. He turned to Marah and Luke, smiling, as the screen flickered to life. Then he leaned against one of the side walls to watch.

Luke and Marah glanced at each other. They both frowned, unsure, before turning their attention to the screen.

The first thing they saw was the front gate.

The camera turned, and they took in the trees, the house, the forest, more trees. Finally, the camera found James, Brigid, and Griffin. It stopped and zoomed in closely. The screen showed each of their faces one at a time. First Griffin—his eyes serious and his face vacant of his usual mischievous smile. Then Brigid—her face streaked with dirt and her eyes filled with fear. Finally,

James—determined, but both Luke and Marah could see the pain on his face.

The camera zoomed out so they could see James' whole body, then zoomed back in on his arm. It took them a minute, but Marah was the first to understand what the camera was showing them. She sucked in a breath.

There was a cloth wrapped around James' upper arm, stained blood red. Luke sighed heavily. Marcus only chuckled.

The camera zoomed out again so that they were able to see more. James, Griffin, and Brigid. The trees. The lasers crossed in front of them.

Luke shook his head. He couldn't watch this anymore.

But neither of them could take their eyes away.

They watched as Brigid took both James and Griffin's hands. The three of them disappeared, then reappeared on the other side of the lasers.

Marcus smiled. "Teleporter. Interesting."

Marah and Luke kept their attention on the television screen. They watched in silence as James, Brigid, and Griffin walked through the field. Marah held her breath, waiting for something to happen. For something to pop out at them.

Nothing did, though. Finally, the three of them came upon a pile of boulders, climbed to the top, and stood there for a moment. Luke raised an eyebrow.

Then, the rock lifted into the air, Brigid, James, and Griffin hanging on tightly.

Luke snorted. "Floating rocks," he muttered. "How original."

Marah relaxed a bit as she and Luke watched the other three jump across the rocks with ease. Finally, the three of them met on the last rock and looked down at the tree beside them.

Luke raised an eyebrow. "They're going to jump?" he asked Marah quietly.

Marcus laughed aloud.

Both Marah and Luke glared at him before turning back to the screen.

They watched closely. Brigid stepped to the front of the rock first. She started to jump, but the rock started to shake. Marah sucked in a breath. Brigid fell backwards, then stood up quickly and jumped.

They saw Griffin and James exchange glances. Then, Griffin jumped off as well. James started to stand, but before he could, the rock started to shake again.

The shaking was getting worse, and James was slipping off of the rock, his face twisted in pain.

"Come on," Luke whispered.

"Please," Marah breathed.

Then, he was gone.

The camera swiveled, and there he was. Lying on the ground, motionless. Lifeless.

And the screen went black.

Luke stared at the darkened screen, unable to believe what he had just seen. Marah hung her head, her tears streaming hard and fast.

Marcus strutted to the television screen and shut it off. He turned to face them, smiling that same evil smile. "Like I said. Your friends are already dead."

Marah shook her head, sniffling softly. She looked up at Marcus. "How could you?" she asked softly.

"Easily," Marcus said, his lips curled into a scowl. "But I am not the one who set all of this wonderful equipment up for you."

Marah and Luke exchanged glances.

"What?" Marah asked.

Marcus only smiled. "We'll get to that later. More importantly, if you don't tell me what I want to know...the same that happened to your friends will happen to you."

Luke shook his head. His disgust was evident. For once, Marah was glad he was tied down. She didn't know what would have happened if he wasn't. Nothing good.

"Why in the world would we tell *you*?" Luke asked.

Marcus let out an aggravated breath. "I already told you. Tell me, or you die."

"Maybe we'd rather die," Marah whispered.

Marcus stared at her. Luke raised one eyebrow.

"You'd rather die?" Marcus asked incredulously.

"I'd die before I told you anything. And if you kill them," she said, motioning her head towards the television screen, "Then I don't want to live anyway."

Marcus shook his head. "You'd rather die," he repeated. "How would your parents feel about that? How would the people in their *precious* city of Jericho feel about it?"

Marah shrugged. Luke said nothing.

Marcus smiled. He shook his head, still not seeming to believe what Marah was saying. "So the oh-so-powerful rulers of Jericho sent their children after me. Sent their children to die. Sent them to die on the quest they should have gone on," Marcus muttered to himself. He chuckled. "Perfect. They'll never forgive themselves."

Marah kept her gaze steady, but Luke could feel her shaking.

"You're sure you don't want to tell me?" Marcus asked.

Marah swallowed hard. "We're sure."

Luke nodded.

Marcus smiled. He even laughed. "As you wish."

* * *

Griffin dropped out of the tree and took off running. He heard Brigid's voice behind him.

"Where are you going?" she yelled. "Griff—" She stopped, and he knew she had seen. She dropped out of the tree, but could not move past that. She just stared, watching Griffin run to James. Hot tears ran down her face.

"James," Griffin whispered as he ran. "Please, no."

Finally, he reached him. Griffin dropped to his knees and grasped James' good arm. He stared at James' face, his closed eyelids, the blood stained cloth around his arm. He was so...still.

Griffin tightened his grip on James' arm. "James?" he asked. His voice caught, and he choked on the tears he hadn't known were there. "Can you hear me?"

James did not stir.

"Please, please," Griffin whispered. "Come back."

Griffin reached for James' neck, his hands shaking so badly that it took him several times to find his pulse. Finally, he found it. He was still alive, but the pulse was weak.

He returned his hand back to James' arms. "Come on, James. Wake up."

"Please," he whispered. "Please."

But still, nothing.

Griffin shook him softly. "James. Wake up."

Nothing.

He shook him harder. "James," he said, louder. "James!"

Griffin held his still shaking hand on his head. "Come on," he whispered.

Then, James opened one eye. He groaned. "What happened?"

Griffin let out a sigh of relief. "You fell."

"Why does this keep happening?" James groaned.

"Not my fault," Griffin said. "You're the one that keeps getting hurt."

James stared up at the rock above him, his eyebrows creased in confusion. Griffin followed his gaze, then looked back down at James.

"How are you still alive after that?" Griffin asked.

James shook his head. "I have no idea. That's a really long fall. I should be a lot worse off than I am."

Griffin shrugged. "Hey, I'll take it."

"Me too," James nodded, cringing with the effort.

Griffin stood up, then held his hand out to James. He took it and winced in pain as Griffin pulled him to a standing position.

"You alright?" Griffin asked.

"Pretty hard fall, but I'm alright," James said.

They headed back towards Brigid, who had a mixture of concern and confusion on her face. Griffin came to her first. "He's alright."

Brigid ran the few steps to James and jumped to hug his neck. She let out a breath of relief.

James laughed. "Somehow."

"That's amazing," Brigid said, shaking her head.

"Where to next?" Griffin called back to them.

James shrugged. "Forward."

* * *

Marcus was still laughing.

Luke rolled his eyes. "Get on with it, would you?"

Marcus just stared at him. "Fine with me."

Marah kept her gaze in her lap, letting her tears fall and watching them pool on her legs.

"But one last thing," Marcus said. He smiled. "Remember that thing I had of yours?"

Marah looked up, and Marcus stepped closer to her.

"Missing this?" he asked. He pulled her necklace out of his pocket and dangled it in front of her face.

She refused to look at him or the necklace. Refused to show any emotion.

Marcus shook his head. He reached out and caught one of her tears on his finger. Her skin burned with his touch. He rubbed the drop in between his fingers, then flicked it away. Finally, she met his eyes.

Marcus sneered. "I think you're going to enjoy this."

He walked back to the doorway, gave them a slight wave, and disappeared behind the wall.

Marah sucked in a breath.

"Marah?" Luke whispered.

"Yeah?"

"It's going to be okay."

Marah was silent for a moment. "How do you know?"

"I...I just know."

Marah nodded, and they were both silent.

Then, "Luke?"

"Yeah?"

"Thanks."

Luke smiled.

All too soon, Marcus returned. He still had Marah's necklace, but he now held something in both hands. In his other hand, there was a jagged orange stone, about the size of a baseball. Marah and Luke stared at it, and Marcus looked much too happy to have it.

He held up the stone. The light in the room reflected off the orange rock and bounced along the walls. Marcus turned it in his hand. "This, my friends, is sunstone."

"Sunstone?" Luke asked skeptically.

"Yes, sunstone. As in the opposite of moonstone. As in nothing good for the two of you."

Luke raised an eyebrow. "What is that supposed to mean?"

"That's what I'm about to show you," Marcus said, growing impatient.

Marah and Luke exchanged glances.

Then, Marcus' cruel smile returned. He lifted up Marah's necklace and the sunstone at the same time. Slowly, he brought them closer together.

Finally, he touched the sunstone to the small moonstone gem on Marah's necklace.

Marah's scream was piercing.

35

They walked in silence for only a moment.

Griffin was in the lead, Brigid in the middle, and James behind her. Each step was careful, and planned. They could not risk another close call. There had been too many already.

"Quiet?" Griffin asked.

He had spoken too soon.

Nearly a second later, Griffin stumbled backwards as a brick wall, at least ten feet tall, shot up in front of him.

"Where the heck did that come from?" he shrieked.

James sighed.

They did not have long to think about it, however. All of a sudden, a horrible screeching noise echoed through each of their minds. They fell to the ground, clutching their ears.

Brigid screamed, though the other two could not hear it.

James fell slowly to his knees, his eyes closed in agony.

Griffin leaned against the brick wall, his hands clawing at his ears.

But it didn't stop.

The screeching continued as if it would never end. All three of them were screaming now. The noise was horrible—worse than that. And there was nothing they could do to stop it.

James had finally found something to distract him from the pain in his arm. But his arm was nothing compared to this. The noise echoed through his mind; it consumed every part of his consciousness.

The three of them could not hear their own screams. They did not even know they were screaming. They were trapped within themselves, trying desperately to block out the sound. But somehow, it was inside of them, with no way of getting it out.

Then, the noise was gone just as quickly as it had come.

James' head throbbed, and his ears were still ringing. Brigid groaned.

James opened his eyes slowly. He looked at Brigid and Griffin, lying on the ground, their eyes closed.

"You heard it, too?" he whispered.

Griffin only nodded. He sat up slowly. "What was that?" he asked, rubbing the side of his head.

James shook his head. "I have no idea."

Brigid pulled her knees to her chest. She rested her chin on the top of her knees and studied James and Griffin. "Something tells me that it was Marcus."

James nodded. "Probably."

"We need to hurry up and get to Luke and Marah," Griffin murmured.

James and Brigid nodded. The three of them stood up and stared at the wall in front of them.

"This place is starting to get annoying," Griffin said.

"Starting?" Brigid asked.

"Let's just go around it," James said.

Griffin nodded. "Yeah."

They turned to the left, but before they could take a step, another wall shot out of the ground, right against the first.

"Okay," James said. "Nevermind."

They turned to go around the right side, but another wall came up.

"Great," Griffin muttered.

They turned again, their backs to the first wall. But another wall shot up, completing the square. The three of them were closed in completely.

Brigid gripped James' arm. "What are we going to do?"

"We really should have seen this coming," Griffin muttered.

"How do we get out?!" Brigid demanded.

"Calm down," Griffin said. He smiled. "This is where my talent comes in."

He motioned to one of the corners of the box they now found themselves in. One of the boulders they had had to jump onto only a few minutes before was lying on the ground.

Brigid furrowed her eyebrows at it, then realization dawned on her. She smiled at Griffin.

Griffin grinned. "This is the fun part."

He walked up next to the boulder and pretended to push up his sleeves. Brigid and James watched him in amusement.

Griffin wrapped his arms around the sides of the rock, his hands not coming close to the middle of it. It looked impossible. But sure enough, Griffin lifted the rock easily. He grinned over at James and Brigid. "Watch out."

He walked to the middle of the square and faced the last wall. He twisted his upper body, then turned back as fast as he could, letting the rock go as he did so. The boulder flew at the wall and hit directly in the middle.

The wall came crumbling down, and Griffin laughed in triumph.

James patted him on the back. "Nice one."

They climbed over the rubble, Griffin beaming the whole way.

But, as soon as they stepped into the open field, the time for celebrating—and even speaking—was over.

An arrow whizzed by James' head.

He turned around—just in time to see hundreds more flying at him.

"Get down!" James screamed.

They dropped to their stomachs with only seconds to spare.

"What the—" Griffin began.

Another set of arrows flew over, seeming to come out of the brick wall.

James strained his eyes, going over every inch of the brick. Then he saw it. Small compartments all over the wall were open, and arrows were shooting out of them every minute. And more were opening.

Arrows.

Ninja Stars.

Rocks.

"We need to get out of here," James said.

Griffin looked up. He sighed. "But the house is that way." A rock flew by him, inches from his face. "Nevermind."

They waited on the ground, sliding back and forth to avoid the dangers. Finally, there was a pause, and the three of them stood up.

"Go, now," James said. They took off running—in the opposite direction they were supposed to be.

James sighed. He turned his head slightly. He could see the house—Marah and Luke—growing farther and farther away. But he had no choice.

He turned back just in time to veer off the path of another arrow. He glanced at Brigid and Griffin. They returned his gaze, neither of them breaking stride.

They came upon two trees and had to separate. Griffin on one side, Brigid on the other. James through the middle. They tried to come back together, but it was impossible.

"James!" Brigid called, looking for a way to come back to him.

James glanced at her. "Just keep going!"

She nodded and picked up speed.

James couldn't see Griffin or Brigid anymore. Trees, boulders, walls—everything was blocking his path, forcing him to keep twisting throughout the field, getting farther and farther away from the house.

Arrows shot from every direction. It was impossible to tell where they were coming from anymore. He didn't have time to think about it anyway.

He kept pushing, kept running. He could no longer feel his legs—it was as if he had turned them on autopilot. But there was nothing else he could do. If he stopped—he died. If he slowed—he died.

Trees blurred past him. He saw flashes of Brigid and Griffin, but they were getting farther and farther away from him. It looked like he was on his own right now.

But, the more he ran, the more difficult it became to dodge everything coming at him. Things were coming from every direction—arrows, arrows, and more arrows. He glanced back and forth worriedly—it was by sheer luck that he hadn't gotten hit yet. What had happened to Brigid and Griffin? Had they been hit?

He pushed forward, trying not to think the worst. He dodged another arrow, then realized that it too had turned. James let out a frustrated breath. He had hoped that lesson of Wane's wouldn't have been needed.

A specialized arrow. Like he had needed another problem.

James ran even faster, trying to stay ahead of the arrow. Unlike Brigid and Griffin, his talent was of no help in this situation. He kept running, but he knew that he wouldn't be able to go for much longer. Especially with all the blood he had already lost. And regular arrows were still coming at him—along with the specialized arrow still on his tail.

He couldn't keep this up for much longer. Something was going to have to happen. And James had a feeling that that something wouldn't be good for him.

But then, everything just...stopped. No more arrows shot towards him. The specialized arrow dropped to the ground and stayed there. For the first time since they had arrived, it was silent.

James stopped, breathing hard. He turned around to see how far he'd gotten. Except for a few small boulders, he was in open grass. He could see the white house in the distance. He sighed. Who knew how long it would take him to get back there?

But why, he wondered, had everything stopped? Then it hit him. Defense mechanisms could usually go for as long as needed...until someone turned them off. Marcus, for some reason, no longer needed them. And what did that mean for Marah and Luke?

James groaned with the little bit of breath he had left. He saw Griffin out of the corner of his eye, several feet away. Griffin met his eyes and nodded. He gave James a perplexed look. James shrugged.

James turned and looked in the opposite direction. There was Brigid, perched atop one of the boulders. She held her head in her hands, her fingers intertwined in her blonde hair.

"James."

James started. His hand went immediately to his ear. Wane.

"Wane?"

"Who else?"

James grimaced. "It's about time."

"You had to do this one on your own."

"Well that went well, didn't it?"

Wane chuckled. "You're still alive, aren't you?"

"True," James said. Then his face fell. "Luke and Marah might not be, though."

There was a pause. "What are you talking about?"

"The ground opened up when we first got here and they both fell through. They survived that, because they talked to us through the necklaces. But they're in the house, and we think they may be with Marcus."

Silence. Then, "Did they say that?"

"No. We haven't talked to them since they first got there. But there's nowhere else he could be."

"Okay. What's going on now?"

"Well, they had a bunch of defense mechanisms, but they all shut off."

"They shut off?"

"Yeah," James said. "Wane...what is this all about?"

Wane didn't answer for a moment. "I told you. He betrayed us."

"Then why send us?"

"Because...because this is your life now. You are to be the new leaders of Jericho. And it's not going to be easy."

"Why so soon?"

"You were ready. You all are more talented than you realize."

"We could have been killed."

"But you weren't. Everyone is tested at some point in their lives."

"And this was our test?!" James demanded.

"James...everyone has a destiny. The difference is whether or not they choose to accept it...whether or not they choose to pursue what they were born to do. This..." Wane paused, and James stared at the scene in front of him. He felt the blood seeping through his sleeve. Wane took a breath. "This is yours."

James was silent as Wane's words sunk in.

"My destiny?" James asked. "This?"

"No one said it was going to be easy. Especially for those who are destined for such great things. You are one of those people, James."

"I don't know..." James stuttered.

"You have no idea what you're capable of. I can see it in you, James. You will be great. You already are."

* * *

Marcus pulled the sunstone away from her necklace, smiling wide. Marah held her head down and squeezed her eyes shut. Her head was throbbing from that awful sound.

Luke sucked in a breath. "What was that?" he breathed.

Marcus chuckled. "Didn't like that, did you?" he asked. "Sunstone and moonstone don't exactly agree with one another."

He dropped the necklace into Marah's lap. "But now. On to your wishes."

Luke stared at him, but Marah still refused to meet his eyes.

"It was an honorable try, attempting to come after your parents' enemy. But now they'll have to come after me themselves," Marcus said. He shrugged and returned to the doorway.

"Oh, and you wanted to know who set all of this up? It was your beloved Wane. How do you feel about dying for him now?"

Both Marah and Luke's mouths dropped open.

"Wha—what?" Marah asked, her face filled with despair.

"Goodbye," Marcus said, his smile terrifying. He pressed a button on the back of one of the television screens and was gone.

The television flickered to life. The screen was black, but the white numbers glared back at them.

2:00.

"Luke..." Marah began, "What is that?"

Luke sucked in a breath. "Nothing good. We need to get out of here."

"How?!"

"I need to burn the ropes."

"Can you do it in two minutes?" Marah asked, her voice escalating.

"I have to try, Marah."

"Please hurry."

1:30.

"I'm almost there," Luke murmured.

Marah nodded. "Keep going."

"I'm going as fast as I can."

"I know, I'm sorry," Marah whispered.

Her voice caught and she said, "Do you think Wane really did it?"

Luke paused. "I don't know, Marah. I...I don't know."

1:00.

The ropes slid off Luke's wrists and fell to the ground. "Done."

He jumped up, slid his chair away, and reached for Marah's wrists.

0:45.

Luke struggled with the ropes that bound Marah's wrists, but they would not budge.

"It's not going to work, Marah. Whoever tied this tied it well."

"I guess you're going to have to burn it like yours," Marah said.

"I'll do it as fast as I can."

0:30.

Luke focused on the ropes and they started to burn. He had to go slowly, so as not to burn her skin, and there was a lot of rope. Slowly, the layers of rope began to fade away.

"Almost there," Luke whispered. His voice was strained, and Marah knew that his energy was slowly draining.

0:15.

"Luke...just go," Marah whispered. Her voice caught on her tears. "There's not enough time."

"No."

"We're not going to make it. You have to go."

"I'm not leaving you, Marah."

0:10.

He kept burning the ropes. His energy was fading, but there was no way he was stopping. Not now.

"I'm almost finished," he whispered. "Just hold on."

0:05.

The ropes fell off her wrists and Luke let out a sigh of relief. Marah jumped out of her chair as fast as she could. Luke grabbed her hand and they sprinted towards the doorway.

0:01.

36

James stood, staring at the white house. He glanced at Griffin and Brigid. They needed to start if they were to get to Marah and Luke anytime soon.

Brigid looked up and met his eyes. They exchanged nods, and she stood up. James looked to Griffin, but he had already begun making his way through the rocks.

James breathed in deeply and took a step, but that was as far as he got.

The explosion seemed to shake the entire property.

James watched in shock as the big white house exploded, sending debris everywhere. He heard Brigid's scream and saw her fall to her knees.

He felt numb.

Marah and Luke were in there.

"No," he whispered to himself. "Please, no."

The dust faded and he looked at what was left, immediately wishing he hadn't. The house had been reduced to a pile of rubble, with a few small flames still blazing.

The world seemed to grow smaller. The air became thinner, and every breath was a struggle. Everything they had survived, for this?

They couldn't be gone, he told himself.

Griffin turned around and stared at James. The despair on his face was painful to look at. James met his gaze anyway. Griffin shook his head. He said something, even though he was too far away for James to hear him. But James read his lips.

"No one could have survived that."

James closed his eyes. He barely had the strength to stand, but he couldn't move. Not even to fall to the ground.

He held his face in his hands. His cheeks were wet, but he hadn't felt the tears.

Everything was still—silent. None of them moved. They didn't have the strength or desire to do it.

Griffin turned his eyes away from James. He stared at the place where the house had been—the place where his friends had been. He didn't want to see it, but he couldn't take his eyes away. He stared, not having the energy to do anything else. His body did not move and neither did his mind. He could only see two things. The last time he had seen Marah and Luke. And the house exploding. Those two images replayed in his mind without mercy.

Brigid kept her gaze on her knees. She gasped for breath. She clutched her necklace in her hand, sobbing silently. She couldn't take it anymore...seeing James get nearly killed, almost dying herself...and now, Marah and Luke. Gone, just like that. She cried until there weren't tears left. Already she thought of the things she should have told them. Wished for more time. Everything they had learned...everything they had been through...for it to end like this? It couldn't.

Slowly, she lifted her head. She pulled a few blades of grass out of the ground, twirling them through her fingers. She looked over at Griffin, then James, but neither of them met her eyes.

James stared at the rubble, without actually seeing it. Instead he saw Marah smiling, Luke laughing, them both screaming as they fell from his sight forever. He shook his head, trying to stop the images. He should have gotten there faster.

It was all his fault.

James used his last bit of strength to bring his hand up to his ear. "Why would you send us here?"

Wane didn't answer for several minutes. James waited.

Finally, "What happened?"

James sighed. "They're gone, Wane."

"What are you talking about?"

"They're gone!" James exclaimed. "The house blew up!"

He held his fingers to his temples and tried to calm down.

He heard Wane curse under his breath. "Tell me exactly what happened."

"All the defense mechanisms stopped out here. Then as soon as we started to head towards the house to get Marah and Luke, it exploded."

"Everything stopped, and then the house exploded? And nothing happened after that?"

"Wane! Don't you get it? They're *gone*!"

Wane said nothing.

James fumed, no longer able to form the words that he wanted to scream at him.

"It all stopped. And then the house blew up," Wane repeated.

"I told you that already."

Wane cursed again. "He found it. How did he know?"

James shook his head. Wane wasn't making any sense. "Know what? What do you mean?"

"It wasn't…" Wane stopped, breathed in heavily. "It was just another stage of training, James. Nothing else."

James stared at the scene in front of him, not quite able to grasp what Wane had just told him. It wasn't training. It couldn't be. "What? No, it wasn't training. We finished training already," James said. He knew he was rambling, but he couldn't stop himself. "We were coming after him. He's here. He was supposed to be."

"No..." Wane started. He paused, and everything that had happened replayed in James' mind. The ground falling through as soon as they had arrived, the lasers and arrows seeming to shoot straight at them, the house exploding with Marah and Luke inside. Wane took a deep breath.

"He wasn't supposed to be there. He shouldn't have been there."

Acknowledgements

Many thanks to God my Father, the most important acknowledgement by far, for loving me and blessing me far more than I will ever deserve.

Many thanks to my sister, Ryan, for believing in this book, and listening to me talk through my ideas day after day and almost never getting tired of it ☺ Thank you for all of your ideas, for your excitement about the book that matched mine, and for never letting me give up on it. Thanks for being the best sister a girl could ask for. I don't deserve you.

To my parents, for believing in me, for reading and critiquing as many times as I asked you to, and for telling everyone you knew about it. Without your love and support, none of this would have been possible. Mom, thank you for loving me and believing in me. You're the best and I am so blessed to have you as a mother. Dad, thank you for loving me and this book. All of your suggestions made it so much better and I absolutely loved talking through it with you. Your enthusiasm is so encouraging, thank you for everything!

To my friends, thank you for your excitement and encouragement, and for always being there for me. I am blessed to know every single one of you.

To Mr. Kessinger, for believing in me and pushing me to publish this book on my own. Without you, I would still be stuck waiting.

To Lathan, for your excitement about my project and for designing such a wonderful website for me.

To Noah and Jacob, and our writers club, you two never fail to bring a smile to my face. Without you, writing this would not have been nearly as much fun. Thank you for your endless encouragement, and for believing in my book. I will always believe in yours.

To Abby and Lindsay, thank you for your encouragement and support. You both are such wonderful friends, and I'm blessed to know you. Without your help, I'd still be sitting, hopeless, in front of Photoshop ☺ You two are the best.

To Matt Williams and Shari Horeth, thank you for believing in my project and my success from the moment I met both of you. Mr. Williams, thank you for being such a wonderful mentor. Thank you both for all of your help.

To Justin, thank you for being an amazing coach and friend. Your excitement about this book and your encouragement meant the world to me. You are such a blessing and I already miss you so much!

To my wonderful Mauldin cheer team and coaches, thank you for believing in me and giving me the opportunity to be a part of something so great. I love each and every one of you.

To Mrs. Yon, thank you for reading this book when I first finished it and supporting me every step of the way.

About the Author

Reed Piller lives with her family in South Carolina. The Dark Side of the Moon is her first novel, and she is hard at work on the second in the series, Once in a Blue Moon. To learn more, visit www.reedpiller.com.

Coming Soon…

Once in a Blue Moon
The Dark Side of the Moon Trilogy
Book 2

Made in the USA
Lexington, KY
20 February 2014